A MILWAUKEE INHERITANCE

Also by David Milofsky

Playing from Memory

Eternal People

Color of Law

A Friend of Kissinger

Managed Care

A MILWAUKEE INHERITANCE

THE UNIVERSITY OF WISCONSIN PRESS

The University of Wisconsin Press
728 State Street, Suite 443
Madison, Wisconsin 53706-1428
uwpress.wisc.edu

Gray's Inn House, 127 Clerkenwell Road
London EC1R 5DB, United Kingdom
eurospanbookstore.com

Printed in the United States of America

This book may be available in a digital edition.

Library of Congress Cataloging-in-Publication Data
Names: Milofsky, David, author.
Title: A Milwaukee inheritance / David Milofsky.
Description: Madison, Wisconsin: The University of Wisconsin Press, [2019]
Identifiers: LCCN 2019008116 | ISBN 9780299325701 (cloth: alk. paper)
Subjects: LCSH: Milwaukee (Wis.)—Fiction. | LCGFT: Fiction. | Novels.
Classification: LCC PS3563.I444 M55 2019 | DDC 813/.54—dc23
LC record available at https://lccn.loc.gov/2019008116

To

JEANIE

JENNIE

and the memory of

RUTH DORSEY MILOFSKY

"You can talk, you can talk, you can bicker you can talk, . . .
you can talk all you want but it's different than it was."
"No it ain't, no it aint, but you gotta know the territory."

MEREDITH WILLSON, "Rock Island," from *The Music Man*

A MILWAUKEE INHERITANCE

Everyone knows you have to have eight units to make a go of it as a landlord. So it was almost as if my mother was willing me to fail when she left me her old threedecker in Milwaukee along with a death bed request that her tenants could stay on at their present rent until they were ready to leave.

My wife wasn't happy about this. Not that Moira ever figured Mom would die and leave us a fabulous fortune, but a run-down rental that didn't make enough to cover the mortgage hadn't figured into her plans. We moved back to Milwaukee several years before from Boston, part of a nostalgic idea I'd had while in law school about returning in triumph to a place where I'd lived mostly in poverty and unhappiness. We had a house on the lake and my best friend from high school had found me a place in his downtown firm. This was as good as it got in my view, but Moira didn't share my enthusiasm. She had liked our life on the East Coast and resisted change.

But I had promised my mother that I'd take care of the house because I knew she felt strongly about this. I had only been home a few years when she was stricken, and on the last afternoon of her life she sat in her garden with me and Moira. Her legs were covered with a knitted throw someone had made for her, but it was at best a bittersweet moment because Mom had had a hard life, filled with disappointment and the deaths of loved ones. Still, she was cheerful as we sat there among the begonias and zinnias. She put her hand in mine and looked at me fondly. "All in all, I've had a good life," she said softly.

She was fifty-five and dying of advanced breast cancer. "Only you would say so," I replied.

She nodded and tears formed in her eyes. Then she asked me not to evict her tenants or change anything in the house. "I saved it for you, Andy," she said. "I know you aren't going to live there, but I'd hate to think of someone else owning it and tearing out walls and making those people go somewhere else."

At the time, Moira was as moved by this as I was, but it did little to change her general view of Milwaukee or my inheritance. Today, we were finishing lunch in our new kitchen surrounded by a sea of granite and stainless steel. Beveled windows let in what there was of the afternoon light. I was about to go over and look over our new property. "Face it," she said. "You're just not a landlord."

I smiled. "I guess I am now."

"Come on, Andy, that place is falling down around itself. And if you can't raise the rent, how can you fix it up? Maybe you should just sell it, no matter what you promised your mom." Then she seemed to soften. "At least the neighborhood's not that bad," she said.

Which was true. The only thing my mother ever knew about real estate was that it made sense to buy on the edge of a good neighborhood. Even if hers was the most decrepit house on the street, from the front porch you could see the stately towers of Newberry Boulevard where huge homes crowded each other for space along a wide street that led right into Lake Park. I remembered her glee at being in close proximity to the wealthy, her idea that they'd cringe if they knew an old fellow traveler was just a short distance away. That day we had walked down into the park and drank coffee at the restaurant overlooking the lake. It was nice to think of her being so happy at pissing off the enemy.

"The neighborhood's great," I said. "And it's getting better all the time. We could consider it an investment and in time it could pay off."

"Investment?" Moira laughed. "Place would probably fall down before it became worth anything."

"Maybe, maybe not, but it's not going to cost us much and we can afford it for now. Anyway, I can't sell it."

"You can't sell it, but you can lose money if something goes wrong?"

"That's right," I said. "I could do that."

"I'm getting a migraine," Moira said and went into the other room to lie down.

Besides being near Newberry, the neighborhood was characterized by other duplexes, a few single-family homes, and a commercial block around the corner that had seen better days. The university extension was a few blocks up the street and they were expanding steadily, putting up new buildings and bringing in more students and faculty, which was promising for the future. If things moved our way in the next few years the value of the house might actually increase, but this wasn't the important thing to me. I wasn't selling. I'd made a promise to my mother to hold onto the place and I intended to keep my word.

Part of the problem was that I could see what had attracted Mom to the house. We were a lot alike in that way. There were three usable floors and an attic with a cupola with enough light for her to paint. Even now there were forty canvases leaning against the walls up there, testimony to a life lived mostly alone. After my father died and I left for school on the East Coast, art became her constant companion. I figured you could have worse partners in life, but I knew she was lonely.

Despite its charms, however, I had never lived in this house. After we moved to Milwaukee from New York, it had been just the two of us in a succession of apartments and floor-throughs on the lower East Side, each just slightly better than the last, though the degree of improvement might have escaped most people. Mom had a teaching degree, but she took a series of part-time office jobs in order to paint and spend time at home with me. After I left, she managed to put together a show that was successful enough to allow her to buy the house. She had hoped that eventually Moira and I would bring back some grandchildren and live there with her. A slow-growing malignancy scotched that plan and the grandchildren had failed to materialize. Which left me back home but alone in the world with a property to manage. The thought made me unaccountably cheerful, something I didn't fully understand, but the psyche's a funny, unpredictable thing and I've learned not to question it.

I hadn't mentioned it to Moira but the truth was that I already knew one of my mother's tenants, though "knew" might be too strong a word. Perhaps I should say I knew of Frank Pignatano; I knew about him. Everyone on the East Side did. Frank's father was the head of the major crime syndicate in town, so Frank came to us with that burden. Moreover, though he tried hard, he was not a prepossessing kind of man. Short, perhaps 5′6″ in stacked heels, he was a wiry little guy who wore his white T-shirt rolled above the bicep, with a pack of Camels inside. He had black wavy hair and was always in the bathroom at school combing it back over the ears in a duck's ass and then teasing a little curl that looped down over his eyebrows.

Frank attended Riverside under the provisions of a Wisconsin law known as the Huber Act, which allowed convicts to attend high school or go to work during the day while they spent their nights in jail. Frank was actually in juvie but what had gotten him there was the fact that he had supposedly used a tie pin to blind another boy while some of his henchmen held the kid down. I was never able to verify this story, nor would I have tried, but he had done something that got him sentenced, that much was sure. And the story explained Pignatano's subsequent nickname, Frankie the Pin. Frank wanted people to think he was a tough guy but actually he was a punk and couldn't have taken most of the girls at school if his gang wasn't around to help. But high school kids are cruel, or at least they think cruelty is cool, so the tie pin story made Frank if not famous then at least notorious, which at our school was probably better.

My only contact with Pignatano had come later, when he had been released from jail and was hanging around Francesca's pizzeria working on his curl. I was walking home one night with Darryl Eigen, a boy so reckless it baffles me now that I ever knew him. Darryl signed up for the Marines after graduation and served in Desert Storm. Later he reenlisted because, as he told me on one of my visits home, he "liked killing" and wanted to learn about the latest automatic weapons. His father was a city librarian but Darryl had picked up none of his father's bookish habits. He liked to fight; he liked violence. He was perfect for war in the desert. But that was later.

On this night, we were walking home on Locust Street when I became aware of a group of boys suddenly next to us. They had appeared like a dark cloud, out of nowhere, and then what seemed like a strong wind put me on the ground, stars in front of my eyes. I learned later that I'd been hit with brass knuckles but at the time being knocked out presented itself as a novelty.

I don't know how long I was unconscious, but when I awoke Frank Pignatano was standing over me. When he saw I was awake, he said in what I remember as a gentle voice, "This isn't about you. Go back to sleep." I closed my eyes obediently and when I came to again, I could see the gang farther down the street with Darryl in their midst, bobbing and weaving for all he was worth.

It turned out I had a fractured jaw and my mother, outraged at this, brought a detective to my bedside with a mug book. After looking at dozens of grainy photos, I told him I had no idea who hit me. I said I had never seen the guy before.

But all this was almost twenty years ago and that was the last contact I'd had with Frankie the Pin who, through an odd concatenation of events, was now my tenant. My mother thought Frank was cute and gave him some latitude regarding the rent. When I checked I discovered he was two months behind.

My wife wasn't amused. "You're renting to a criminal and he's behind in the rent? What are you, the welfare department? Why don't you just evict him?"

My mother actually had leanings in the direction of welfare but it would have done no good to say anything about that now. My own motivation was different. I was both scared of and fascinated by Frank, even if the fateful night with Darryl had been years ago and we were both now pushing middle age. "He'll pay," I said hopefully. "I just have to go up there and talk to him."

"You're taking security?" I knew she was only half-joking. When we were in Boston Moira found my stories of an urban boyhood exotic, Runyonesque, but now that we had moved here she was neither amused nor tolerant. She didn't like Milwaukee with its huge brooding buildings, dark trees hiding the skies, and aggressively friendly neighbors asking questions about her family. She thought it meant they were concealing something about themselves.

"I don't think that's necessary. We were in school together," I said, as if that explained something. But Moira wasn't listening and the truth was I didn't blame her.

Although I would never have admitted it to my wife, I was secretly charmed by my mother's bequest and didn't see what harm it could do to play along. We didn't really need the extra money and as long as it didn't become a long-term commitment, I welcomed my new association with Frankie Pignatano. It was a connection to what I thought of as a colorful part of my past, which for the most part had been anything but that, a blue-collar boyhood, a result of the poverty visited upon us by my father's early death.

I had fled all this in the first place by going as far away as I could for college to escape the drear reality of the East Side. But after college and law school, marrying Moira and working for a couple of years as a legal aide attorney, I turned down a job my father-in-law had found for me in a nice Boston firm with offices on Commonwealth Avenue and returned to Milwaukee. Something drew me back home, something that wasn't completely unrelated to Frankie the Pin and all he personified.

Yet when I climbed the stairs of what was after all now no longer my home but merely a rental property I had inherited, I felt less scared than shy. I worried that Frank would remember me as that frightened boy cowering on the sidewalk; I was equally afraid he wouldn't remember me at all.

I needn't have worried. Frank flung the door open wide and gave me the big hello, even slapping me lightly on the cheek as I had seen mobsters do in the movies. "Andy," he cried out. "Long time, eh?"

It was a question that required no answer and now Frank called over his shoulder, "Honey, come in here and shake hands with Andy Simonson. We were in school together. Old friends."

Had this visit been calculated to extend the nonpayment of rent, it could not have been more successful. We were boon companions, partners in crime, as much as if we had actually boosted a car together or knocked over a few liquor stores in days gone by. I liked the illusion since like any good dream it was adjacent to reality but not completely unrelated. It was almost enough to make me forget for a moment that I was an officer of the court, Frankie had done five years in Green Bay, and that in real life we were working opposite sides of the street.

The years seemed to have had little effect on him nor had his stay in the joint caused him to bulk up, like many convicts. He still had the d.a. and wore a short-sleeved silk shirt, rolled to show his nonexistent biceps. He was slim as before but seemed to limp a bit as he ascended the stairs, perhaps from some late-night brawl in a bar or, more likely, premature arthritis. It was hard to tell but along with his manufactured energy there was something slightly weary about his affect that spoke of the passing years as much as living in a down at the heels apartment when you might have thought he'd merit a concierged condo down on the lakefront.

As we entered the adjacent living room, Frankie's girlfriend extricated herself from the deep cushions of the couch, showing a liberal amount of thigh as she did. She smoothed out her flame orange skirt and turned to face me, a slight pout on her small round face. Now she walked toward me, moving her lips in a way she knew would be effective with any man. She held out her small hand and we shook fingers. "I'm Cindy," she said. "Nice to meet you. You guys want something to drink?"

It was a small gesture but one my wife would never have made because of the implied suggestion that this woman should wait on us while we engaged in man-talk among ourselves. I found it almost unbearably attractive, bringing to mind as it did the girls with big hair and tight mohair sweaters I had known and lusted after in high school, many of whom had become pregnant before graduation and dropped out to take jobs as aestheticians. There was a kind of rough honesty to those girls. You want it, you're going to pay for it one way or another, they seemed to say. And while I had often flattered myself by thinking I was more high-minded than this, now I wondered at the choices I had made, choices that seemed logical at the time.

"Nah," Frank said now. "Andy ain't staying. Go watch TV so we can talk here." He slapped Cindy on the ass sending her out of the room. Then he pointed at an overstuffed chair. "Sit," he ordered. "Take a load off."

I sat and surveyed the room. The wall facing me looked as if a bomb had hit it, with the drywall and studs fully exposed and a small metal chimney extending through the wall. A wood stove sat on a thin metal tray that I was pretty sure wasn't conforming to anyone's code. As if to distract me, Frankie said lightly, "So, Andy. I hear you went over to the other side."

He smiled to let me know he wasn't serious, but I was again flattered by the assumption of a shared past. "No big deal," I said, lying. I was proud of my law degree, proud of where I'd come from and where I'd gone. "I'm in the trust department at Charney and Gates. Me and forty-five other lawyers."

Frankie nodded as if he knew what I meant. Then he said, "I wanted to tell you I was sorry about your old lady. She was quality all the way, real class. I liked her a lot. I just wanted you to know that."

Tears came to my eyes, which surprised me. I wanted to say, "If you liked her so much why didn't you pay the goddamned rent?" but I just mumbled, "She liked you too, Frank. She told me you were cute."

This made him laugh. "Yeah? Cute? Hey, that's great, I like that. Cute!" He shook his head and we sat silently for a moment.

Then I said, "What's with the hole in the wall, Frank? And I see you're a little behind in the rent." Getting tough with the tough guy, I liked it but I could feel my hands clammy with sweat.

Frankie gave me that half-smile again, only part of his lips moving about his pointed teeth. Half-sneer, half-smile. "Now you're really sounding like a landlord, Andy. That's another thing I liked about your old lady. Every time I went down there with a rent check, she looked surprised, like she'd forgotten all about it, like she'd forgotten I was her tenant. You know what I mean, like we were friends and it wasn't a business relationship. But you're a smart boy, aren't you, Andy? Always were and now you got that East Coast law degree and a hot wife to go with it."

I felt myself flush at this and wondered how he knew where I went to law school and whom I'd married. I willed myself not to feel intimidated. Instead, I smiled and said, "I just want to know where we stand, Frank. I can put you on a schedule, whatever works for you, but I've got a mortgage on this place so I've got to get the rent out of it."

Something I said must have resonated with the other man as he hunched his shoulders now and then shook out his hands as if they were wet. "Sure you do," he said. "I ain't gonna be a hardon about it, either. I mean, why? We're old friends, right?"

The way he said this I couldn't tell whether he was serious but I decided to take him at face value. "Right, Frank. We went to school together."

"Exactly. Hey, how about I give you a check tomorrow and every two weeks until I catch up. That work for you?"

As if it were the vig and I was his loan shark, but something was better than nothing. "Sure," I said, "no problem." Then I looked pointedly at the wall.

"Hey, it was cold as hell in here," Frank said. "I didn't want to bother your mom, sick as she was. I knew a guy who had some of these stoves. He fixed me up but I gotta get him back here to finish the job, put in the drywall, plaster, paint the wall like new. I'll call the asshole today. How's that?"

Arguing about this would have been pointless. I had asked for the rent and mentioned the stove; either he'd pay and fix it or he wouldn't. I'd deal with that later. For now, I'd made the contact and told him my concerns and that was enough for one day. I rose to indicate that I was satisfied, and Frank walked me to the door. As I walked down the stairs, I noticed the ratty, stained runner and water stains on the wallpaper and realized I was lucky to have a tenant at all in this dump, even one as unreliable as Frank Pignatano. The light was out in the hall and there was an odd odor in the vestibule. Whatever Mom's virtues, she hadn't been big on home improvement. I wondered idly if Moira was right about the house, though it seemed unlikely that what was wrong with it was beyond repair.

Frank called out after me, "And don't be a stranger, Andy. I'd like to meet your wife, maybe have you two over to dinner sometime."

The idea of Moira and me sitting down with Frank and Cindy for a meal almost made me smile, but I just nodded and waved back. This was Frank's way of delivering a pleasantry. He knew it was never going to happen and that was fine. Despite having a sense of power at actually facing him down after a fashion, a stranger was exactly what I wanted to be to Frank Pignatano. I didn't think my new associates at the law office would approve, and I knew my wife wouldn't. Despite the hail fellow well met act, I suspected Frank felt the same way about me.

"Whenever you want," I called back and headed home.

I had my reasons for returning to Milwaukee, reasons I had tried to explain to Moira even if I knew she wouldn't understand. I knew all that bullshit about not being able to go home again, but I didn't feel I was going back to the same place I had grown up—and wouldn't have wanted to. I had no desire to live in another floor-through on the lower East Side, eat TV dinners and take the bus when I had to go somewhere. That was another life and one I had fortunately escaped. At the same time, while I was glad to go east to school and grateful for the opportunities my education gave me, I'd never bought into the Ivy mystique, never wanted to join Tiger or Collegiate and go to wild parties on the Street when I was an undergraduate at Princeton.

And later when I was in law school I didn't care about the scarred tables down at Morry's or drunken Saturday afternoons singing "Boola, Boola" at the Yale Bowl. It would be an exaggeration to say I was on a mission, but it was something like that. It might have been different if I'd been born into that life, gone to Groton like my classmates and knew a comfortable life awaited me in the Connecticut suburbs or on the Main Line. But I was running scared from the past and in some vague way it seemed the best way to combat that was to reenter it by a side door.

While my friends from law school went off to New York or Boston to join prestigious firms, I turned down a job my father-in-law arranged for me through his political connections that not only would have paid more than I was making in Milwaukee but was more in line with my training and interests. I didn't fully understand Boston politics, but I knew it was an engine that ran on a complex web of backslaps, winks, and personal favors. My father-in-law was named Ed McQuaid and he had been one of Tip O'Neill's operatives in Cambridge at a time when that mattered. His nickname was Eddie Pockets because of his skill in coaxing campaign contributions out of reluctant voters, and I assumed Ed had called in a few IOUs to get me a job offer. But that wasn't enough to persuade me to accept it even though I knew neither he nor his daughter would forget or forgive my rejecting his generosity.

I had tried to explain things to my father-in-law, but he really couldn't see why anyone would prefer the Midwest over Boston or why his large Irish family would seem overpowering to someone who'd grown up alone with a single mother in a run-down apartment. Still, what was done was done and there was no calling it back. My problems now had more to do with working with my new colleagues and clients, dealing with my tenants and my wife's dissatisfaction with life in general, in inverse order of importance.

I'm not sure what I expected Moira's reaction to Milwaukee to be. While I was appreciative, and a little surprised, that she hadn't raised more hell at leaving Boston, I had hoped she'd be a sport about our new home, especially when we bought the home near the lake and got her an Audi to drive around town. Whatever my reasons for returning to Milwaukee, however, Moira hated almost everything about her new home. She didn't like Milwaukee's architecture, compared the art museum unfavorably to the BFA, turned up her nose at the local schools, having graduated herself from Miss Porter's and Smith, and refused to attend the symphony because she said it would only depress her to be reminded of the Boston Symphony. She was mildly impressed that the park outside our windows was designed by Frederick Law Olmsted and that Frank Lloyd Wright houses dotted the East Side, but Lake Michigan, which locals touted as the Great Inland Sea, was, she reminded me, a lake, not an ocean like the one she had left in Massachusetts to come to this cultural wasteland.

What's more, my homecoming had been somewhat underwhelming. My friends were pleased that I'd come to my senses and left behind the cesspool of the East, but life hadn't stopped while I was gone and the stream of existence hadn't altered since my return. I fit in easily, as I always had, which I found mildly disturbing. Because in my mind I had gone east to make a point, though I could no longer remember exactly what it was.

Even if the city as a whole wasn't overwhelmed by my return, however, there were some definite benefits in returning to Milwaukee, starting with my old friend Tom Williams who had gotten me a job at one of the best firms in town. Tom had stayed home when I left, attended Marquette law school, joined Charney and Gates after graduation, and rose quickly, making partner before he was thirty. Now at thirty-five he was on the management committee and thus able to do a favor for his high school friend. It probably wasn't very different from the favor my father-in-law had tried to do for me in Boston, but I preferred to owe Tom rather than Ed McQuaid.

Everyone has prejudices so I didn't really blame Moira for resisting the city, but I loved it and especially enjoyed being poor no longer. Even if Moira disdained the cultural opportunities of Milwaukee, we went where we liked, bought what we wanted, and seldom worried about the cost of anything. After a childhood of powdered milk, Spam sandwiches, and clothes from Sears, this was not an insignificant change for me. I also liked the idea of Milwaukee being a small town or a collection of small towns wrapped in a big city. I liked the fact that merchants would still run a tab for you, that the drug store would deliver, and that no one ever refused to take a check.

Perhaps because of the poverty of my childhood, I disliked drawing attention to myself and cultivated invisibility. Living here, I felt concealed, hidden away from the world as I never had in New Haven or Boston. Others may have been drawn to New York, Boston, San Francisco, or L.A. for the bright lights and glitter, but it was precisely the anonymity of Milwaukee within the national community that I liked. The absence of recognizable landmarks and famous writers, artists and composers. Milwaukee wasn't even on the weather maps you saw on the evening news, as if weather didn't happen between Chicago and Minneapolis.

The Milwaukee Repertory was good, but not that good. The local paper had won a few Pulitzers back in the day but no one really cared. And while the universities, like all universities, bragged up their few distinguished professors and departments, no one ever worried if they were as good as Harvard or Yale.

That's not to say that the locals didn't recognize or value quality; it just didn't impress them very much. It wasn't the way Milwaukeeans evaluated themselves or anyone else. And while there weren't a lot of famous people in town, there were celebrities who were *from* Milwaukee. Spencer Tracy, say, or Fredric March or Alfred Stieglitz, all of whom had left for one reason or another. Those who remained were relatively obscure and determined to remain so. You'd meet someone at lunch and discover inadvertently that he'd been a finalist for the National Book Award in poetry or learn that someone else had graduated from Juilliard before coming back to the Midwest. People like Moira's father might look down their noses at us, if it gave them satisfaction, amid the dog eat dog struggle of a daily life we'd never want. But you could live here, burrow into whatever interested you, make dramatic mistakes, and feel content in the knowledge that the wide world would never know or care. This was narcotic to me.

19

I could have tried to explain all this to Moira or dismissed her disdain of the city as the bad temper of an East Coast elitist, but that wasn't really true or fair to her. Moira had turned her back on four generations of Bostonians, a large family, most dramatically her father, as well as an old boyfriend named Billy Phelps, to follow me out here. No one she knew could understand how she could leave all that for what passed for civilization in the Midwest. But I knew why; we loved each other. Even if I found her complaining unpleasant, the fact that she had given up something to come with me was undeniable. I owed her.

To make matters more complicated, we were trying to get pregnant. I say "we" because that's the convention, but if and when the operation were successful it would be Moira who was pregnant, not me, Moira who would have to put up with the weight gain, morning sickness, and go through the pain of delivery. You'd have to say that on the whole my part in the process was small if unavoidably important and perhaps as a result I felt most of the time like a bit player, standing ready to respond when needed but not central to the drama.

Moira's doctor had assured her that the average time for couples to conceive was a year, but she possessed a vein of fatalism and after six months of trying she decided she was doomed to be barren and alone in Wisconsin, that my sperm were probably not energetic enough, lacking the essential motility to swim through her uterus to new life, and that, to put it mildly, something was terribly wrong. I didn't take this personally, or not too personally. After all, we'd been married for nearly ten years before she took on this crusade and when I thought about it at all, which wasn't often, I'd reconciled myself to a life without children. Most of the people I knew who had kids complained about them constantly and while I had grown up with the idea that a life without children wasn't a fulfilled life, experience had taught me otherwise. Was having me really such a great step for my mother, who had previously been a working artist in New York free to come and go as she pleased? It sounded odd to regret my own birth, but it had been at best a mixed blessing for Mom.

Moira and I had traveled, worked in various places, and had a full life together, so I felt no urgency to alter it now. When Moira got this way, however, I'd discovered there was no good way of persuading her that whatever happened would be for the best. Though essentially a good-natured person, when her Black Irish pessimism emerged the only workable strategy was to wait it out. In the meantime, she would sit splay-legged on the bed, chin in her hands, black hair falling over her forehead and cry. It was an affecting sight but I had learned to fight my natural tendency toward sentimentality because her moods seldom lasted long.

"Look at the bright side," I said one morning. "If we don't have kids we'll have more money. We can retire sooner."

"You're thirty-five, Andy. Why are you talking about retiring? I thought you loved the law. You always said you were passionate about it; it made me jealous."

I had said that when I was still in school and was inspired by famous jurists of the past. Brandeis, Learned Hand, William Douglas. It was hard not to feel excited about the law when you were reading opinions by those guys, but equally difficult to feel much one way or another when you were helping Rose Hoffman draw up her will in such a way that none of her five children would inherit anything. I had originally thought I'd be a civil rights lawyer fighting for the downtrodden, arguing cases that future generations of students would read about in their casebooks. I hadn't imagined then that my path in the law would involve helping wealthy misanthropes conceal assets. But I didn't want to admit this to Moira, so I backtracked.

"I still like it," I said. "I just mean we could spend more time together."

Moira gave me the half-smile that meant she wanted to believe this but didn't, or didn't today. Now she groped herself. She had read in a women's magazine that in addition to taking her temperature, vaginal mucous was a good way to gauge fertility. She rubbed something between her fingers and held up her hand for my inspection. "What do you think?" she asked.

I wasn't sure what I was looking at but tried to be clinical in these situations because the fact was I found the whole thing off-putting, especially since whenever she decided the time was right I was expected to be ready to perform immediately. Fortunately, her beauty left me in a constant state of arousal, but there was something comical about the exploration of her nether regions. "Looks fine to me," I said now.

Without further comment, Moira lay back on the pillows. "Then come on," she said.

Sex had always gone well for us and in a short time Moira began to respond, moving subtly against me and then harder until finally I came and collapsed on top of her. For a moment we lay together in exhausted fulfillment, for once without irony or dissatisfaction with anything between us.

"Oh, Andy," she said and kissed me on the cheek. "I love you. It's just that I hate this city."

I left the house whistling. Morning sex will do that for you. It may sound self-involved but while I needed Moira's love and affection, I didn't really need her to love Milwaukee. To me, the city was like an unattractive child. It took time and patience to learn to love it. With gray skies six months of the year and blocks of unattractive apartment buildings marching north and south on undistinguished avenues, there was much that was ugly about this place. I saw that, but I also saw other things. Not just the lake, huge and gray-green on our eastern border, and not even the large parks laid out by dour German socialists who took public service as seriously as religion. I liked what Milwaukeeans called *gemutlichkeit,* the tendency of a complete stranger to interview you about every aspect of your existence and seem truly interested. There was an openness I considered midwestern that I had never found in the East, where doors were kept locked and people were similarly protective of their inner selves.

People in Milwaukee weren't constantly looking over their shoulders, examining their mirrored reflections, because no one was watching. This tendency extended to the small-talk that I found to be the pitch and gravel of life, the impulse to extend oneself in small ways, something Moira thought superficial and I found reassuring. No doubt we were both right.

The city's ease and friendliness did not extend to my law firm, however, where thirty associates ran around all day with clenched teeth worrying about their futures while the firm's partners luxuriated in Olympian superiority behind closed doors with frosted glass panels.

This morning I had hardly settled in when I heard a knock and Tim Harter seated himself in my clients' chair. "You're late," he said. "And trust me, Williams noticed."

Harter was of medium size with a round face and thin butterscotch hair which lay lacquered against his scalp in what I assumed was a purposeful arrangement. He had thick glasses held together with tape, no doubt because he was too busy to get them repaired. I liked him but was glad not to be similarly driven. I looked at my watch. It was eight-thirty, not late, but I knew Tom Williams never arrived later than eight. No one had formally given me hours when I was hired. The assumption seemed to be that we were professionals and would work until the work was done. But it was a competitive situation and whatever leeway my Yale degree had conferred in the beginning had long since lapsed.

"Did I miss anything?" I asked. Harter looked at me with the cagy eagerness a fox might reserve for a chicken.

"There was a staff meeting," he said. "Well, not a formal meeting, just a group of associates and partners who happened to be around."

"Unlike me," I said, but my good humor gave me away. I couldn't regret making love to my wife, even if it had caused me to be late to the office.

Harter shrugged and sat back in the chair. "No one took attendance; they were just talking about billing. Apparently, we're not fucking enough people regularly enough, if you get my drift."

This wasn't hard to understand. Milwaukee wasn't Boston but the game was the same in any large law firm. A partner might charge a client $700 an hour while most of the work was done by an associate who billed less than half of that. At the initial meeting, the partner would be present to establish the billing structure while afterwards the client would deal almost exclusively with associates or paralegals. So far this had worked well for me because of the Ivy League patina, but it was tricky, a love-hate relationship with my clients who were suspicious of easterners. It helped to the extent that it was common knowledge I was a local boy who had the good sense to come back home after getting my degree.

"So I didn't miss much," I said. "But I'd better get in there now?"

Despite Harter's warning, I wasn't really worried about being late or Tom Williams's disapproval. We had known each other since the third grade, gone with the same girls, competed together on the basketball team, and lived in each other's houses when things were stressful at home. It didn't mean Tom would always give me a free ride, but it was hard to be intimidated by someone whose mother still sent you cookies at Christmas.

When I walked into his corner office, Williams was bent over peering into the kind of fancy new telescope all the heavy hitters were buying as furniture that year. "Checking out the galaxies?" I said. "Got to aim high in our business."

Williams shrugged and smiled. He was a tall ungainly man who looked much as he had at fourteen, all knees and elbows with an increasingly high forehead. "Actually, I've been watching my dream girl over on the twenty-sixth floor of the First Wisconsin Center."

"Some things never change," I said. And it was true. Before Tom was a big shot in suspenders and a Brioni suit he got his kicks following girls' dresses up the stairwells at school. "What did you need to see me about?"

For a moment, he looked stunned, as if I had put him on the spot about something. "Nothing, really," he said. "Everything going okay, your cases, clients?"

"I don't know. You tell me. Any complaints so far?"

"You've only been here a couple of years. It takes time to learn to mistrust you." He smiled, big teeth filling up his face, letting me know he wasn't serious. In another situation it might have been awkward for your boss to be an old friend but to me Tom was insulation from the rest of the world. Our lives had gone in different directions but our friendship remained solid so when he offered me a job I didn't think of it as a favor but rather as an extension of all that had gone before.

"You remember a guy named Frank Pignatano from high school?" I said now.

"Frankie the Pin? Scary little shit as I recall. Father connected with the mob or something? What about him?"

"It turns out I'm his landlord. He was living on the second floor of the house on Hackett and Mom made me promise to keep all the tenants."

I expected Tom to be surprised but it takes a lot to surprise a lawyer. He just smiled and cracked his knuckles. "Interesting," he said. "Millie's even got her hooks in you from the grave, doesn't she, Andy?"

Tom's tone was jocular but there was an edge of seriousness in his voice. We both knew part of the reason I had gone away to school was to get away from my mother. We'd been close, closer than close, and now that she was gone it was hard for me to think of the house, her house, as just a piece of real estate. It was more like some kind of trust that I'd been named to watch over and protect. I knew I had to get over this but it was hard. I had trouble even looking at pictures of my mother without feeling sad. So I had things to work out but not today, not at this moment. So I kept the tone light. All my friends were on familiar terms with my mother, but Tom had a special place in her heart. After I left town he became a sort of surrogate son and her death upset him almost as much as it did me. "I don't know, maybe. But I can't just throw the guy out."

"Especially with his connections," Tom said, laughing now. "They'd be fishing you out of Lake Michigan."

"Right. Hey, thanks for your counsel and advice. Can I go back to work now?"

Tom spread his arms wide, indicating the office, Milwaukee, the whole world as far as I knew. "Absolutely, get out there and bill. This place doesn't run on good intentions."

I was having lunch at Plotkin's on Oakland Avenue. It was one of the pleasures and limitations of returning home that everything was familiar to me. It was comforting that there was little that seemed new about my new life. This might not have been true, or as true, if I had moved to one of the suburbs growing like ganglia to the north, but I wanted to live near the lake, no matter what Moira said. What was the point of coming home if you avoided everything you knew was good about the place?

I had been going to Plotkin's since I was a kid and every waitress in the place brought my usual without my asking. I knew the hole in the west wall was from a fight in junior year when Joe Rose knocked Jimmy Reardon's head against the wall. I remembered hanging out on the corner outside on warm summer nights and fights and girlfriends I'd had even if their names and faces were no longer sharp in my mind.

In the old days Milwaukee had been a city of ethnic rivalries. "What" you were mattered more than who you were or wanted to be because where you came from, who your people were, *was* who you were or would ever be in most cases. Genetic determinism was the order of the day. Family mattered, religion mattered, the part of town where you grew up mattered more than the job you did. In fact, if you happened to rise above the expectations people had of you, you would need to spend a good part of your time letting them know you were still the same deep down and that success hadn't gone to your head. It was modesty borne of paranoia.

Deep in thought as I was, I hadn't noticed Vince D'Amato come into the restaurant, something that was remarkable considering Vince's size and heft. When he played football at Riverside, Vince probably went two-forty, big for a high school kid, but now he looked considerably larger than that. His face was broad and pockmarked and looked as if a stamping machine had run across it. His rug of black hair sat low on his forehead and now he stood in front of my table casting a shadow.

"Too good for your old buddies, Andy?" he said. He grinned maliciously and without waiting for an invitation sat down.

"Never too good for you, Vince. How's crime treating you?" Unlike Frank Pignatano, Vince actually was a tough guy. He had been involved in various illegal activities around the area since he was in junior high. This was so well known that it wasn't even worth joking about.

Now he leaned forward, his large arms taking up most of the table. "Always a comic, Andy." He punched my shoulder playfully. Then he turned serious. "Hey, I just wanted you to know we're proud of you, all of us around here on the East Side, even if no one ever says so. In my business, you hear things. I even hear about you down to the courthouse when I'm there. People talk about you going off out of state and now coming back. That's a big deal to people here; that you wanted to come back to us."

He sat back, apparently exhausted by his speech, but I was touched. "Thanks, Vince," I said. "I didn't know anyone gave a shit, to tell the truth."

He shrugged. "The way people are on the East Side. The last thing they'd want you to know is that anything you do matters, but I'm here to say it does. Okay?"

"Great," I said. "You want to stay and eat."

Vince made a face. "I can't eat this Jew shit," he said. Then he punched me again, perhaps a bit harder this time, to show he wasn't serious. "Catch you later, but remember what I said."

Finishing lunch, I was struck by the odd antimony of my situation. Wherever I went, there was some elemental way in which I'd never been able to leave Milwaukee. I had thought that going east to school, marrying well, and getting a law degree would accomplish that, would erase the memory of poverty and loneliness I'd grown up with. But it hadn't. If I stopped and allowed my feelings in, it was right there where I'd left it all those years ago. Sitting in Plotkin's eating corned beef I realized that while much had changed in my life, most of it was superficial. The bedrock facts of life never altered, and it seemed to me now that they never would.

Although she disdained most things about Milwaukee, Moira had a paradoxical gift for making friends and in a short period of time she had gathered a group of women around her whom she saw nearly every day. When I got home one of them, Patsy Steiner, was in our kitchen drinking coffee. Patsy was a small, wiry woman with a brown face and a helmet of black hair who was arresting because of her obsessive honesty about everything. With Patsy, you always had to be on your toes, even about the simplest things.

"How are you, Patsy?" I asked.

"My hair's falling out," she said. "Unusual in a woman my age, but there you are." Patsy was dressed as always in blue jeans, running shoes, and a shapeless sweater with the sleeves pushed up. She wouldn't have worn the shoes if she wasn't a runner because she disapproved of fashion, but she had been a marathoner before her knees gave out. I wasn't sure she actually had any other shoes. I sometimes went running with her and because of her modesty and loose clothes had been surprised by Patsy's shapely legs and ass in shorts. I had always liked thin women, but I pushed this image out of mind now.

"Looks okay to me," I said.

Patsy was not the sort to let something like this go by. To prove her point, she parted her hair with her fingers to reveal a nascent widow's peak. "It's thin in back, too," she said. "One of my students mentioned it to me. Livened up my lecture on Hopkins, I'll tell you that."

"'No worst, there is none,'" I said, hoping to impress her.

Patsy smiled. "Very good, Andy. You can take the boy out of the Ivy League, but you can't take the Ivy League out of the boy." She taught at the university and liked to tease me about my education.

Moira came into the room looking unreasonably attractive in a bright turquoise tunic. "Are you flirting with my husband again?" she asked.

"Always," Patsy said. "I've never met a lawyer before who's actually read Victorian poetry and remembers what he read."

For all her learning, Patsy had never understood that sarcasm wasn't true wit. She was always trying too hard and her breezy reply implied something, though I wasn't sure what. I'd always been loyal to Moira, but out of habit I wondered idly if I had a chance with Patsy. With her boyish clothes and gamine look, there was something oddly alluring about her but why did I even notice? I was happy with my wife, content with my situation generally. Not for the first time I wondered if man existed for any reason other than to seduce any woman he could. It was at once a disturbing and exciting idea.

"Patsy and I are going to the art museum," Moira said now, breaking into my thoughts. "She says they've got some killer new Alsatian marble to add to the permanent collection of tom-toms and Indian pottery."

"You shouldn't make fun of the Native American collection," I said. "People who know about these things say it's one of the best in the country."

Moira shrugged. "I'm sure," she said. "But when you get down to it, who cares? Want to come along?"

"I've got to get back to the office," I said. "I just came by to pick something up." This wasn't really true. I didn't know why I had come home in the middle of the day, but maybe I didn't need a reason. Perhaps home was just something that exerted its own pull, gravitational and real.

I took the long way back downtown, looping down Lake Drive to Lincoln Memorial and then along the lake, vast and beautiful on a sunny afternoon, past the Yacht Club and the Art Museum jutting out into the air as if it was going to fall into the water. I replayed the conversation with Vince in my mind and wondered whether he or anyone was really pleased that I was back. And if so, why? I wasn't sure how Tom and Vince and Moira and Patsy could all coexist somewhere in my psyche, and yet I had recently seen them all and moved easily in conversation and association with them. Not that this was so unusual, but now more than ever human relationships seemed to be a confusing, interlocking maze that never really seemed to lead anywhere.

I came in through the back door and leafed through my messages before venturing outside my office. All involved questions about trusts, estates, and wills I'd either prepared or was supposed to be working on. I stuffed them in my pocket and wondered why I ever got into the law, something I thought about more often these days, though the answer was easy. I liked living in a big house near the lake and driving a nice car. These weren't things you were supposed to admit, but having grown up as I had I was without guilt with regard to material things. Now the phone on my desk buzzed. I shared a secretary named Sherry with the other associates, so I tried to save her trouble by not putting more work on her than was necessary. But this had the opposite effect and she frequently stuck her head in the door to ask if I didn't have something for her to do. "Yes?" I said now.

31

Sherry was whispering into the phone. "Andy, there's a very scary guy out here who wants to see you."

It was unusual for anyone to simply arrive at my office without an appointment. What I did wasn't really a walk-in business, and few of my clients were under seventy or traveled anywhere without a walker and an oxygen tank. "Scary?" I said. Sherry had gone to Catholic schools and was unnerved by many things. "What does he want?"

"To see you," she hissed. "Should I call security?"

Sherry seemed sincerely disconcerted by my visitor, but this was the most interesting thing that had happened to me professionally in some time and I was reluctant to let it go. "Does he have a name?"

"Everyone does," Sherry said. "But I forgot what it is. He says he knows you. Frank. Something eyetalian, I think."

Frankie the Pin in my outer office, I thought. What were the chances? "Well, just send him on in here," I said.

Although it wouldn't have been obvious to Sherry, Frank had cleaned himself up for this occasion. Instead of his characteristic sleeveless muscle shirt, he was wearing a black double-vented suit with a crimson shirt open to the breastbone in order to display an impressive set of gold chains. A violet pocket square drooped out of his breast pocket. He stepped a few feet into the office, stuck his hands in his pockets and looked around. Then he let out a low whistle. "Class," he said admiringly. "Real class, Andy."

I probably should have been pleased that Frank approved, but the fact was I found this embarrassing. Compared to others in the firm, my office was simple, even Spartan. No telescopes here or leather furniture. But Frank was clearly impressed by the Audubon prints and faux Stickley furniture Moira had assembled to decorate the place. I gestured toward a chair and wondered why Frank had come. Maybe to pay his rent as I hadn't yet received the promised check.

"What can I do for you?" I asked and moved a yellow pad next to my elbow.

32

But Frank was in no hurry. He sat in my clients' chair and patted his thighs. He looked around the room again and shook his head. Then he straightened his collar and sat up, ready for business. "I need a lawyer," he announced.

This didn't surprise me. I assumed a guy in Frank's business would always need a lawyer, but I had somehow imagined a team of attorneys in Armani suits on retainer ready to serve him at a moment's notice. Why come to me? "I don't do criminal law," I said with some regret. "But other people here do. I could give you some names."

Frank waved his hand in front of his face as if I were a troublesome gnat. "It ain't like that," he said. "This is, what you call it, civilian."

"A civil case?" I wondered if protocol dictated that I call in Tom Williams at this point, but at least this was my general area.

"Right," Frank said. "Civil. You remember that bitch you met at my place, when you came by about the rent?"

I felt it would not be lawyerly to agree even tacitly that she was a bitch but nodded anyway. "Cindy?" I said, surprised that I remembered her name. Actually, it was the orange skirt—or more precisely the way she filled it up—that I remembered.

"Her," Frank spit out. "Bitch, cunt." He looked around the office angrily as if she might be hiding behind an ottoman.

"Take it easy," I said. "What's the problem?"

Frank seemed uneasy, wary. He cut his eyes and looked at me. "So is this that lawyer shit now, confidential, whatever? You know what I'm saying?"

He wasn't my client, but I doubted he'd appreciate subtleties and it was unlikely that I'd be called to testify about a fight he was having with his girlfriend. At the same time, I felt there was some element of performance about all of this. Frank knew more than he was letting on about legal proceedings. Anyone who had done time in Green Bay had to understand the system pretty well. It was the same instinct that led politicians to speak ungrammatically and shorten their names. "I won't tell," I said.

He shook his head. "That ain't good enough." He thought for a moment. "What you get an hour down here—four, five hundred?"

This was a good deal more than associates made at our firm, but I didn't want to reveal this to Frank, at least not yet. "That would cover it."

He nodded, took a roll of bills out of his pocket and peeled off five of them. "So I'll hire you for an hour and tell you what's going on. After that, you can decide if you want to be my permanent lawyer."

I looked at the bills on the desk and wondered why he'd dragged his feet about the $300 a month rent, or if that was performance too, a feeling he shouldn't be held to the same requirements others were. "Fine," I said, wondering if I was doing the right thing. "You're my client for an hour. So tell me what's going on between you and Cindy."

Frank sat in his chair and examined his boot for a moment. Then he said, "I kicked her ass out of the house."

A lovers' quarrel. This didn't really seem like a legal matter, but I assumed there was more to it than this. I tried to look interested. "These things happen," I said.

"That's what I thought," Frank said bitterly. "I was with her three years, moved her in before your old lady died, bought her everything she wanted, took her to Vegas, spent a shitload on the bitch and now this."

I thought again of him withholding rent while spending thousands gambling in the fleshpots of the country but tried to stay professional. "Now what exactly, Frank?"

"The cunt's suing me," he said. "Palimony or something. Says I owe her big time."

I was only vaguely aware of the laws regarding palimony and thought of it as primarily involving celebrities, movie stars, and rock singers who lived together as man and wife and then split up. It wasn't the kind of thing that came in the doors of Charney and Gates on a regular basis, and I had the feeling the prudent thing would be to send Frank away. "You made promises?" I said, helping him along.

"I made dick," Frank said. "I didn't tell her nothing, didn't sign nothing. It's all bullshit, Andy."

I nodded, beginning to understand. "But she's saying you made promises or agreed to pay something to her on a long-term basis?"

"Yeah, I don't know, maybe. All I know is I got a call from her lawyer and I'm hip enough to get it that this ain't a good sign, know what I mean?"

I did, but I also knew that I shouldn't go further with this without talking to a senior lawyer. I wasn't even supposed to open a folder on a prospective client without approval from on high, but I figured I could get around this by explaining this was just a conversation with a friend. Which was as far as I wanted to take it in any case, but the truth was I was getting interested.

"Okay," I said. "I get it, but that's all I can listen to for now without talking to someone else here. Give me Cindy's lawyer's name. I'll talk to Tom Williams and see what we can do for you."

Frank shook his head slowly. "I don't want anyone else in on this, Andy. Not even Tommy Williams. I understand you got to tell him, that's okay, but you're my guy, all right? I ain't really interested in this getting around with my crew, you know?"

I didn't know if I could be his guy or not, but there was no need to get into that. What was interesting was that, more than being scared by whatever action his girlfriend was going to take against him, Frank Pignatano was embarrassed that this could be in open court and make the papers. Having spent his life trying to impress people with his toughness, Frank hadn't succeeded in scaring his girlfriend at all. I wanted to know more about that.

I walked Frank to the door and he stood in the doorway, hands curled at his sides, getting ready to do his cock walk out the door. He stretched his neck and looked around the outer office to make sure no one was listening to us. "Okay, so you ain't telling no one else, am I right?"

I nodded. "I've got to mention it to Tom and then I'll get back to you, but that's it. If I can represent you, that is. If I think I can do anything for you, I will. Otherwise, I'm going to suggest someone who'd be better."

Frank poked me in the chest. "I don't want anyone else, Andy. I told you that. It's bad enough I had to tell you about it. Pain in the ass."

He opened the door and we walked into the outer office. Sherry cringed at her computer, but I smiled in what I hoped was a reassuring way as I watched Frank leave. Then I turned to her. "Can you get Mr. Williams on the phone for me?" I asked.

My mother worked at various jobs in her life, but she never allowed any of them to define her. What she was, what she said she had always been since experiencing a lightning flash of insight at the age of seven, was an artist. For her, this had little to do with making money, though early on she had sold some of her paintings through galleries. What her work spoke of instead was a way of life, or more exactly a way of seeing life, perhaps a calling. She tried to pass this on to me, though not in any overt way such as demanding that I take art lessons or even appreciate art in any specific way. We would sit on the back porch drinking coffee and she would hold her hand up and trace the outline of a tree or flower in the air, wordlessly, just holding it there for me to see. Often enough I didn't, but she loved me anyway and maybe that was the real point in the end.

Whether it was or not, art made my mother sure of herself in a way that few other people I ever met were able to match. She knew who she was; it was that simple and that complex. It had nothing to do with what the world saw in her or valued and nothing to do with conventional ideas of success or failure. While she wasn't exactly disappointed when I became a lawyer, I imagined a kind of spiritual sigh in recognition that what she had spent her life on had not been transmitted to the one person most important to her.

It has always bothered me that because of life demands my mother wasn't free to paint full-time, not because I thought she was a great artist but because few people are called to do anything and those who are should be allowed to do it. But she was philosophical on the subject. "Maybe this was as much as I would have done no matter how much time I had," she said one afternoon toward the end. Then she reached over and ran her hand through my hair. "I regret not having more time with you," she said. "Not spending more time painting. I've done enough of that."

Sitting in a red overstuffed chair in the attic room she had used as a studio, I had to admit she'd done a lot. In addition to the forty canvases that lined the walls, there were ceramic tiles from her days as a potter and a half-dozen small sculptures, which sat on surfaces around the large sunny room. There was a limit to the amount of work Moira wanted to hang in our house so being here was my way of staying close to the only parent I remembered. This room was my private gallery. Oblong and intensely colorful, the paintings mirrored in the cut glass changed as the light lowered during the day. It represented my mother's artistic autobiography, going as it did from the representational pieces she'd done as a student in New York through her later experiments with Cubism and Expressionism. I had different feelings about the various periods; I didn't necessarily love everything equally. But taken together the paintings and sculpture especially were impressive and stood as evidence of a life fully lived, independently and often alone.

Trees in somber colors stood isolated on a gray background, a house, cars, a train station. Occasionally a group of people sitting together around a table, having a meal or talking. But that wasn't her world. Some still lifes and a few nudes also alone in their nakedness. None of this struck me as sad or depressing, though it was somber.

From where I sat I could look out through the beveled windows at the haloed oaks that lined the street far below. I liked to think it gave me perspective but perspective on what I wasn't quite sure. I liked the feeling of seclusion I got watching people who were unaware they were being observed. A lithe young woman walked among her lilac bushes, head tilted upward toward the light. A painter prepared a surface across the way, his hands sweeping along the wood like the hands of a clock. There was a larky lack of self-consciousness to their gestures, a pleasure in awkwardness that gave rise to an odd instinctual grace that wouldn't have been present otherwise.

I tried to avoid tenants when I made my visits to the attic, preferring to experience it all alone, but on the way downstairs I ran into Ginnie Walker, who lived on the first floor with her lover, a realtor. Ginnie taught sports medicine at the university and, unlike Frank, I had been pleased to find her as a tenant after Mom died. I had always heard lesbians were easier to deal with than either men or single women. From the beginning, however, Ginnie found fault with everything in the house. Mom would have smiled sweetly and ignored her requests, but I had a built-in desire to help women so this was hard for me. It didn't help that Ginnie was beautiful with large inviting breasts that often floated free in a loose T-shirt. Now she was wearing khaki slacks and a crisp white shirt with her breasts straining the fabric. "Going to class?" I said lightly.

"I was going to call you," Ginnie said.

"A social call?" I said, bantering with her for no good reason.

She looked puzzled and decided to ignore my comment. "We told you before, we need a light."

"You don't have lights?" I asked, looking around her, as if the empty hall would reveal something.

"Not in the house," she said. "Outside. In the driveway. It makes Sandra nervous to walk from the house to the car in the dark."

I doubted Sandra, who was built like a linebacker, had anything to worry about from potential rapists, but saying this would be unkind and wouldn't help matters. "Have you had problems? Noticed anyone lurking out there at night?"

Ginnie looked annoyed. "That's not the point. We don't want to have problems down the line, okay? Jesus."

I shrugged. "It'll have to wait a while. We're stretched pretty thin right now." It was true. I'd already put in new drywall and carpet and painted their place after Mom's death. Given the fact that Frankie didn't pay and I didn't want to raise Ginnie's rent, I was running at a deficit and Moira had definitely noticed.

Ginnie put her hands on her hips and sighed. I waited for her to stamp her foot, but the truth was I wanted one of my tenants to pay the rent on time and the others to stop raising hell about everything. "Look, Mr. Simonson," Ginnie said now. "I'm sure you're a gentle person in other situations, but I don't see why you're giving me shit about this."

The problem, I knew, was that I wanted her to like me, to react to me as women had all my life. I wanted to charm her in a harmless way, but she wasn't going to be charmed, at least not by me. It was mathematical, an unbridgeable truth without regard to whether I wanted it that way or not. Time to give it up.

"I'm not that gentle," I said. "Here or anywhere. But I didn't say I wouldn't put in another light, only that it would have to wait. Maybe a month. Until then you two could walk together to the car or park in the driveway. Or something else, I don't know what. Okay? Got to go. Have a nice day."

When I got home Patsy was gone and Moira seemed in a more congenial and forgiving mood. She even liked the new museum exhibition, but she bristled when I mentioned my conversation with Ginnie.

"So you've got a couple of demanding women on the first floor and a gangster upstairs who won't pay his rent. That's just great, Andy. Tell me again exactly why you wanted to be a landlord?"

"I didn't," I said patiently. "You know that. It's just that as it happens, I am one. Right now." This didn't seem the time to tell her about Frank peeling bills off his roll in my office that afternoon.

"And you can't change that, get rid of that dump before it falls down and the tenants sue you for damages?"

The house was actually sturdily built and most of the problems were cosmetic. But we weren't really talking about that. "No," I said. "I can't."

"Can't or won't?"

"Does it matter?" I walked over and put my arms around her.

She didn't answer directly. "You know I loved your mother, Andy. Not that that's so unusual, because everyone loved her. But I did. She was an amazing person."

I nodded. That was part of the problem, most of the problem. Had Mom been any less admirable, any less a fighter or an East Side character in her farmer's overalls and red bandana, it wouldn't be so hard now to disregard her last wishes. But she was, and as disreputable as her house and tenants were, they actually gave me back a small part of my mother, a part I didn't want to lose.

"But whether we loved her or not," Moira continued, "she's not here anymore and we can't go on trying to please her fucking tenants just because that's what she would have done."

Her point was so reasonable it was hard to disagree, especially when she spoke without irony, but she didn't really understand. Mom wouldn't have done a thing to accommodate the lesbians. She would have smiled sweetly and gone on her way and they would have liked it. It was that sweetness that I couldn't manage. "I know," I said. "This won't go on forever."

41

"How long?" Moira asked, an edge in her voice.

How long was love, how long was filial responsibility? That long, but I wanted to stay married too. "Maybe a year or two."

"A year," she said, incredulous. "Two? Jesus, it's already been that long. I'm going for a walk, I can't take this shit." As she left the room, she threw over her shoulder, "Someone from your office called. For Tom Williams, I think."

"Hey," I called after her back. "Thanks for letting me know." It was part of Moira's ongoing resistance to our move to Milwaukee that she treated my professional life like a hobby. It was flattering in a way since her assumption was that I was so much more gifted than my colleagues that I could ignore my responsibilities and still make six figures no problem. But usually she delivered messages sooner or later, often leaving notes scrawled on return envelopes from the gas company or a department store. The house was quiet with her gone, but Moira's mood swings didn't bother me. We'd been together long enough for me to distinguish a rhythm, a kind of loose pattern in these things. If I left her alone for a time she'd start to feel differently independent of anything I could do or say. This represented some learning on my part since my tendency was to try to fix things, but now I felt at loose ends, aimless and without direction. It was late afternoon, that time when it's no longer possible to pretend that this will be a day of accomplishment, when the onset of evening and the run of meals, television, an ineffectual run at a novel, and then bed presents itself as numbing repetition, but I was powerless to break the pattern.

Tom hadn't been in when Sherry called earlier but I knew he'd still be at the office, that secretaries would be typing and filing and eating at their desks, that work would be going on and that I should be there to witness it. That was how you made partner; no one had to tell me that. Still, standing in my living room after Moira left, I felt no urgency about returning Tom's call. I sat in a recliner and turned on the TV, flipping through channels, perhaps reassuring myself that I was still my own man, a free agent, at large and not tethered to the law firm.

This worked for a half-hour or so. Then I got in the car and drove back downtown. I didn't exactly feel guilty for spending most of the afternoon admiring Mom's art, but there was a reasonable expectation on the part of my employer that I'd put in time in the office, meet clients, most important care about it all as desperately as Tim Harter did. We were all professionals and no one was required to punch in or out, but associates were supposed to bill two thousand hours a year, which worked out to around forty a week, and this didn't include vacations and downtime. It was hard to do the hours if you weren't in the office. So far I'd managed to make my quota, but I knew a reckoning was on the way.

When I got to the office, the usual roar of activity had lessened to an aggressive hum that resonated beneath everything. Some doors were closed, a few secretaries had been allowed to leave. I surveyed the pink message slips strewn across my desk and organized them as to order of urgency. None were important to me; the only one that required action was from Williams, whom I now saw had called three hours earlier.

"Sorry," I said when I reached him.

"I had a nice talk with Moira," he said.

"Really?" I was surprised. She generally had little time or patience for business and didn't like most of my Milwaukee friends.

"Well, relatively. She didn't hang up and gave you the message."

"I'd call that progress."

Tom laughed. Nothing bothered him, a trait I envied. When it was time to do something, he could pull the trigger but between now and then he would spend no time worrying about it. "So in your voicemail you said you'd had a meeting with Frankie the Pin," he said. "We need to talk about this. Meet me downstairs in half an hour."

43

Downstairs was actually a faux Irish bar a block away called Donovan's with shillelaghs on the wall, Guinness on tap, and signs everywhere saying things like "Erin go bragh." I'd forgotten why we started going there, but it was better than staying in the office. By the time Tom arrived, I was into my second draft and a pleasant haze was descending on the room.

He shrugged out of his jacket and blew the foam off a schooner. "So tell me how this happened with Frank," he said. "Last I heard you were his landlord but not his lawyer. Is this a way to recover that back rent?"

"I doubt it," I said. "That's probably a question of principle with him, and I'm not really his lawyer. I mean, I didn't agree to anything. He did peel a few hundreds off a roll for my hourly fee. Want your cut?"

Tom laughed. "Keep it," he said. "You've got an expensive wife."

"He's got a problem with his girlfriend," I said.

"Who doesn't?" Tom said. "I always figured guys like him had women hanging around constantly and they'd just change them out when they got bored."

"I guess that's what Frank thought he was doing. Maybe you two saw the same movies. Anyway, he threw this girl out but she crossed him by deciding to sue him. Palimony."

"Son of a bitch," Tom said. "How'd she know about that?"

"Probably saw it on *60 Minutes*, who the hell knows?"

"Ah, the miracle of telecommunications," Tom said. "So she's not afraid he'll put her in a lead overcoat in the Milwaukee River?"

"According to Frank she's hired a lawyer."

"Impressive, "Tom said.

"Breach of contract," I said. The street lights outside were beginning to come on. A few years back someone had decided to install fake gaslights and now the area looked like a stage set. Whoever did it must have imagined old Milwaukee actually looked like this. It didn't fool the locals but was supposed to appeal to Milwaukee's nonexistent tourist trade.

"And he wants us to represent him?" Tom said. He was drawing four-leafed clovers on the bar napkin, intent on his work.

The bar was filling up now. There was a trio with an Irish tenor in the front and the crowd around the bar was getting noisy. "No," I said. "He was pretty specific about that. He wants me to represent him. No one else."

Tom looked up from his drawing, interested now. "And did you inform Mr. Pin that we have some quaint rules in our firm about associates taking on clients on their own? Unless he wants you to draw up his will, which given his occupation could be a great idea."

"I told him I couldn't even open a file on my own without your say-so. I also asked him if his old man didn't have lawyers on retainer to keep him and his lowlife friends out of jail."

Tom smiled. "Same old Andy," he said. "Kicking ass and taking names. It does my heart good to hear it. What did Mr. Pin say to that?"

"He wants it to be separate from the family business. I doubt he's even told his dad about this. I think he's embarrassed being sued by an old girlfriend. Doesn't make him look like the ass man he wants to be."

"I can see that," Tom said. "Pretty reasonable from his point of view. Make a settlement offer and pay her off so she'll go away and leave him alone. Nice and clean and who needs to know?"

"Something like that," I said. "Anyway, he says he wants me to handle it, that if you don't let me he'll go somewhere else. For what it's worth, I think he means it, though I'm not sure why. The idea he can keep his old man and everyone else from knowing about this is bullshit. Milwaukee's still a small town in a lot of ways and I think this girl could have a big mouth."

"You've met the young lady?" Tom asked.

"Once," I said. "She's what you'd expect for Frank and I wouldn't have thought she'd sue him for damages. But if she's got representation she's already told at least one other person about it."

Tom nodded and drank some beer. The tenor had started in on "Danny Boy." Before long, grown men would be crying, arms around each other and joining in on the chorus. I had never understood the American romance with Ireland, the American take on a country that had great literature, soft green vistas, violent revolution, and grinding poverty. Most Americans thought only of a benign reality consisting of green beer on St. Pat's and Notre Dame football. This didn't go far to explain the thousands of young people who emigrated annually because there were no jobs and no hope of any.

It was now nearly seven and Moira would be back from her walk and wondering where I was, but Tom was in no hurry. "I have to say this wouldn't be our usual client, Andy. You know that. It's not really what we had in mind when we hired you. We tend to represent CEOs, not gangsters."

"Everyone deserves a defense," I said. "It's America."

"Right," Tom said and drank more beer. "You want to do this?"

"It sounds interesting."

"More than the usual run of widows and orphans?"

"Wealthy widows and orphans," I added. "Wills and contracts, all that, yeah, this sounds more interesting to me. But I'd keep my usual caseload and, like I said, I figure the girl will settle once she gets over being mad. She probably just wants money."

"A lot of money?"

"Maybe, but Frank'll be good for the fee. Like I said, I think he's really embarrassed and wants to make this go away as soon as he can."

"You think? I never knew the guy at school and doubt I'd recognize him on the street now." Tom took another swallow, his way of thinking. Then he put down the glass decisively. "Okay, this is how it goes. I'm the principal on the case and I open the file, but Frankie doesn't have to know that. You handle discovery, all the interrogatories, the girl's lawyer, the works. I've got to meet Mr. Pin at the initial interview but after that I'm in the background. I'll work it out with the partners and you handle everything else. That okay with you? Like I said, this isn't really our area and I don't know the first thing about palimony, but I think we can make it work."

"That sounds fine," I said. "Unless we go to court."

Tom nodded. "We really don't want that, but you said you're guessing it won't go that way."

"I don't think so."

Tom stood to leave. "Thinking can get you in trouble, Andy. Always has, your Achilles heel. Since we were kids." He patted me on the shoulder to show he wasn't completely serious, but I knew in a way he was. "Better get home to the wife now," he said and walked away.

I sat at the table for a few more minutes and listened to the music. It was "Irish Eyes" now and the place was wet with nostalgia, but I didn't care. For the first time since returning to Milwaukee, I felt like a lawyer again.

It snowed overnight, the kind of thick wet blanket that would have snarled traffic in New England and made kids late for school, if they went at all. I remembered the mayor of a town just west of Boston who'd announced one January morning after an all-night blizzard that the city would not send out plows or hire workers to shovel. "God made the snow and He'll take it away," the mayor said. Which He did, but not until April.

Milwaukee was different, the whole Midwest was. Here even a big snowstorm was a hiccup, a brief interruption in the forward progress of the city. Though the so-called Sewer Socialists who had run the city for thirty years were gone now, their influence lived on. The cardinal sin here would be a condition that prevented men from getting to work, which meant city crews were out at four a.m. and the streets were cleared overnight and if things really got bad plows could be attached to city dump trucks and buses while passenger cars trundled along in their wake. In Milwaukee bad weather didn't close schools or interrupt the normal flow of business.

I knew all this, but it seemed extravagantly irrelevant from where I stood, at my bedroom window looking out at the pure white vista of the park. From here, all hints of civilization were obliterated, the park buildings, tennis courts, even the park benches. Everything man-made was gone and I could imagine this was how it might have looked to settlers two hundred years ago. It was a way to start over, mentally at least, and I felt my mind clear away everything that might have weighed on me at another time on another morning. The idea of obliteration being calming was a little strange, but that's how it was working for me today.

I could hear Moira singing softly in the bathroom but even that worked its way into my fantasy where there were no angry tenants, no dissatisfied clients or disgruntled partners, nothing except the bland and beautiful whiteness of the snow under a perfect blue sky. But it was only seven and I knew peace like this couldn't last, which it didn't. At breakfast Moira announced she was going to see the doctor.

"Why?" I asked. "He said you were fine, that it's normal to take a while." Generally, we avoided actually saying the word pregnancy but danced around it with synonyms.

"I don't even know what normal means," Moira said. "Every day I see women on the street in muumuus with huge stomachs dragging three kids along behind them. You get the feeling they just pop them out effortlessly without even trying. So why not me? I take my temperature and tell you to wear boxers and come right home if it looks good and all the while I'm feeling worse and worse, like nothing will ever work."

I put my arms around her. "It's just one thing," I said. "Everything else works great and it always has."

She nodded and pulled away. "Yes, but not this and I hate it and I hate myself because of it. It's awful to think of sex as a job, especially when you fail all the time, but that's how it feels to me now. Anyway, it's easy for some doctor who has nothing at stake to say everything's fine. What does he have to lose? This isn't fine, Andy, and it's not going to be."

She was right, but that's why you went to doctors. They weren't emotionally involved and could look at things objectively. Still, I would never have thought of sex with Moira as being a job. We'd been together for more than ten years and it still seemed fresh and new to me, even if I didn't like the constant emphasis on fertility. "Do you want me to come with you?"

"Why?" Moira said. "We already know about your sperm. I just want to ask him some questions." She stopped, deep in thought. "Maybe I should just go back home for a while. Daddy knows a specialist at Mass General."

I recognized this as provocation, her ace in the hole whenever things got tough. In her view, doctors in the Midwest were hopelessly backward, still indulging in bleeding and cupping, unlike the great minds of the East. This wasn't true but there was no point in challenging her. And considering her general attitude toward living in Milwaukee, I knew I should be grateful she was passionately involved with something, anything. "Maybe you're pregnant already," I suggested.

"Right," Moira snorted. "You wish."

"That's right," I said. "I do."

When I got to the office there was a message saying John Alexander had called regarding Cindy's action. Alexander was a lawyer in a smaller firm, a good guy and smart. It struck me as an interesting choice for Frank's girlfriend because I knew she didn't get Alexander's name off late-night TV. He was an A-list guy and it made me think there might be more to this than Frank had let on, more to Cindy who it seemed had some connected friends. I took a deep breath and thought for a moment before returning the call. I looked around my office and wondered what kind of support I'd have if this case went anywhere. But this was getting ahead of myself. I couldn't feel bad about coming back to town and landing where I had. Beyond the exaggerated respect colleagues had for my Ivy League background, I wouldn't have Tom Williams watching my back at another firm. I had Tom to thank for a lot of things, not least his friendship.

Alexander and I played phone tag most of the day, but I finally got him late in the afternoon. "Sorry, Andy," he said. "I was in court all day." He hesitated, as if he had to remind himself, then he said, "I'm calling on behalf of Cynthia Braithwaite."

For a moment I thought we'd gotten mixed up in someone else's case, but then it dawned on me. "You mean Cindy?" I asked. "As in Frank Pignatano's girlfriend?"

Alexander laughed. "Yeah, and also as in Arthur Braithwaite's daughter."

The name was vaguely familiar but I hadn't been back long enough to know many people. "Isn't he a partner over there?"

"His name's on the door," Alexander said. "My boss, actually."

Great, I thought. Not only did Cindy have a good lawyer but her father was one too and a principal in an important firm. I wasn't sure where to go with that. "I was wondering how Cindy got involved with a classy guy like you," I said.

"Back at you with your client," Alexander replied.

"He's my tenant," I said. "I inherited him along with the house from my mother. She thought he was cute."

Alexander appreciated that. "I wonder if the guys who knew him at Green Bay felt the same way."

"I think his posse looked out for him in the joint," I said. "Or maybe friends of his dad's. Actually, back in the day we both went to Riverside and I sort of knew him, but we didn't really hang out."

"I get it," Alexander said. "Didn't take too many of those AP classes, did he? Let me tell you, Cindy's father wishes she'd never met Frankie."

"Not that bad a guy really," I felt obliged to add.

"Sticking up for your client," Alexander said. "I like that in a lawyer."

"So let's cut to the chase," I said. "What's it going to take to make this go away, John?" I figured we might as well see what we were in for. I knew Williams would want to know that just for starters.

"Miss Braithwaite is heart-broken," Alexander said. "And she's insulted by the way Mr. Pignatano treated her."

Cindy hadn't really struck me as the sensitive type when I met her, but there was no point in disrespecting her now. "You mean her old man is?" I said.

"It comes to the same thing," Alexander said. "Let's just say neither of them is in a conciliatory mood."

I looked out my window toward the lake, ice blue in the distance. The snow had stopped now but it was cold and steam rose from the water just offshore. Drivers in the street below revved their engines and I could hear tires spinning. October snow always caught everyone off balance without snow tires or tune-ups. Dead batteries and fender benders were all pieces of that world out there I wasn't a part of at the moment. "You didn't answer my question, John. I know you have to posture for the client, but just between us girls, what's it going to take?"

I heard Alexander's exhalation of breath. "I don't know, to tell the truth. They're both pissed off but for different reasons. Arthur grew up in the Third Ward and moved his family to Whitefish Bay after he made some money just so his daughter wouldn't ever have to deal with guys like Frank Pignatano. He sent her to Holy Angels and some finishing school out East only to have her come back home and move in with a gangster."

"That's a little harsh, but it makes a kind of sense when you put it that way. I have to say I wouldn't have pegged Cindy as a Holy Angels girl."

"President of her class," John said. "Adolescent rebellion, sure, but Cindy says they were in love."

"Maybe they were," I said. "Then they fell out of love. Hey, these things happen; people get divorced, after all. But bottom line the old man has to want something, so what is it—money, a pound of flesh, what?"

Alexander laughed again. "Trust me, this guy doesn't need more money, but that'll come into it as a way to hurt Pignatano. What he says he really wants, though, is satisfaction."

"Jesus," I said. "Don't we all?"

I imagined a duel on the lake bluff overlooking Bradford Beach at seven a.m. Seconds, the works. Old Braithwaite had probably been captain of the fencing team in college. But I knew there was always a certain amount of posturing at the beginning of a case. If the lawyers could handle that and keep the clients quiet, it was usually possible to reach a negotiated settlement before going to court. I had found humor was a good way to lighten the load. "Translate that for me, John," I said. "Are we talking pistols at twenty feet or broadswords?"

Alexander laughed again. "I know, it sounds kind of ridiculous, but Cindy feels promises were made. They spent a couple of years making a home together and now Frank has tossed her out and in the process humiliated her in front of her friends and family. She wants him to pay for what he's done."

It wasn't much of a home from what I saw, but this was easy to understand. Still, we weren't social workers. When lawyers used words like satisfaction and humiliation it usually got down to a dollar figure eventually, but eventually could take a long time and cost a great deal. It was obvious that Frank had seriously underestimated his live-in lover. "So, breach of contract, is that what we're talking about? I'm not conceding anything, just asking the question."

"I understand," John said. "Yeah, for starters."

"No common law marriage in Wisconsin, John."

"Of course," Alexander said. "We'll talk about the rest during discovery."

So no quick settlement, I thought to myself, and wondered how much of my time was going to be taken up by this case. Not that I really minded, but there were those widows and children whose estates I was supposed to be supervising, not to mention a wife who wasn't happy with me right now. "You're not seriously thinking of going to court over this, John. I always heard you were the kind of guy who liked to help clients find common ground."

"You sweet-talking sonofabitch," he said. "But you're right, generally. Like I said before, though, in this case my clients don't want to settle, at least not right away. Arthur feels his name has been dragged through the mud. I'll be honest, this is nothing new. He's been pissed off ever since Cindy moved in with the guy, but he'd more or less accepted that and wouldn't have done anything if they were still together. Frank throwing her out the way he did is what brought this on."

"Not a classy thing to do," I admitted.

"This is just a friendly call, Andy," Alexander said. "But I'm telling you, Braithwaite's on a mission. I don't really think Arthur knows what he wants, but I know he wants a lot of it."

I hung up the phone and went back to my examination of the skyline. I could just see the new art center expansion off to the right and behind that the yacht club. A container ship cut the lake in half on its way into port and I wanted to be on it. I wished I would never see Frank again and suddenly doing wills seemed pretty inviting. But the die had been cast and there was nothing to do about it now. I could have told Frank to go away when he first appeared in the office, but I hadn't and having gotten into this situation there was nothing to do but go and talk to my client about my conversation with Alexander.

In addition to working at the firm, associates were expected to be members of what was euphemistically referred to as "the community," either through pro bono work or being active in the various professional groups in the city. What this meant practically for most of us was that we did as little as possible but always in the right places. I wasn't really cut out to be a big brother to anyone, so I served on the Symphony Board and spoke at elementary school career days when asked. What took more time was continuing legal education, which was also required to stay accredited. Tonight I fought traffic and drove to the South Side to hear some lawyer from Chicago talk about estate planning. By the time I got home it was ten o'clock and Moira wasn't happy.

She was wearing the heavy Canadian reindeer sweater I had bought her on a trip to Ottawa and leaned against the fireplace, arm hugging herself. She had the intense dark look on her face that I liked, but I knew in this case it would likely be from anger rather than passion. "You could have called," she began.

"I did," I said. "You were out. You didn't get the message?"

"You could have called again," she said with inescapable logic. I hadn't called repeatedly and devoted myself to reaching her, no matter what else I might have been doing. She had me there. I sat down and took off my shoes. They were spattered with mud and chevrons of salt residue ran along the sides of the soles. The pristine snow of the morning was long forgotten, now replaced by a gray/black border of slush on every street and sidewalk. Over time the traffic would make this worse, and given Milwaukee's weather it wouldn't melt until May. The only hope was that it would snow again and begin the cycle anew.

"What did the doctor say?" I asked, changing the subject.

Moira sat down and let out a volcanic sigh. "He says everything's fine and that I should check my mucous every day."

"That sounds like something I could be involved in," I said. And for the first time in days, my wife smiled.

"Can't you ever be serious?"

"Why? Anyway, you're serious enough for both of us. You've got that covered."

She nodded. "I don't even know why I get so upset," she said. "I never really wanted to be a mother before."

This was true. When we were in school we had disdained people with careers and plans for a family. We talked about traveling around the world on a tramp steamer and never living anywhere for more than a year or two. We'd work at nothing jobs long enough to earn some money and then take off on another adventure. This lasted for two or three memorable years. Then reality set in. I was through law school, her father was offering me a job I didn't want, and Mom got cancer. She was alone in the world and for the first time in memory she'd called and said she really needed me to come out to help her.

"I'm old and sick and you're young and strong," she said. "I need you to do this for me, Andy. I really do."

I could have taken a leave of absence from my job in Boston and come out for a few months rather than subject Moira to the move, but it didn't really help to look back and second-guess myself. I could never have predicted that our relationship would deteriorate to the point that we'd be sitting in a cold living room, staring daggers at one another and worrying about unborn children, but that was the situation. Maybe it would make sense in the morning when I wasn't so tired.

"Maybe we should go and check that mucous now," I said. "Just to be on the safe side?" It always helped to joke when I felt morose.

"You're so bad," Moira said.

"Be honest," I said. "It's what you like about me."

The next morning I walked through what was left of the snow, a muddy scrim on the park walkways, feeling optimistic about a job well done. Even Moira was in a better mood after a night of subdued passion. I trusted in zygotes without really knowing what a zygote was.

Perhaps it was the anticipation of paternity that got me thinking of my father, whom I never knew except through pictures and family legend. He was, I'd been told, tall and slim, as I am, and a moderately talented actor who grew up in Portland and made his bones at the Williamstown Summer Theatre before coming to New York to fail and meet my mother, who was working out of a studio in Chelsea.

"He was a starving actor who actually starved," my mother had told me once. "He didn't understand the whole thing was supposed to be a metaphor," she said mordantly. He died of what they now called Crohn's disease but was referred to then as spastic colitis. In the end it didn't matter what they called it, but before my father passed from the scene my parents managed to fall in love and in that giddy union of youth and hormones make me.

New York was a great walking town then, as it is now, and since walking was free, it made up a large part of my parents' recreational moments, when Mom wasn't working or Dad failing at auditions. I imagined him as a kind of poor man's Hank Fonda, perhaps because one of his few jobs was as understudy for Ensign Pulver in *Mister Roberts* during the play's long run at the Alvin. They would, Mom remembered, walk crosstown from 10th Avenue and then up Lexington to 82nd Street where they'd cross the park and come back home on the West Side, often stopping for something cold along the way if it was summer or a hot drink if it was winter. In Times Square they'd look at the five-story sign advertising a popular soft drink.

"You like it, it likes You," the sign proclaimed and ever after in affectionate moments my parents would look at one another, raise an imaginary glass, and say, "7-Up."

I tried preserving this tradition with Moira, but it fell flat as she'd never heard of 7-Up. As I walked through the snow this morning in my Red Wing Birdhunters I imagined my long-dead father striding along with me, wearing a canvas Bean coat like mine and a jaunty Borsalino, something an aspiring actor might have sported, as if all of life were a lengthy audition for some future role. As attractive as this fantasy was, however, the truth was I had no idea what my father had been like; as much as I would have wanted to, I had no memory of the timbre of his laugh, no sensory impression of the smell of his after shave or tobacco on his coat. I had nothing, really. I had his name, though no one had ever called me junior. For reasons known only to her, my mother had cleverly hidden most of the pictures, though as far I could tell they'd been happy together.

"The past is gone," she'd told me. "Why dwell on it?"

So except for the occasional comment, usually thrown out in an antic moment—as in, "That's just like your father"— any sense I had of him was my own creation, wish fulfillment, projection, or all three, and no less valid for that.

Still, I sometimes wondered what it would have been like to grow up with a father, to be someone others could refer to with either affection or scorn as "Andy Simonson's boy," an older man to push against or lean on, someone to take me to scout dinners and on fishing trips, to throw balls at me on the diamond or tennis court, someone to be there in a solid daily sense. I missed that and envied anyone who actually had a father, even Frank Pignatano, whose father was the local don, though I had to admit that being the scion of a crime organization was not quite the same as taking your place in the family hardware business.

I was meeting Frank at the Pavilion in the park, a space that doubled as a senior citizen center and short order restaurant. You could look at the lake and eat breakfast while hearing the click of dominoes in the background. It was a good place to consider the future and the past, but my motives this morning were not so lofty. I needed to talk honestly with my client and at least here I didn't have to worry about him scaring the secretaries.

Frank was sitting in a chair near the big picture windows with his boots up on the molding. Though he was wearing a leather jacket and a silver choker below diamond earrings and spiked hair, from this vantage point he looked almost contemplative. I was pretty sure this was an illusion, an impression that was verified when he heard me coming and turned, ferret-faced, and demanded, "You talk to that bitch yet, Andy?"

58

I told him I'd spoken to Cindy's lawyer and summarized our conversation. "It looks like they're serious, Frank," I said. "They're calling it breach of contract, saying you had an agreement with Cindy and you broke it by throwing her out."

He looked at me incredulously. "That cunt," he said. "What contract? I never even wrote her a Valentine's Day card."

It occurred to me that it might have helped if he had, but I could see contracts had a rather limited meaning to Frank. If it didn't involve rent or killing, it didn't interest him. "Contracts aren't just written," I said. "There are verbal contracts too. In those cases you wouldn't have to write anything down, you might just have implied something and you'd still be obligated. For example, did you ever promise her anything, ever say you'd be there for her, ever say you'd be together always, that you'd take care of her, anything like that? Ever?"

He looked suspicious and for the first time uncertain. "They say I did?"

"It doesn't really matter what they say, Frank. I'm your lawyer, and I'm trying to represent you, which means I have to know what went on between the two of you. How can I defend you if I have surprises coming at me because you're holding back? So think about it. You lived together, what, two or three years? In that time do you remember promising Cindy anything?"

Frank looked puzzled. "Who the hell knows? I probably said lots of things when we were fucking or if I was in the bag."

This was great. Now we had memory lapses in addition to everything else. "Okay, but except for those times, you don't remember consciously promising her anything?"

He shrugged, so I pressed on. "Come on, Frank. You've got to help me here. Was there anything recorded that you know of, anything on tape?"

Frank nodded knowingly. He understood bugs, wiretaps. "You think she taped us in bed?" he asked. "I'll kill that bitch." Even so, there was a tone of admiration in his voice.

"I didn't say that," I put in hurriedly. "I'm just asking questions, trying to figure out where we are. Do you remember any telephone conversations, anything someone else might have heard, at a party, a restaurant, when you were out together? Were there any witnesses to promises you might have made to her?"

"Witnesses?" Frank smiled wickedly. "I ain't worried about any fucking witnesses, Andy."

Imagining bullet-ridden bodies on a warehouse floor, I said, "I don't want to hear it, Frank. I'm an officer of the court and if you threaten anyone with intent I have to report it. I just want to know if you know if there are any records of conversations, promises, agreements you might have made or Cindy might reasonably think you made? If not, no problem. It's your word against hers."

"Great," he said. "I like the odds."

I wasn't sure I did. I pictured Cynthia Braithwaite of Whitefish Bay crying on the witness stand because of her treatment at the hands of a depraved gangster while Frank sat hunched in the corner in a Johnnie Walker suit. If it got that far, we'd do what we could to keep Frank's past from the jury, but such things were always difficult. For the moment, I kept quiet and let Frank think of himself as a sympathetic witness. What harm could that do? After all, my mother had thought he was cute, but she had unusual tastes, to say the least. Still, if we got him a conservative haircut and a Brooks Brothers suit, he might clean up pretty well. He'd have to look better than he did now, though that wasn't saying much. But I was getting ahead of the game. With luck, we'd never get to court. With luck, we'd find a way to settle no matter how angry Cindy and her father were. I patted Frank on the shoulder and ordered breakfast. I wanted to hold onto as much of the morning's good feelings as I could under the circumstances.

The office had an obscure rhythm that I found comforting, even if I couldn't describe it, measure it, or even be absolutely sure it was there. It reminded me of a lecture I'd once attended on chaos theory, in which the lecturer talked about the idea that everything had a pattern even when things seemed completely random. Sometimes I'd sit at my desk and leave the door to the outer office just slightly ajar in order to sense the energy of the place, even though I knew that much of that energy was misused or directed at screwing people. That was the way the legal machine worked and that wasn't the point. The law was an enigma, sometimes fascinating, often boring, but always running somewhere. This was part of what had drawn me to it and kept me engaged now.

I ran through my appointments mechanically, paying attention to clients, nodding in the right places, but reserving the part of my mind that mattered to thoughts of Moira, our unborn child, and, occasionally, Frank Pignatano. Along the way, I got a call from Ginnie at the house asking again about the light in the driveway, and I promised I'd get back to her on the weekend. This time she seemed less tough, almost sweet. Sweet works with me.

Around three my phone buzzed. My secretary said, "It's Arthur Braithwaite. You want him?"

I hesitated for a moment, and then picked up the receiver. "Mr. Braithwaite, this is a surprise." There was nothing specifically improper about my speaking to Cindy's father, but it was unusual to get a call from a family member on the other side. Generally, communication would be between lawyers. Braithwaite knew this so I wondered what he wanted with me.

Arthur Braithwaite had a deep voice and I suspected he was talking over the speaker in his office, perhaps with others listening in. "I understand," he roared. "Of course, I understand very well and in ordinary circumstances I wouldn't be getting involved, but this isn't any ordinary situation. We're talking about my daughter's honor, Andy. May I call you Andy?" He continued without waiting for an answer. "Frankly," he said, "I just find it hard to believe that a young lawyer with an important firm, a lawyer like you, with great promise who graduated from an excellent law school, would want to defend something like this Pignater."

I had a feeling he knew Frank's last name very well but didn't bother to correct him. "Everyone deserves a defense, Mr. Braithwaite. I'm sure we'd agree on that."

"Absolutely," Braithwaite boomed. "Fundamental to our system, but that wasn't my point. I just thought this fellow would get someone from Cain, Sloan. They usually take care of those people, don't they?"

Fred Cain was the best criminal lawyer in town. The word was that he'd never lost a case so it wouldn't surprise me if Frank's father actually did have him on retainer. From that point of view, Braithwaite should have been pleased Frank had come to us. "Well, he chose me instead," I said.

"So he did," Braithwaite said. "Let me ask you, Andy, are you a father?"

"Not yet," I said.

"I didn't think so," Braithwaite said. "It changes the way you look at things. But you've met my Cindy, haven't you?"

I remembered her, smear of red lipstick, chewing gum in a short skirt in Frank's apartment. Her blueblood roots had not been obvious to me then. "Yes," I said. "I had the pleasure of meeting her once."

"Lovely girl," Braithwaite said. "That bastard just broke her heart, so speaking as a father not a lawyer now, Andy, you can understand how I feel. I just thought I'd give you a call out of consideration for another Yale grad, that's all. I mean, just to let you know that my honor is at stake here. Remember, son, reputations can hang by a thin thread, a very thin thread. They can be affected by all sorts of things we can't foresee but when they're gone, they're gone forever."

He couldn't have known that mentioning the Yale connection would be counterproductive with me and I didn't care much about my reputation either. What this conversation did was make me more sympathetic toward Frank and, if anything, more interested in defending him. It became a class issue and inflamed my blue-collar roots. "I understand that, Mr. Braithwaite," I said. "And frankly, I don't give a shit. I hope you're not threatening me, Sir?"

Here I imagined an intake of breath, but it could have been the phone. "No, no of course not," Braithwaite said hurriedly. "Wouldn't dream of that, just thought I should talk to you, that's all." And then he was gone.

My windows had gone black, the suggestion of something sinister and intriguing, night in the city, a time conducive to deep thoughts, or at least it had always worked that way for me. I decided to walk over to Donovan's, thinking Tom might drop in sooner or later, though I hadn't seen him at the office. For some reason I thought back to the time we were kids in high school and used to sneak into the parish house and nip at the priest's private stock of sherry. I wasn't Catholic myself. I didn't know what I was and Mom had never told me, though I thought she'd been raised as something more High Church than Unitarianism, which took in a lot of territory. Tom was Catholic in name only, but he'd put in some time as an altar boy and had become a favorite while there, probably because of his Irish good looks. One of the priests had given him a drink once and Tom never forgot. Catholic kids who went to the public high school had to attend something called Confraternity of Christian Doctrine classes to maintain their Catholic roots while in the hands of infidels. Tom never actually went to CCD himself, but he used to hang around on Wednesday nights just to be in position to hit on the girls when they came out. I often went with him and if we got lucky we'd take the girls to the lakefront and share a little of our stolen sherry. Thinking of all this now made me feel lonely, though given the recent scandals in the Church I had a feeling the priests would be more careful nowadays about sharing their stock with altar boys after mass.

In Donovan's I positioned myself in a corner behind a pint of Guinness and some beer nuts. On reflection, I realized that Arthur Braithwaite's was probably not an empty threat, that he likely could hurt my reputation, what there was of it. So why wasn't I concerned? I believed what I'd said about everyone having a right to a vigorous defense, but Fred Cain would probably have wrapped the whole thing up in five minutes on the phone. So why had Frank called me? Maybe because it just seemed there was more to this case than I was seeing, probably more than Frank was telling me, maybe more than he knew himself. And, okay, Arthur Braithwaite was the proud father, insulted not so much himself as for what he might have imagined was his daughter's honor, but calling me without consulting his attorney was going further than most lawyers would. It was part of the professional code to not get personally involved, especially in cases concerning your family.

I wasn't ordinarily foolhardy, but I didn't like being pressured. I'd inherited a pugnacious streak from my mother, who took no crap from anyone and had paid for it in various ways throughout her life. I remembered one of few times she'd made a big sale, maybe a thousand dollars, which would have paid our rent for a couple of months. We were over at the gallery celebrating when the buyer showed up drunk and demanded to know when Mom would install the piece in his garden. He was having a party or something and wanted it right away. Mom looked him up and down. Then she took his check out of her pocket and tore it into little pieces. "I don't want people like you to have my art," she said. "I'd rather starve to death."

Which we came close to doing at times, but what she did that afternoon made an impression. John Alexander and I might have worked something out, met and talked amicably about the whole thing, reached a compromise fair to both parties. But Braithwaite's threat had pissed me off.

Color distracted me. I looked to my right to see Patsy Steiner studying me intently. She was wearing a turquoise scarf around her shoulders fastened with a scarab pin. "Hey, you," she said, in what I imagined was a come-hither tone. "What are you doing here?"

I turned on my stool and looked. It seemed like a question I'd more likely ask her. Donovan's wasn't exactly a working-class bar, but it wasn't a university hangout either. Not a tweed jacket in the place. There was a hint of humor in Patsy's expression, upturned mouth and slightly raised eyebrows. It was as if I'd never really looked at her before. "I might ask you that," I said, aware of a slight slurring of the vowels. "My office is right over there," I made a show of pointing but I had no sense of direction in there. I really had no idea what was where relative to my barstool.

"My Irish Literary Revival seminar meets here sometimes," she said. "You've heard of it?"

"Who hasn't?" I said, though I wasn't sure what Yeats or Synge would think of the faux Irish decorations Donovan had put on the walls. Anyway, Patsy was here now. "Want a beer?" I asked, indicating the pitcher.

She seemed to hesitate but then sat on the next stool and poured herself a glass. Maybe it was the soft lighting in the bar or the music that was starting up in the front, but I was now aware not only of Patsy's expression but her figure. Beneath the shawl she was wearing an off-the-shoulder blouse that emphasized the curve of her breasts and her ass fit nicely on the seat. One thing that had never figured in my marriage to this point was other women, not because I hadn't had chances but because no one but Moira interested me. Yet here I was drinking Guinness with her friend Patsy as night came on, aware of a slight tingling on the back of my neck that could be sexual interest, the beer, or nothing at all.

Neither of us mentioned Moira as we sat together, but it was warm and pleasant in the room and I liked the complete absence of any kind of tension. Patsy smiled at me and poured another glass and now I realized I knew almost nothing about this woman except that she used to run marathons and taught English at the university. I had only seen her perched at our kitchen counter drinking coffee and heard her disembodied voice on the phone. I looked at her curiously, expecting the truth to be revealed.

"I'm embarrassed to say this, Patsy," I said, "but I don't even know if you're married."

She smiled, her eyes nearly black in the dim light. "Used to be," she said. "It was a while ago, right after grad school. I didn't like it."

She could have been talking about Italian food. It seemed a little too casual to be real. "Kids?"

"What is this, '20 Questions'?" She laughed to show she wasn't really upset.

"I guess so," I said. "It just hit me that even if I've seen you fairly often, we hardly know each other."

This seemed to please her, the idea of being mysterious, unknown. I understood that. She arched a shoulder and then in a passable imitation of Marlene Dietrich said, "And vot would you like to know about me then, Darling?"

"If I knew, I'd tell you." Then we sat there without talking for a while, but I had the feeling a lot was going on in the space between us. We were in a tavern together as night came down, our knees brushing slightly beneath the table and neither of us doing anything about moving. Patsy was a friend of my wife's and you might have said it was nothing, an innocent meeting between friends having a drink. Except in my experience these things were never completely innocent. I hadn't come to Donovan's intending to pick anyone up and neither had Patsy, but we hadn't backed away when opportunity presented itself. But in the dim light of the bar she seemed irresistible. I was drawn by the small dimple in her chin I'd never noticed before, the slight line between her eyes, the curve of her forehead, the pout of her lips, by her. What was puzzling me was that I wasn't unhappy and Patsy had never struck me as a home-wrecker. The opposite really in her native ponchos and Nikes. So what was going on here? Whatever it was, I knew that now things had changed between us and I'd never see her in our kitchen drinking coffee and feel the same way again.

"Does your seminar always meet on Fridays?" I asked.

Patsy nodded. "So far," she said, as if the time of the class was flexible.

"Well, then, maybe I'll see you again?" I said, rising from my seat.

She gave me a knowing look. "Or somewhere else?"

I wasn't prepared to go that far. I leaned in to give her a social kiss, a brush on the cheek as I might have done had I run into her at the supermarket. But she turned and kissed me full on the mouth, the gossamer hint of tongue behind her lips, light on my mouth. I felt importantly unaware of signals that must have passed between us. I looked at her questioningly, but Patsy just looked amused and wasn't about to help me out.

"Right," I said then. "Or somewhere else."

Moira wasn't enthusiastic about any efforts to improve my mother's house, so she predictably objected to installing lights in the driveway no matter what Ginnie had said about safety. She had seen an article somewhere that said the way to get value out of an old house was to let it fall down around you and then sell it for the land. "You're three blocks from Lake Michigan," she said logically. "That's the only reason that old dump would be worth anything. Why put any more money into it, at least until you can get that gangster to pay you some rent?"

Despite her brusque affect, I knew Moira had nothing against my gay tenants or even providing better lighting for them. It was just the house itself and what she thought it represented. "How much more do we have to pour into that place before we consider it a loss and sell it?" she demanded.

Conversations like this never went anywhere, in part because I knew lights were the least of it when it came to improving the house. The back fence was falling down, the garage was on the point of collapse, the paint was chipping on the second floor, and we'd need a new roof soon. Worse, pride of ownership had taken me over and I now had the idea of doing the kind of significant work on the place we could never afford: refinishing the floors, putting in built-in cabinets, and remodeling the bathrooms and kitchens. "This won't cost much," I said, dodging the question.

"Maybe you could just get someone to burn the place down," she said. "At least then we'd get the insurance."

"It's a possibility," I admitted. "I could speak to Frank about it. I'm sure he'd know just the guy."

Part of the reason I didn't take Moira seriously in this regard was that I understood that, despite her complaining about it, the house wasn't what was really important to her. She wanted to be pregnant. She had decided this was the solution to her malaise and it had now become an idée fixe, an obsession, even if I doubted that a baby would magically resolve everything between us. She was simply unhappy, though there was nothing simple about it. She was unhappy with Milwaukee, with the constant gray skies, with the absence of what she considered to be culture here, with the distance from her home and family, most of all with the way her life had turned out, and telling her that at thirty-two nothing was set in stone wouldn't help.

Moreover, while others might see me as a success, it was all relative. Moira was disappointed with the choices I'd made, which ended up being her choices as well. And behind this was the possibility that she'd made a mistake in coming back to Milwaukee with me. She might have begun to think her father was right.

"You know, there are lawyers in town who'd kill for a partnership at Charney and Gates," I said one day. "It's one of the best firms in Milwaukee."

"I don't doubt it," Moira said. "But you're not a partner yet. Daddy got you a job at one of the best firms in Boston. And you turned it down."

"Which would have been better, right?"

She shrugged but in her mind the answer was so obvious that there was no point in talking about it.

"Look," I said. "I just don't like seeing you unhappy, but Milwaukee's my home. You knew this when we decided to come out here."

"I didn't know it would be like this," Moira said.

"Like what? You've got a beautiful home on Lake Drive, we can travel, do whatever we want and sooner or later we'll have a family."

"You think so?"

"I do. I'm sure of it."

"Nice for you," Moira said. "I'm not so sure. Anyway, you're not responsible for me being happy. I'm fine."

She was right about that. In one sense it wasn't really my problem, but I had a Sir Galahad complex, always eager to help a damsel in distress. This probably resulted from youthful efforts to be my mother's little man when what she really needed was a functioning husband. I hadn't been very good at rescuing Mom and it didn't look like I was going to be any more successful with my wife. I had to back off and let her live as best she could, but this wasn't my nature. I had never been good at accepting hopeless situations, which was another way of saying I wasn't good at being hopeless.

When I walked the three blocks over to the house the next morning the contractor I had lined up was stalking up and down the driveway, hands in his pockets and a doubtful look on his face. His name was Eddie Howard and we'd known each other in high school, though I hadn't seen him since and had picked his name out of the Yellow Pages on a whim. "I can try to mount a light on the garage, Andy," he said now. "But to be honest with you if you drive any nails in there the whole damned thing could collapse."

I wondered if he'd been talking to Moira as the similarity in their views was ominous. Eddie had grown into an imposing man, at least 6′5″ with impressive biceps honed no doubt from years of manual labor. "Let's take a chance, Eddie," I said. "Look at the bright side. If mounting lights knocks down the garage, I can give you an even bigger job rebuilding it."

He smiled. "You know, Andy, you always were kind of a crazy sonofabitch. That's why I liked you when we were kids. How the hell did you ever get to be a lawyer? I mean, did they cover negligence where you went to school?"

"It's a mystery to a lot of people," I said. "Including me, but I'm the only one who'd be liable in this case."

I left Eddie to his work, but before going home I stood at the end of the driveway admiring the house. I couldn't really disagree with either Moira or Eddie about its long-term prospects or general level of disrepair, but I was fond of the place. I liked the way the roof shot into the blue sky and the exaggerated pitch of the gables. It had taken Mom twenty years to be able to buy a house and I wasn't going to let this go easily. Now Ginnie walked over to stand next to me.

"I just wanted you to know we appreciate your doing this," she said. "I know you didn't think we really needed the lights, and you were probably right."

She wouldn't have admitted this if Eddie weren't already hammering away in the back, but I was in a generous mood. "No one should be scared to come home at night," I said. "The cost isn't really that big a deal."

She put her hand on my shoulder and squeezed. Ginnie was tall for a woman and attractive in a healthy outdoors kind of way. She had a good grip, probably from working out at the university. "You didn't have to do it is all I'm saying," she went on. "You do a nice job of hiding it, but deep down, you're a good guy."

"You might get an argument from some people about that," I said.

She smiled. "Maybe," she said. "But only people who don't really know you."

Depositions were the most interesting part of the progression of a case to court or settlement, a kind of slow, meandering crawl in an undetermined direction. This suited my temperament because depositions were similar to trials but less structured and gave the lawyers a chance to ask all manner of question, fishing for bits of information that might be helpful even if unallowable as evidence. They gave you an opportunity to study potential witnesses in an informal setting, to press them a little, see how they might perform in court and decide whether you wanted them testifying for your side.

Depositions could also serve the function of convincing one party or the other that they had no case—or at least not one that was worth the time and expense of pursuing. And if you missed something in the interrogatories or the deposition, it was possible to reconvene the deposition and try again.

The deposition of Cindy Braithwaite came the following Tuesday morning at John Alexander's office. I brought Frank with me, even if officially he wasn't allowed to say anything. I wanted him to see what he was up against and I was curious as to how Cindy would react to seeing him again. John's office was on Water Street, where his firm took up two floors in an old building with high ceilings and marble fireplaces. From the conference room there were views of City Hall, the Performing Arts Center, and the Milwaukee River wide and green behind it. The room was large with lots of wainscoting and leather club chairs lining the walls. A court reporter was there to transcribe testimony and Alexander made us wait ten minutes before bringing in his client.

When they did come in I was struck immediately by the change in Cindy's demeanor. I remembered a big-bosomed girl with pouty lips and a short skirt, but this young woman was wearing a brown tweed suit whose skirt just brushed her knees over a demure eggshell blouse with a tie at the neck. Her hair was pulled back into a chignon and all in all she looked as if she'd just dropped by on her way to a Holy Angels reunion. Looking at her, she could have been a girl I went out with or one I would have wanted to date. The Holy Angels girls had a kind of class that students at the other Catholic schools lacked, not that they didn't all have their charms. The churches in Milwaukee were tribal. Italians went to St. Joan Antida and the girls there were supposed to be easy, though in my experience this wasn't true. Polish girls went to St. Mary Czestochowa while Irish girls attended either St. Pete's or Dominican and gave as good as they got, being aggressive and quick with a retort if you got out of line.

Holy Angels was different, almost Episcopal in its sense of entitlement and privilege, and the fact that knowing this Arthur Braithwaite had sent Cindy there only to see her end up with Frank made me sympathize with him for a quick moment.

I snuck a look at my client in his leather jacket and d.a. and was again struck by the contrast between plaintiff and defendant. We'd have an uphill battle with almost any jury, but I already knew that because I knew Frank. Still, there was something bruised and vulnerable about him, perhaps because he was so anxious to be tough, and I began to understand why my mother had been drawn to him.

73

Alexander placed a box of Kleenex on the table next to Cindy, as if he were the stage manager at a performance. Frank was in the corner with his arms crossed tightly on his chest, a menacing look on his face that seemed at the same time somehow comical to me.

John looked at both of us and smiled. "Should we begin?" he asked.

Depositions, in addition to being theater, have their own rhythm and shape. I began by asking factual questions, hoping to put Cindy at ease before going into weightier matters, though it was hard to see anyone being at ease with Frank glowering at them. I could imagine John Alexander licking his lips but ignored this and plowed on through Cindy's age, address, and place of employment until I arrived at her relationship with my client.

"Cindy," I began. "Do you remember the first time we met, at the apartment you were then sharing with Frank?"

This seemed straightforward enough but she looked over at her attorney for guidance. John nodded and she said, "You came about the rent."

"That's right. Well, that day it seemed to me that you and Frank were happy together. Was I right in thinking that?"

Tears welled up in the edges of her eyes now. "We were fine, until . . ." She hesitated and looked at Frank, who was smirking at her. "Until he did what he did."

I waited for a moment. "And from your point of view, what was that?"

She looked at me as if I were an imbecile. Then she dropped the schoolgirl manner. "He kicked my ass out of the house. The house that I furnished for him with my daddy's money. You're his lawyer, for Christ's sake, don't you even know that?"

For a fleeting moment I wished she had used some of that money to pay the back rent, but this wasn't about me. I looked at Alexander, who was suppressing a smile, and then at Frank, who was enjoying himself more than a defendant should. "I do know that," I said. "But everyone has a different view of things and I wanted to get yours."

"Yeah?" she said. "Well, my version is that he broke my heart into little pieces and then danced on it with some skank he picked up at a Mexican bar on the South Side."

This sounded like something out of a country and western song, but we were meandering and I knew Alexander could cut the deposition off at any time for a variety of reasons. "I'm sorry to hear that," I said. "But that's not why we're here. People break up all the time, good people, honest people. It's not against the law."

"He's not good and he's not honest," Cindy said. "He's a snake. He said we'd be together always, that he'd take care of me, that we'd have babies together."

"Bullshit," Frank offered from the corner.

"Bullshit not," Cindy shot back. "You did and I can prove you did."

There was a sudden silence in the room; even the typist's manicured fingers on her machine seemed muted. I looked at John Alexander, but he was giving nothing away. "Let's back up for a moment," I said, buying time. I looked at my notes to further slow the pace. "You know, Cindy, that people who are in love often think that love will last forever. And you did say you were in love with Frank? Before all this happened, I mean."

"Right," she said. "I'm not ten years old. But it wasn't like that."

"Like what?"

"Like some stupid romantic Top 40 kind of thing," she said. "I mean, I knew who he was, what he did and that he'd been in Green Bay."

Now I became aware if I hadn't been before of her toughness and intelligence. She didn't want to be patronized. I'd have to remember that.

"Top 40?"

"Sure, all that bubblegum bullshit about loving forever, writing your initials on a tree, wearing my ring, you know what I mean?"

"But isn't that what you just said," I persisted. "That you were going to be together forever."

"Yeah, but what I mean is he promised, it was like a contract because, face it, after I'm with Frankie most guys would think I'm damaged goods. I mean, I'm not exactly going to be the mistress of honor for the debutantes at the Town Club Ball."

This brought Frank to his feet. "I'll show you some damage, bitch," he yelled and started to come around the table.

Alexander and I jumped to our feet and got in front of him, but Cindy didn't seem upset. "You keep your client under control or this is over," Alexander said, just because he had to say it.

I put my hands on Frank's shoulders and pushed him back down into his chair. "He'll be okay," I said.

"I mean it," Alexander said. "No more threats."

I nodded. Protecting your client was an important part of the game, and Alexander and I both knew it, just as we also knew if Frank had really tried anything John Alexander couldn't have done a thing about it. "Okay, John, he'll be okay," I said. Then I continued my questioning. "Cindy, you say Frank made a promise, but whether or not other men will be interested in you isn't really his problem, is it?"

"It would be if he were a gentleman," Cindy said, holding her ground.

The idea of defending Frank as a gentleman seemed so ridiculous as not to be worth mentioning, so I moved on. "Before you used the word contract," I said. "What did you mean by that exactly?"

Cindy looked at me. "You're a lawyer. Don't you know what a contract is?"

I smiled and I could tell Alexander was enjoying the badinage too. "Yes, I do," I said. "But I also know there are different kinds of contacts, written and oral."

"This was oral," Cindy said. "He always liked that."

"Damned straight," Frank put in from the side, and it occurred to me that it was absurd to be trying a case in which the plaintiff and defendant were still flirting with each other.

"So what you mean is that he made you a verbal promise but there's no record of it?"

Cindy shook her head. "I didn't say that. There's a record, just not written down." Now she held up her phone and smiled. "See," Cindy said. "I made a tape of what he said and got some copies of it, just in case."

"Shit," Frank said and I couldn't disagree.

"In case of what, Cindy?" I asked.

"Come, on," Cindy said dismissively. "You know who this guy is, who his scumbag family is. In case they try to get funny with me."

I turned to Alexander and said, "And of course the defense will have a chance to examine this alleged recording of a conversation, which could be inadmissible?"

Alexander nodded, but he knew I was bluffing. The existence of a real recording with anything on it about a promise Frank had made to Cindy would be devastating, whether we could stop it from getting into court or not.

We broke off soon after that, making a date for Alexander to interview Frank, but in the elevator Frank was uncharacteristically quiet. "You never knew about this?" I asked. "The tape."

"If I knew I'd've told you," he said. "But that bitch is smart, I'll give her that. She could have recorded it off the phone without me knowing or some other time. Who the hell knows?"

"Recorded what? Do you know what you might have promised her?"

"Beats the hell out of me," Frank said. "I probably said a lot of shit."

"Well, that's great," I said. Then, trying to be helpful, I added, "We'll have a better idea once we listen to the tape."

"Yeah," Frank said. "We'll have a better idea how tight she's got my balls in a vise."

I left Frank and started walking with no clear destination in mind. The way some people are inspired by nature, by trees and birds and the wind in their hair, I am by cities, by the ebb and flow of neighborhoods, the crush of people on the streets, the noise and smell of buses, smoke in the air and grit in your eyes. It's odd but it makes me feel more alive somehow. Not that I don't see the panhandlers and whores, urban decay and failure all around, but for me it's fecund, part of the growing, dynamic life of the city. I liked to look at the second stories of downtown buildings, often a remnant of years gone by with the names of forgotten owners of buildings scrolled across the lintel put there by optimists before the brutal rush of modernization took hold and changed everything. There are trellised roofs, dormer windows, and sometimes ornate balconies high above the street, waiting for the right Rapunzel to come along and let down her hair.

As I walk, I wonder what happened to old man Siebert whose name is above a lingerie store on Third Street or Tagler and his sons who had a warehouse on Wells that is no more. It's the same in any city, of course, nothing remarkable about Milwaukee in that sense except that it *is* simply by being unremarkable, or so it seems to me. Still, walk up Fifth Avenue in New York and wonder at the contrast between the gilt front of the Scribner Building—which housed Max Perkins, Hemingway and Fitzgerald, and the Scribner's Bookstore in the old days—and consider what's there now and what's to come.

I walked across the Wisconsin Avenue Bridge, past the old Gimbels building with its gargoyles staring sightless out at the river and the Riverside Theater, whose days as a first-run movie palace were long gone. Now I felt my head begin to clear. Looking the other way up Wisconsin in the distance I could almost see the public library and remembered meeting girls there in the stacks. Then north past the museum to Courthouse Square, where Alexander and I would face off if the business about Frank and Cindy ever came to that.

I paused on the hill and then took a seat on a bench someone had thoughtfully placed there and considered the prospect before me with the convention center on the right, the Journal Building on the left and City Hall directly in my sights. For reasons I didn't understand, I thought of my father, though he'd never even been in Milwaukee and had nothing to do with the place. My memories of him, as I've said, were vague and indistinct, the way he wore his hat slightly tilted back to reveal a stretch of broad forehead; a worn leather jacket that I inherited and wore briefly before losing it when I was with a girl one drunken night in Lake Park years ago; a pair of work boots with rounded heels that I wear from time to time just to get the feel of him; little things. But every so often I'll be surprised by memory or notice unconscious mannerisms I recognize as his. The way when I put my shoes on, first holding my leg below the knee, gripping it tightly and pulling it toward me as Mom told me he did toward the end when he was too weak to hold his legs up without aid. Or the way the skirts of my robe flap around my long thin legs as his did when he was too sick to get dressed or go out and was kept hostage in our apartment. Without ever seriously thinking about it, these and a dozen other small details are fixed in muscle memory, my way of paying homage to the father I only slightly knew and now barely remember.

These thoughts and the walk up the avenue had an effect and the faint tickle of an idea began to emerge. Something about this case was not as it seemed and while I couldn't say exactly what it was, I trusted my instincts in these matters. Okay, Frank had dumped Cindy and she was hurt, but bringing the resources of one of the most important law firms in town to bear on this didn't quite make sense, even given the fact that one of the partners was the father of the plaintiff. I knew why I was involved, but I wasn't sure about Alexander. And what about the recording? Maybe it existed and maybe it didn't; maybe it had nothing to do with romance, but the simple assertion of its existence had an obvious effect, as the other side had known it would. I also wondered why we hadn't heard from Frank's father or his representatives. Frank might not be the ideal child, but he was a son and in an Italian family that was important. What's more, I knew he had to be involved in some way in the old man's affairs. What affected one thus affected the other to a degree. It seemed odd that no one seemed to care about that.

My head was clear now and I felt better. With new energy, I walked away from the courthouse down Kilbourne, heading to the office.

Tom Williams was waiting when I arrived, his long legs taking up half the space between my clients' chairs and the desk, his size twelves resting on a corner of my occasional table. He liked plain tip brogues and from where I stood the tips seemed to extend to Chicago. He was wearing red suspenders with blue ducks on them and a club tie. For a guy from the East Side, he'd come a long way. I liked the way Tom dressed, the casual dishabille of it, something I could never quite manage though I'd tried. Looking at him, anyone would think he was the Ivy Leaguer, not me. He didn't move when I came in.

"I always forget what shitty offices we give the associates," he said, gesturing vaguely at my walls with their Impressionist reproductions.

It was hard to argue with this so I didn't. "I was at a deposition," I said, pushing my briefcase along the floor.

"I know," Tom said. "Old Braithwaite called Billy Doyle to raise hell about it and Billy called me."

Doyle had his name on the door, which meant he merited attention if not respect. I knew him as a pot-bellied old man with bad feet who wore drip-dry shirts and gabardine suits he bought at Sears. It was a kind of reverse snobbishness, an in your face assertion of someone who had so much money that impressing others was out of the question. But he'd always been decent to me, more than decent really. It turned out he had once bought one of my mother's paintings, and there weren't a lot of lawyers in town who could say that. "Am I missing something?" I asked. "What's Billy Doyle got to do with my case?"

Tom shrugged. "Nothing and he'd like to have less. But he and Braithwaite have known each other forever, went to law school together, belong to the same fraternity or something, old Milwaukee money. Bill told me he doesn't even like the guy but when you've been together that long it doesn't matter really."

I waited for the essential connection to be made and when Tom said nothing further, I asked, "And?"

"And he thinks it's an embarrassment to the firm and I'm here to tell you he thinks so because we're friends, like he and Braithwaite are."

"I'm not embarrassed," I said, my ears getting hot. "I'm afraid I'm going to get my ass handed to me, but I'm not embarrassed."

Tom nodded his head and sat quietly for a moment. Then he launched himself out of the chair to a standing position. He looked at me and shook his head again, a slight smile creasing his face. "Maybe you should think about that," he said. And then he was gone.

Without Tom in the room, my office seemed to have grown exponentially. Sitting in one of the clients' chairs I unlaced a shoe and immediately thought of my father again. I wondered if he'd be proud of me or if he'd have thought I went over to the other side with my big house, fancy car, and law degree. I decided he'd understand, but who the hell knew?

Sitting there, I was barely aware of what was going on around me, a clock ticking somewhere, a siren a few blocks over, oddly of children's voices screaming in fear or delight. I wondered if I were hallucinating or in some kind of fugue state. From my window I could see a gaggle of kids being prodded along the street by nuns, their habits like dominoes from this distance, the whites blinding in the afternoon light. They must be from St. John's, I thought, the apostolic outpost in this commercial jungle. It could be a field trip, though there were no fields nearby. Reassured as to my sanity, however, I laced on a pair of hiking boots I kept in my office closet specifically for this purpose and headed east up Wisconsin Avenue, from which I could traverse a path through Juneau Park and then to an abandoned railroad right of way through the interlocking parks that bordered the lake.

Lake Michigan, the great Inland Sea, no matter what Moira thought. It's as close to a sea as most Milwaukeeans ever get, so why not? It has waves, tides, a sea port welcoming ships from Europe that come to us through the St. Lawrence Seaway, as well as a receding beach and shorefront castles on Lake Drive whose owners are constantly rebuilding their sea walls in defiance of the inevitable. But all that was of only abstract interest to me as I walked since I'd never owned lake property and never would. I did like having this gray-green mass forming one boundary of my life and walked on the shore as often as possible. I picked my way along the old tracks that were not entirely obliterated by fill thinking of the iron horses of the past bellowing along my route. Of course now it was very quiet except for runners and apparently lovers, judging by the number of condoms littering the ground. I found all this oddly comforting. Sweating, whether through exercise or love, seemed healthy, and I remembered a poem I read in college, Keats, I imagine: "Ah, love, ah happy, happy love. Forever panting, forever young." I panted a bit on the inclines and thought of the poet, dead when he was younger than I was but so wise.

I came home through the park, enjoying the breeze off the lake, the slight smell of cinders in the air. Runners went by, some in uniform on their way somewhere at various paces, while women with strollers lined the park walkways. The next generation and none of mine among them. My neighbor Nell Prendergast was standing between our houses as if on sentry when I crossed the street and appeared to be upset about something on or near the sidewalk.

Generally, I tried to avoid Mrs. Prendergast. She was the sort of woman my mother used to describe as "having ideas about things" especially if they were the sort of things that sullied her sense of propriety and historical rightness. I supposed she was like Billy Doyle, old Milwaukee money; I knew she'd lived in her house for thirty years, staying on after her kids had left town and her husband Buddy had passed. I'd liked Buddy who once played right guard for Harvard and had the thickened nose and ruddy complexion of a serious drinker. After Buddy found out where I'd gone to school we had a standing bet on the Harvard/Yale game, something he took more seriously than I did, which could be why he died owing me $20.

Mrs. Prendergast was a cousin of one of "the Uihlein girls" and I thought there was some Schlitz money behind her but it was hard to tell for sure. Standing there in her ratty cardigan, straw hat, and broomstick skirt she didn't look like she was rich, but often that was a dead giveaway.

Now she spoke to me in a high, fluty voice. "So, Mr. Sorenson, how goes it in the law?" This was your basic unanswerable question and didn't require an answer.

"Nice to see you, Mrs. Prendergast," I said.

She picked up her walking stick and pointed at the street. "Disgraceful," she said.

This could have referred to the city's socialist mayors, the rabble across the street in the park, the rise of the lower classes, or all three; it was hard to tell for sure. "What's disgraceful?" I asked and immediately regretted it.

"Well, the way they let the city disintegrate," Mrs. Prendergast said.

Who "they" were was a mystery but you could assume whoever they were they weren't our kind of people. Since I wasn't really our kind of people either, I had limited sympathy with my neighbor's point of view, but peace across the back fence was important. I looked more closely and noticed some cracks in the pavement abutting the street and a small pothole that hadn't been filled, apparently left over from last winter, which had been a hard one. After living in New England, I was always impressed with Milwaukee's public works department, but I doubted I could convince Mrs. Prendergast of this.

"I just thought that since you're in the law you might be able to call someone," she said. "This used to be a very nice neighborhood."

83

Her suggestion was both flattering and condescending. On one hand, she believed I could just pick up the phone and get a crew out to our street, that I had that kind of influence downtown; on the other, she seemed to think I was her errand boy, available at a moment's notice. I decided to feel flattered, given the choice. I was in too good a mood to let anything bother me. "I'll see what I can do, Mrs. Prendergast. I'll call in the morning." And before she could respond, I pirouetted around her and went into the house.

We had been married for ten years and for almost two of those Moira had been focused on becoming pregnant. Since I had removed her from Massachusetts, taken her from the bosom of her friends and family, the implied suggestion was that I owed her a child in return. This made no sense, but I was in no position to object. I'd done my best to oblige, but the truth was I'd never had a passionate desire to be a father. An only child, I'd grown up mostly with adults and even as a child had no particular fondness for childish things. I disliked children's books, didn't watch cartoons, and resisted circuses and amusement parks. Even now I was the only person I knew who had never seen *The Wizard of Oz* or read *Wind in the Willows.*

And there was the experience of observing older friends with kids now in their teens or twenties, most of whom seemed mired in sullen determination to prove their parents wrong about a multitude of things despite years of private lessons, orthodontia, cars, and expensive schools. The most convincing argument I'd heard for having children came oddly enough from a childless friend who commented wistfully that it gave you the chance at one more intimate relationship. This sounded attractive, even if I wasn't doing so well with the intimate relationships I already had.

At base, I didn't understand the yearning some people had to reproduce, the idea that one of you somehow wasn't enough for the world. It was as if creating your own biological cluster made you more valid, even invincible, a way of putting off death and cheating mortality. Freud and others had said that true maturity could only be reached through parenthood, but I had my doubts. What was maturity anyway? All this was academic, however. Whether or not I wanted to be a parent, Moira did with a steady unswerving passion.

Which is why I was sitting in the waiting room of a fertility clinic at eight a.m. on a Thursday morning, clipboard on my knees writing out my medical history.

This wasn't the first such office we'd visited. Moira generally considered medical practice in Wisconsin to be medieval, a step removed from the barber's chairs where surgery had been practiced with razors in previous centuries. But in this case one of her friends had suggested a doctor she knew, so we agreed I'd visit the man and see what he had to say. After the customary blizzard of paperwork I was ushered through a white door and led down a corridor where I was shown into a cubicle to wait.

I'd already had the lab tests and a physical. I knew the drill. Moira assumed it was probably my fault that we'd failed to conceive, and I couldn't say for sure that she was wrong. The only thing that left me unconvinced was the fact that I'd managed to knock up Susie Wilson, a high school girlfriend who'd then gone down to Chicago for an abortion. But I'd never mentioned this to my wife and besides that was years ago. Things could have changed.

Finally, the door opened and a short thin man with a high forehead entered. He smiled nervously, as if he knew who had the problem, then offered his hand. "Mr. Simonson, I'm Dr. Walters." He didn't ask how he could help, which I took as acknowledgment that he might not be able to.

When we were seated, Walters looked quickly through the chart while I read his diploma wall. There were degrees from Marquette and the University of Texas, a state even more suspect in Moira's view than Wisconsin. "You've been at this for some time," he began, as if we were building model ships in bottles or remodeling the kitchen. "Very frustrating, I know."

He nodded in a way that seemed convincing and made me like him more. The circles beneath his eyes were pink and I wondered if these kinds of consultations made him nervous too. It seemed unlikely, but who knew for sure? Now he shut the folder with finality and looked seriously at me.

"Fertility is a very democratic field," he began. "So examining one partner only tells us a part of the story. The problem can be with either the male or female, but the number of complicating issues is greater in women. That being so, I can't really say anything without examining your wife, too."

"She's got a doctor in Boston," I said, as if this explained anything. "That's where she's from."

He nodded. "Well then, you said your wife is thirty-two? So I assume her doctor has done imaging tests to look at her ovaries and her fallopian tubes. Probably an ultrasound and blood tests to find any hormonal irregularities."

I nodded I as if I understood what he was talking about. "I can ask," I said.

"You do that," he said. Then he looked down at the chart on his desk. "As far as you're concerned, in men problems usually involve sperm shape and male reproductive hormones. Your sperm shape and motility are normal as is your sperm concentration. There are no testicular abnormalities, no infections of any kind."

He paused and though this was a clinical recitation of my private parts, I felt like shouting and throwing my arms in the air in victory. I restrained myself. We weren't out of the woods yet and it seemed like an oddly intimate conversation to have with another man, even a doctor. Still, it was reassuring to get the green light on my sperm count and made me feel curiously proud of the microorganisms within.

"Could it be something else?" I felt obliged to ask because I knew Moira would when we met later.

Walters shrugged. "It's unlikely. Sometimes there are sexual issues, erectile difficulty or what we call retrograde ejaculation where," he hesitated here, "where the semen doesn't go in the right direction."

Under the circumstances erectile difficulty seemed like a perfectly normal reaction, but for whatever reason we'd never had that problem. "Where would it go?" I asked.

"Most often into the bladder," Walters said quickly. "But I'm sure that's not what we're looking at here."

"Okay," I said. "Then in your opinion what is it? Do you have any idea what the problem is?"

Walters seemed to understand. I guessed that he got this a lot, couples blaming him because he wasn't able to produce children for them. He wrinkled his forehead and looked at the ceiling. "It's an inexact science," he began. "Sometimes situations simply resolve themselves, though it's true that you've been trying for a relatively long time." He reached into his desk and got a form. "You might take a look at this and if your problem continues we can do an ultrasound of your testes, but I don't think that will be necessary."

I looked at the sheet. Three pages of boilerplate with a long list of things that could interfere with pregnancy. It seemed more likely than not that something here would apply to us. Suddenly, I felt sympathy for Moira. It's hard to want something, something simple that ordinary people have without even thinking about it or even wanting it, people with no particular gifts, people less intelligent and good looking than we were. I thought about the large Catholic families I'd grown up among, families with eight or ten children in which the woman kept trying because she'd managed to produce only boys and wanted a girl. If either of us had ever had a preference, we didn't any longer. We didn't want babies with obvious imperfections, but failing that we'd settle for either sex. Still, nothing happened month after month after month. As much of a pain in the ass as Moira could be about it, I felt for her. The whole fertility drama had not only robbed our marriage of spontaneity but had taken away romance as well and this was something to lose.

"Discouraging," I said when I'd read through the document.

"Yes," Walters said now. "I understand. But beyond just continuing to try as you have or registering with one of the agencies for adoption, you and your wife have to get all the tests and then meet together with either me or her doctor and decide what to do next. For now, I'd say just go on as you are. If this continues beyond another year we can talk about next steps."

"I've heard of in vitro fertilization," I said.

Walters nodded. "We're not there yet," he said. "By far. And as you probably know that's both expensive and unpredictable."

"Not a sure thing."

"Far from it." But my mind was wandering from the room with the white walls and bland furnishings. It seemed odd to talk about fertility in a place this sterile. I thought of Mesopotamia and the Fertile Crescent, ancient cultures and the smell of verdant fields and water just minutes away. Even to talk about "trying" in the sense that Walters had used the word seemed artificial. It would have been oddly refreshing if a doctor showed curiosity about our sex life, asked if we ever made love with Moira on top or standing up, if we'd consulted the Kama Sutra or other manuals for new ideas. I remembered someone telling me I should take warm baths and let my balls soak in soapy water for fifteen minutes before sex. Another well-meaning friend said I should wear boxer shorts instead of briefs. I'd been given herbs and potions and even wore a truss for a couple of weeks, thinking maybe if everything was bound up in there some incredible power would make it all happen. I tried everything, what the hell, and nothing worked. Which had led finally to meeting in this little white box talking about possible artificial insemination.

"In vitro's, the petri dish, right?" I said. "Not to be indelicate, doctor."

Walters smiled. "We don't worry much about delicacy here, Mr. Simonson. But, yes, it's what you'd call the petri dish." He hesitated and looked down again at the folder on his lap. "But like I said, that's way down the road. Give your wife that handout and if you want to talk more, make an appointment with my secretary."

Out on the street, a cold wind blew. I was meeting Moira at a coffee shop to talk about my appointment but when I got there she was sitting in the corner looking at the wall. "So the doctor says I'm okay," I began.

"Of course he did," Moira said, as if the examination I'd just had was somehow compromised.

"I thought this was someone you wanted me to see," I said. "Your friend recommended him, right? Otherwise, why did I go?"

She shrugged and looked at her coffee cup. It was as if the fact that she could no longer hold me responsible for not becoming pregnant had robbed her of something important. I understood. Having someone else to blame for one's misfortunes is one of the essential comforts of life, just as having to accept the ineluctable fact that there's no one to blame is an equally great frustration. Still, I was pleased to have been let off the hook by Dr. Walters. I knew it was a stupid thing to feel good about, but I'd derived satisfaction from dumber things than this.

"He did say he'd like to see you," I said. "That there were some tests you should have, too."

She sighed loudly. "I already had all those tests, Andy. In Cambridge."

"Really?" I pulled the pamphlet out of my pocket and laid it in front of her on the table. "All of these? The imaging of your ovaries and fallopian tubes, an ultrasound?"

"Gee," she said. "They have all that stuff here in Wisconsin? Surprising."

Now she was getting on my nerves. "Look, Moira," I said. "All this is for you. I'm willing to just go ahead and take our chances, see what happens."

"And that's worked really well so far, hasn't it?" she said.

"Look, Walters gave me the name of a colleague if you don't want to go to him. How about if I make the call for you?"

She shook her head stiffly, almost as if she'd developed a tic or a tremor. "I don't think so," she said. Her voice was otherworldly, distant as the still air in the room.

"He also said we could check with adoption agencies, but we haven't really been trying that long. He said a year is average."

Moira pursed her lips, determined. "I'll never give up," she said.

"Jesus, who said we should give up, but if you don't trust the doctors who do these tests who do you trust?"

"I'm going to Boston," she said, a little smirk on her pretty face.

"I thought we settled this already and that going to your friend's specialist was the compromise. What good would going back to Boston do?"

Moira turned to face me, though it was clear I wasn't really essential in this, that the decision had already been made. And now I understood this had been the plan all along, that she'd been holding out on me.

"Daddy knows a specialist at Mass General," she said. "I have an appointment on Monday. I'm leaving tomorrow; I don't know how long I'll be gone."

Of course Harvard trumped whatever hick-town sawbones we could find in Milwaukee and, who knew, maybe the great man there would find something wrong with me after all. One could hope. I felt myself pull away, not a good thing but an old habit when whatever we were talking about threatened our life together. Who was this person anyway, this small beautiful woman I loved but who was finally and essentially a mystery? Because of her obsession with pregnancy, I had put myself out in ways I hadn't even known existed, been prodded and tested, jerked off into a cup for strangers, and in the end it had come to nothing except an out of town consult. And why stop at Harvard? Why not Mayo or Johns Hopkins? There was at base an unwillingness in Moira to think we weren't special and our case wasn't all that unusual or complicated. I understood but I also knew it was a habit of the rich to demand and get special treatment. The guy down the block never knew what was going on in his life and had to deal with things as he found them. Rich people always figured there was an angle they could try. It bothered me that somewhere along the line I'd crossed over into this territory without realizing it. But nothing was going to be gained by pointing this out.

"Okay," I said resignedly. "Have a nice trip and call me after you see the genius at Harvard."

Moira dropped me at my office but I was in no mood to go in and write wills. It occurred to me that I might get fired, that there was a limit to what Tom Williams could cover me for if I continued to avoid work, but I couldn't help that. Instead I walked over to Water Street and stood looking down at the river. Often enough, I found myself here or somewhere like it, feeling part of an endless stream of memories and associations, random and without logic but present in my head like a slideshow. If I drove up Third Street I'd think of the riots back in the sixties I'd only heard of from my mother. I remembered reading about Mayor Maier manning his control post and talking to the reporters about "the Milwaukee Solution," which came down to barricading the blacks in the ghetto, letting no one in or out, and waiting for the kids to burn everything down, which they eventually did. What had once been an interesting shopping street became a succession of burnedout hulks. But who remembered any of that now and who really cared? Life moved on or seemed to for most people, but I was stuck in the past, remembering ancient shopping trips with my mother to Schusters or corner grocery stores where they made their own cheese and ground knackwurst every week. Was this why I had dragged Moira back here, out of misplaced nostalgia, the fantasy that by going back I could somehow go forward, make some progress in life?

I didn't want to admit it if this were true and now things were fundamentally different. Instead of living in a floor-through on Frederick, I had what amounted to a mansion on Lake Drive. I was a downtown lawyer whose practice—except for Frank Pignatano—was limited to dowagers whose exposure to Third Street and all it implied was no more extensive than my wife's. I had more money than I knew how to spend and while I could reminisce about an earlier, simpler time, all of that was behind me now.

Riverside High School, drunken picnics on the beach during the annual bratwurst festival in Sheboygan, cruising up and down Wisconsin Avenue with glasspacked mufflers roaring in my ears, girls with big hair, lost weekends in cheap hotels, all that was gone and it was probably for the best. Except now, having given it up for Moira, my law practice and all that, Moira felt as gone as Third Street even if she wasn't leaving until morning. Since she had said she didn't know when she'd be back, it occurred to me that this might be some kind of trial separation, but I hadn't thought the problems between us had gone that far. What I knew was that it was the first time my wife was planning to leave town on an open ticket without plans for a return. That much was beyond doubt. I picked up a rock and threw it toward the water.

93

The popular conception of law, going to court and making dramatic opening statements, petitioning the governor as the convict approaches the death chamber, wearing expensive suits with flashy lining, all of that had little to do with what I did. I spent my days with clients and doing research. In my firm, the idea was to avoid court if possible by finding a way to settle your cases. Too many things were left to chance if you went to trial, too many variables were beyond your control with juries and whatever judge you drew. By finding a way to settle, you could save money on court costs, which meant you continued to have a billable client. My hours may have been erratic, but I had a good record in this regard, which had kept me out of trouble so far.

Sitting at my desk, talking on the phone, reading, my mind was half on Moira and the rest on what I was actually supposed to be doing. I had offered to drive her to the airport but she said she'd rather take a cab. A part of me wanted to go to Boston with her, another wished she'd just stay away. Her leaving town was about her desire to have a baby and at the same time it wasn't. Beyond anything practical or even impractical it was a way to act out her feelings about Milwaukee, which meant whatever else her leaving meant, it was about me and where I came from, about keeping my mother's house, even about Frank and the kind of life I'd lived before and wanted to live now.

As the hours passed, however, I came to care less and less. Work had the capacity to swallow me up, pull me in, no matter how routine or tedious it was. This was why I'd done well at Yale. I remembered sitting in the law library for hour after hour until my body seemed welded to the library chair, my arms rooted in the table in front of me, going over endless cases and hypothetical situations. And while my fellow students complained rightly that their legal education had little to do with their eventual careers as lawyers, I reveled in the mundane reality of life as a law student and made Law Review in the bargain. It was little different now. The fact that the work I did was not intrinsically interesting and that it was done for people I didn't care about made no difference. The financial lives of my clients drew me in irresistibly and in this fashion the afternoon went by. My wife had left to go back to her father's house, but I was strangely content. I wasn't sure if this was an adjustment or meant I was truly sick, but in a sense it didn't matter.

A blue light was settling over the room by the time I dictated the last letter. Outside I could see the street lights coming on up and down the street. Time to go but I disliked going home alone—or rather going home to an empty house—so I called Tom, thinking we might have dinner.

"Ah, the arrogance of the married," he said. "Secure in your little houses, hunkered down in front of the TV with your dinner on trays in front of you, you figure that whenever you're free we single people will be so desperate we'll jump at the chance to spend a few stolen hours with you. Sorry, Pal, but I have plans. On the other hand, if you think Moira's going to be gone for long, I could tell my friend you're single and ask if she knows someone she could set you up with?"

I thought about it for a second but then hung up. Tom wasn't all wrong about being married, about the sense of insularity it engendered, the feeling of being an actual entity apart from other people. But even if I was alone for now, I didn't feel single, if I ever had. The way I looked at it, the time before I met Moira was just suspended space, years I wasted while waiting for the big thing in my life to happen. Maybe I was preparing to meet her, getting ready, I couldn't say. I remembered clearly though the first time I'd seen her standing in the doorway of the library. She was wearing a long navy coat. When she looked my way with her black hair and heavy-lidded eyes I was a goner, transfixed, locked in place and unable to move. If she hadn't smiled I'd probably still be standing there. But as luck would have it, she did and then she walked away. What I remember thinking is, "Don't kid yourself. That's never going to happen."

About an hour later, someone tapped me on the shoulder and it was the girl from the doorway with big eyes. She motioned to me to follow her into the hall. Once we got outside, she said, "This is really embarrassing, but you look like a nice guy. Could you take me home? It's not far, just over on Church Street, but it looks like my ride's not going to make it and I don't like to walk alone in this neighborhood."

Yale was an oasis in a bombed-out section of New Haven, but for once I was glad they had let the area around the university decay. I got my coat and walked Moira home and that's how it started. She confided later that there had never been a ride, that she'd made the whole thing up because she wanted to meet me. The deception didn't matter because I was in love and the idea that someone like Moira would go to this much trouble to meet me was incredibly flattering. But she was like that; she went after what she wanted with a focus that could be alarming. It was probably why this fertility business got to her the way it did. She couldn't just order up a baby because she had decided she wanted one. Yet I knew that if that was going to be possible for anyone, it would be Moira.

Alluring as this memory was, however, it was the past and seemed more remote all the time. Infatuation, desire, love had little to do with my being alone at seven at night with nowhere to go except home to the television set. I had been raised on reruns of noir films of the forties, however, and found something attractive about being alone and on my own. I had the trench coat and with a slight posture adjustment I could manage the ruffled appearance of a b-movie star, say Richard Widmark or even Ray Milland in *The Lost Weekend.* This didn't work for long, though; I didn't even smoke. As far as I could tell there were essentially two options: a restaurant called The Rendezvous where they served acceptable meat loaf or Donovan's. I chose the bar and felt more cheerful as soon as I heard the pinball machines banging away and Bing Crosby on the jukebox. It was like stepping into an alternate universe but an invented one since I doubted such a life had ever really existed outside like the scene in here, which improved on reality with lighting and alcohol. Anyone who doubts this should stay around a bar after closing when they turn up the lights, but tonight it didn't matter. Given the way I was handling my life, I'd take faux reality, at least for the time being.

To my surprise, Donovan's had a real menu in addition to bar food so I ordered corned beef and cabbage and a beer and sat watching the evening news while I ate. When Patsy appeared next to my table I couldn't have said I was surprised though I hadn't actively been thinking about her. It was Friday and somewhere in my mind I remembered that was when she met her seminar at Donovan's.

She looked as if she'd gone to more trouble with herself than usual. In addition to a form-fitting turtleneck, there seemed to be a spot of red on her lips. It hadn't occurred to me before that Patsy might wear make-up. I might have assumed she'd be against it on principle, but here she was.

"I hear Moira's headed back to civilization," she said, getting right to the point.

I looked over at her. "Have you ever wanted to have kids?" I asked.

A non sequitur but Patsy seemed unruffled by it. "One of me seems to be enough for this world," she said and smiled to let me know she wasn't entirely serious. "Mind if I join you?"

I was pleased that she hadn't repeated some platitude about not wanting to bring children into this debased world, and as I looked at her I noticed something new in her expression, an eagerness I couldn't remember seeing before. It made sense that Patsy would be as lonely as anyone else, as lonely as I was if I stopped to think about it, but I never had. She didn't inspire that kind of consideration with her tough talk and sardonic remarks. "Sure," I said. "Have some corned beef?"

She grimaced at the suggestion but sat down and drank a beer. Then we sat together in quiet companionship for an hour or so, after which we got up and danced to Frank Sinatra and I felt the pressure of her hips in my groin, the soft points of her breasts in the tight sweater pressing against my chest. I wondered vaguely where her students had gone and what they'd think of their professor now. But the song ended without any students appearing and we went back to the table for another drink.

At the end of the evening without either of us saying anything about it, we left together and went to Patsy's house where I spent the first adulterous night of my life in something that felt very much like friendly communion, though I doubt my wife would have understood it that way.

In the morning, I made coffee in her cluttered kitchen. There were tiles on the window sill and some dying plants on a shelf over the sink. A collected Auden sat on the table propping up a napkin rack. There was one stained placemat but somehow the kitchen didn't look sad, just lived-in by a person who didn't take much trouble with food. No Julia Child or Cuisinart or polished bread boards and wine racks, though a half-opened bottle of cheap burgundy was on the sideboard. After a while Patsy appeared in a blue terrycloth bathrobe, hair in her eyes and an ironic look on her face. "You're still here," she said. "I thought guys took off at dawn so they wouldn't have to face the girl in the morning."

I shrugged. "Sorry to disappoint you, but I can make a mean cheese omelet." She came over and kissed me on the earlobe. "I'm not disappointed," she said. "Just giving you some shit. Is that okay?"

"Where's a frying pan?" I said. Then I cracked some eggs in a bowl and cooked while Patsy sat and watched. We ate breakfast together and after that I cleaned up while she read the paper. I liked the fact that neither of us felt the need to "process" what had happened the night before or guess whether it would go on or stop right here. We didn't mention Moira or the fact that they were friends; we felt comfortable in the sunny room, as if we hadn't done anything terribly wrong. I was surprised that I didn't feel guilty, that somehow this barrier had been passed without great emotional conflict, but it seemed undeniable that it had. It bore thinking about. In the meantime, I enjoyed Patsy and appreciated the fact that, whatever was present or lacking, there didn't need to be any declaration of this, any dumping on bourgeois values, any anything.

After a decent interval Patsy stood up and said she had to get ready to teach. She gave me a friendly hug at the door and I left. That was all there was to it. That seemed fine to me at the time but despite our shared insouciance, I should have known that crossing this particular Rubicon would in the end have unforeseen consequences for me.

Time went by, a day, then two or three, and nothing earth-shattering happened. The skies didn't open, no firestorm of guilt or self-doubt enveloped me. Things seemed much as they had before. Moira called a few times and we had brief, polite conversations avoiding the central topic, as if neither of us were sure what it really was. She gave no indication that she was leaving me, or even thinking of it, but the fact remained that she was gone and when we talked she neglected to set a date for her return. For my part, I was reasonably successful at keeping my voice even and noncommittal despite what had happened with Patsy. Under the circumstances that seemed like a significant accomplishment. But at least part of the reason I could be so restrained is that I didn't really know or understand what had happened. It seemed very sudden, perhaps too sudden. Moira left town and within the day I was in bed with her friend. Then it occurred to me that maybe it wasn't sudden at all, but just something that moved at a pace I hadn't been completely aware of or hadn't wanted to acknowledge. I remembered seeing Patsy's body when we ran and her flirting with me in the kitchen weeks before. That could have been the beginning. Still, it was unique in my experience. I'd had no affairs before, nor had I ever been tempted by other women. I loved my wife and that had always been enough for me in the past. It may have been Moira's unhappiness with Milwaukee or her obsession with having children that had caused things to change but that was by no means certain. The truth was I didn't know why I'd done what I had.

In any case, I felt no compulsion to confess to Moira or seek absolution from her. It would be unfair to expect her to understand when I didn't understand myself. Instead, I went to work and when I had time on my hands I decided to act like a landlord. I bought paint at Sears and got up on a ladder and started slapping it on the chipping cornices of the old house, being careful not to go above the second floor. I figured if I fell from there I'd break something but it wouldn't be that serious. I'd live and not be crippled. This reflected pretty accurately my state of mind.

From where I stood on the ladder, I could feel but not see the lake, the brisk damp air on my forehead, the smell of something vaguely like lime. The cornices like white eyebrows, running horizontally above the line of windows, the windows themselves, like milky eyes, reflecting light, opaque in the early afternoon. I didn't want to appear like a voyeur, didn't want to intrude on my tenants, even if I had a right to be there, but the roof sagged under the accumulated weight of years of snow and ice and I imagined the wood rotting steadily beneath the eaves, which would be just another thing to replace, something else for Moira and me to argue about.

As I painted, I thought how important it had been to Mom that I hold onto the place. Decrepit as it was, the house was the sum of her accumulated wealth over a long and difficult life characterized by a racking concern about money. I knew it had been enormously comforting to her to own a house, something that was actually hers and miraculously increasing in value. She loved to sit in front of her fire on winter afternoons drinking wine and feeling wistful and she couldn't have cared less about rotting shingles, peeling paint, or the opinions of others. I envied her this, and wished I was similarly gifted. To simply sell the house for whatever it would bring would be in some way to cash her in, especially since the house had its own special charm and inevitably its place in my life and heart. There was a kind of faded elegance about it, a good location and all that art leaning against the walls in the attic. You couldn't put a price on that.

In the instant of thinking this, however, I suddenly understood in a way I hadn't before Moira's unwillingness to accept my vision. To her, the house and everything in it represented an inability to move past my life with my mother and the years we'd spent together, a dyad against the world. Moira wasn't interested. But putting Moira aside, holding onto the house made no sense to Tom Williams or my other friends either. An aging house, slowly falling in upon itself simply didn't have the appeal to them that it did for me. In the late autumn sunshine, standing on my ladder, I wondered if this was the true reason my wife had retreated to Boston, that the fertility workup was just a premise. I wondered if this old house and all it represented would be an impediment to her ever coming back.

I could feel the pressure of the ladder's rungs on the balls of my feet through my tennis shoes as I stood there thinking and occasionally dipping the brush into the can of paint. Then I became aware of someone watching, a face in the whiteness of the window and the sash coming up violently.

"What're you doing here, Counselor? Stalking me? This is my bedroom, for Christ's sake."

I almost fell off the ladder then and there but recovered in time to see Frank Pignatano just below me in a jock and sleeveless T-shirt, making no attempt to conceal the fact that there was a brunette with large breasts lying in the bed behind him. Despite his cocky smile, I was struck by Frank's narrow chest and flabby biceps. He had a fading tattoo of a cobra in red and black on his right shoulder blade and I wondered idly if this might be a prison tat or some kind of gang sign. Behind him, the girl smiled and wiggled her fingers at me in greeting.

"Sorry," I said. "I was just doing some painting." It sounded lame, I knew, but I honestly hadn't seen a thing, hadn't even thought about whether Frank was in the apartment in the middle of the afternoon.

The girl still didn't move to cover herself and now Frank gestured vaguely in her direction. "Donna, Andy; Andy, Donna." It wasn't much of an introduction but what could you expect with me standing on a ladder, painter's hat on my head? Donna wiggled her fingers again and to my annoyance I felt myself growing hard. In defense, I started going down the ladder as quickly as I could. When I looked up, Frank had head and shoulders out the window. He winked at me, so I called out, "You should be more careful. You're getting sued, you know."

He shrugged. "What're you gonna do," he said, as if we were partners in crime, which in a way we were.

I hitched the ladder on my shoulder and had started walking down the driveway toward the garage when Frank called me back. "Hey, I almost forgot. My old man wants to talk to you."

I stopped short. This was interesting. I'd never even seen Sal Pignatano except for his picture in the papers, but I knew instinctively this was an invitation you didn't refuse. "What about?" I called over my shoulder.

"How the fuck would I know," Frank said and slammed the window shut.

I told Patsy about this at dinner that night. We were eating at Kalt's, a restaurant that tried for a theater ambiance with drawings of local celebrities and forgotten period actors and actresses on the walls, all inscribed lovingly to Howie, one of the owners.

Beyond the pictures Kalt's didn't really have much to do with the theater except that it was adjacent to a shuttered repertory playhouse where I remembered my mother telling me about a play she had once seen starring Shelley Winters. The theater had been dark for years but the theatrical motif of the restaurant derived from the years it had been in business. Apparently as a hedge against seeming dated the owners had supplemented the celebrity caricatures with a subordinate German gasthaus theme featuring fake clay pilasters holding up ornamental steins even though all they served at Kalt's was Schlitz and Miller. For all this, it was a pleasant place, soft lights, jazz, fairly inexpensive, and in the neighborhood. Tonight, I noticed Patsy had put on a new pair of jeans and a fresh turtleneck, which made me wonder if things were getting serious between us.

I described my run-in with Frank and about his father's summons, which made her laugh. Unlike Moira, Patsy wasn't put off by Frank and his associates. She thought the gangland connections were an exotic anodyne to otherwise staid Milwaukee, though I doubted she'd ever seen anyone killed by one of Frank's colleagues. "Maybe you can get to be a made man," she said now.

"I doubt it," I said. "I think that's an initiation rite like a bar mitzvah and it has to happen by a certain age. Oh, yeah, you have to be Sicilian."

She wrinkled her forehead and said, "Like in *The Godfather* that lawyer couldn't be in the mob either, could he?"

"There you go," I said. "A good example."

"My dad was a lawyer back in Jersey who defended this mob guy and when he got sent up he gave Dad the getaway car for his fee."

Patsy had told me her father couldn't make a living from the law and had instead taken up taxidermy, which eventually made him rich when the Eagles went to the Super Bowl and everyone wanted the stuffed variety for their recreation rooms. "An intriguing possibility," I said.

"It wasn't a bad car," Patsy said. "One of those big DeSotos with electric windows and fake velvet seats. A nice ride, cushy, but there were a couple of bullet holes in the fenders."

"Which made it all the more unusual," I said. "A conversation piece. Although maybe not in Jersey?"

When she smiled her face lit up and when she laughed it was a transforming experience. Tonight she looked really happy for one of the first times since I'd known her. In that moment, I wondered why I didn't love her. It seemed easy, much less complicated than my relationship with my wife, and I knew it would have made Patsy happy. Why couldn't that be enough? "Exactly," she said. "You really get it, Andy. That's great about you."

It was strange to be sitting there with this woman whom I'd known before only as a friend of Moira's, to realize this and still not feel uncomfortable, but I didn't. I would have thought either the situation or our shared duplicity should have set something off and made us start sniping at each other. But we were fine together as we sat joking and drinking. It made me wonder about myself, and about Patsy, but I didn't wonder very hard or for very long. Nor did I have any particular curiosity about where our relationship was going or what would happen when Moira came back.

A few days before I had raised this question and Patsy said, "Going? I never know what people mean by that. Does a relationship have to go somewhere?"

"Most women I know would think so," I said. "And a lot of them might feel guilty about being with a friend's husband."

Patsy looked amused.

"You think that's funny?" She was continually surprising me.

"Not exactly," Patsy said. "I mean, not funny ha-ha. Not a joke or anything. And it's not that I've got some kind of Marxist disdain for bourgeois values like loyalty or fidelity. Generally, I think loyalty's a good thing. It's just funny to me that people say, you know, 'I could never sleep with him because I like his wife.' As if it would be fine if they hated the wife. Doesn't that seem kind of absurd to you?"

"But you do like Moira, don't you?"

Patsy nodded and drank some wine. "Sure, I do. I just don't think that has anything to do with this. She can take care of herself so I don't have to worry about that. And to be completely honest, one reason I wanted to be friendly with Moira in the first place was to be around you."

"She was that pathetic, that you couldn't be her friend just because of her?"

"Pathetic? Moira?" Patsy laughed again. "Superwoman is more like it, above it all. Smarter, prettier, classier than the rest of us combined. She didn't need me or anyone else to validate her. She tolerated me, probably because I went to Radcliffe, and I was willing to be tolerated, that's all."

It was all complicated, but I knew that already. I was flattered that Patsy had wanted to be in close proximity to me in case an opportunity presented itself, even if I felt the need to defend Moira. And despite my previous lack of experience, I knew Patsy was right. Openings tend to appear over time even if you do nothing to provoke them. If you truly wanted to avoid such things you'd stay away completely, and I hadn't. Still, I was flattered and surprised that she had focused on me. I considered myself to be about as interesting as the flocked wallpaper in our second bathroom.

"I had no idea you were such a schemer," I said.

Patsy nodded. "I'm good at hiding. Besides, it was possible nothing would ever have happened between us and then what would be the point in talking about it?"

"No harm done then?"

"No harm done anyway," she said lightly. "At least not yet."

It was a new way of looking at things. I had always imagined virtually everything had the power to harm you, which was a good reason to keep yourself locked up and secure from temptation. Secrets had the potential to eat away at a relationship even if they also gave you power and control. But Patsy seemed truly unconcerned. We enjoyed being together, had vigorous sex often, but to her that seemed to be the end of it. There were no impassioned notes or whispered late-night phone calls. No back-door calls at the office or codes by which she could bypass the secretary. Patsy didn't need these things and while I'd always assumed they were essential to any love affair ours seemed to work equally well without them. Live and learn. I suppose you could have said we were adults and carried on our relationship like adults but that seemed too convenient even if it described things well.

"So," she said now. "Are you coming over?"

"I was waiting for an invitation," I said. I paid the bill and we went over to her house and lay together in her bedroom with the down quilts and Burroughs posters on the walls and made love and I was if not happy at least not unhappy. One thing I knew was that I didn't miss Moira and that didn't seem like a good sign to me.

Sal Pignatano's office was located in back of a bakery in what used to be called Little Italy but had recently become fashionable following an influx of Yuppies and empty nesters to the lower East Side. Milwaukee had never been a big organized crime city, maybe because of the socialist mayors and the consequent lack of important corruption in City Hall. All city contracts were put out for bid and Italians weren't even an important minority in town, dwarfed by the Poles and Germans who had controlled city politics for decades.

There was crime, of course, but it wasn't like Chicago or Detroit. The Milwaukee mob was strictly small time, some gambling and girls, numbers and protection payoffs but that was all. You didn't have murders in busy restaurants or barbershops the way they did in New York and Chicago. Maybe someone got his legs broken for not making good on a bet, but I couldn't remember the last time that happened. The Third Ward was only about two miles in diameter and even if the Italians controlled it, which they did, it amounted only to a seat on the City Council and a street fest in the summer at

St. Joan's where the women played bingo with the priests and the men snuck shots in back of the Ferris wheel.

But that was then, in the eighties, when I was growing up. Now Brady Street was clogged with lofts, beemers, and high-end bistros that took reservations a week ahead of time. Even the Italians had mostly moved out to the suburbs, leaving only a few businesses like Glorioso's market and Tagliaferro's bakery, which stood as it always had in the middle of the block on Brady, giving the street a sense of solidity it would otherwise have lacked. I enjoyed the aromatic smell of fresh bread from the street but the woman at the cash register didn't look up when I walked inside. I asked for Sal and she looked mildly surprised, then hunched her shoulder and jerked a thumb toward a rear door.

There was a one-story office suite the size of a double-wide trailer standing just behind the bakery building in the alley and when I stepped inside, it was a world away from the smells and hustle of the front, having the look instead of any business office in town. There was a large beige carpet, Danish modern desks, and Pre-Raphaelite reproductions on the wall. A girl with big hair sitting at the front desk took my name and told me to wait. In a place like this I figured it made sense to follow instructions, so I sat on a side chair and picked up a copy of *Architectural Digest.*

In time another door opened, which apparently led to an inner sanctum, and a thin man with a receding hairline in a camel sport coat and open-necked silk shirt came out and stood in front of me. "Mr. Simonson?" he said. "I'm Salvatore Pignatano. Thanks for coming down here."

He acted as if it had been my choice, which I thought was a nice touch. His speech sounded slightly eastern or foreign, I couldn't be sure which, but there was nothing overtly menacing in his manner, which made me ashamed of my assumptions.

As he stepped aside for me to walk in, I noticed that Sal's gray hair was airbrushed behind his ears and that he was well-dressed in a quietly elegant way that would be noticeable only to those interested in noticing. No pinkie rings or heavy jewelry. This was a man intent on not drawing attention to himself, perhaps because of modesty or because he knew he was continually being watched by the police. The only thing that hinted at something darker were the ropy muscles of his forearms revealed when he removed his coat and an impressive gold Rolex on his wrist. Otherwise he was understated all the way. But of course I was thinking in the cliched terms of old George Raft movies; I had no idea what actual gangsters looked like and was forced to fall back on images from films and TV shows seen and forgotten long ago.

Sal led me into his office where we sat next to each other on Breuer chairs covered in caramel leather. On the wall were degrees from the Extension and Marquette law school as well as photographs of Sal with the usual run of public officials at ribbon cuttings. Sal with past council members, state senators, mayors, governors, and even a presidential candidate. In each case there were the practiced grimaces of public life, a sense that in this job you never know who the hell you were going to have to ask for money, but always Sal was smiling, looking pleased with himself for being there and knowing the score. There was also a plaque from the Italian Businessman's Club as "Man of the Year" in 1985. I wondered what business exactly he saw himself as being part of.

"You're a lawyer," I said, stating the obvious.

"I am," he said, and shrugged though I could tell he was pleased that I had noticed. "Not like you, though. I passed the bar but never practiced. I went to the Extension, and then I got into Marquette to wrestle. Not many Italians there at the time, mostly micks and Germans, but I did okay. I went to law school after Vietnam to please my mother."

"That's something we have in common then," I said.

"Interesting," Sal said, though it wasn't really. "I knew your mother. A fine woman and a good artist; I've got a few of her paintings." Then we were quiet for a moment, as if gathering momentum for whatever lay ahead. I wondered how many people not in the business were invited into this room, wondered if this was where Sal and his consiglieri plotted strategy, if this was where they sweated the traitors who talked to the cops or gangland rivals before hustling them out the door to the alley; wondered if this was the room where poor workers from the neighborhood came to plead their cases to the godfather; wondered, in short, if anything understood in the popular culture about this kind of life was actually true. It was a little like being on a movie lot. But when Sal spoke it was quietly and with a tone of sadness.

"So, my son says you're representing him."

I wasn't sure about the ethics of discussing a client's case with a third party, even his father, but I decided not to stand on principle. "It's a civil case," I said. "Involving an ex-girlfriend."

Sal nodded and shook his head. His manner was somber, even stately. "I was eighteen when I married his mother," he said. "She was sixteen and couldn't speak English. Now no one gets married." He shook his head again. "He could have come to me," he said now. "We have counsel on retainer." He gestured to the empty room as if a legion of briefcased barristers were standing by awaiting his order to spring into action. "In our business . . ." He didn't finish the sentence but I knew what he meant. "Anyway, I want to help any way I can."

I wasn't sure what he could do besides arrange for the disappearance of Cindy Braithwaite, and that would raise questions we didn't want raised. But I knew this quiet gracious man would do whatever he did behind the scenes without his participation ever being noticed by anyone involved. It was hard to square Sal and this room with Frank's tattoos and pimp haircut, his wise-guy attitude, all of it. "I think the best thing is just to do what you're already doing," I said. "Supporting your son."

Sal nodded. "You're right. It's better that I stay out of it, but it's hard when it's your own kid. Do you have children, Mr. Simonson?"

"Not yet," I said, thinking of Moira at the fertility clinic in Boston. "I hope to some day."

"Then you'll know," Sal said, his eyes sad. "You never feel quite as helpless as when your son's in trouble, no matter what kind of trouble it is."

Frank had been in prison and involved with minor rackets in town for years, but his father hadn't given up caring about him. "With luck, we can get Frank out of this," I said, trying to sound more hopeful than I felt.

Sal smiled and I felt suddenly larger, as if I'd been invited into a select circle that mattered. I liked Sal and in that moment, being fatherless myself, I envied Frank for having this man to care about him. "If anyone can, you can," Sal said. "Keep me posted."

Things were never as they seemed. It was a basic truth but one that was hard for me to learn. Frank might be the problem child of Sal's organization, but essentially his father was as concerned as any suburbanite would be on learning his kid was failing algebra. He wanted his son to be happy and like all of us he had definite ideas about what shape that happiness should take. It didn't include Cindy Braithwaite or the brunette I'd seen in Frank's bedroom the day before, though I had a feeling there wasn't much going on in Frank's life that Sal didn't know about.

By the time I got to the car, it was eleven and I hadn't been to the office or even thought about the briefs waiting on my desk. Still, I didn't feel like going there yet so headed in the other direction, driving back up Brady to Farwell and then north toward home. Things had fallen apart somewhat since Moira left but now I didn't have to please anyone except myself with my housekeeping. My diet ran to microwaved entrees and macaroni and cheese when I didn't eat with Patsy, but that was all right. I'd read in books about men who were great cooks and were always whipping up gourmet meals from odds and ends in the fridge, but that wasn't me or any other man I knew. I could crack eggs in a pan or make a bowl of soup if the need arose, but that was about it and it seemed like enough. Scooping a handful of Cheerios from an open box, I headed upstairs.

My home office wasn't much, an extra room with a desk shoved against the wall, a chair and some bookshelves, but it was all I needed when I took work home, which wasn't very often. When I checked, the red light on the answering machine was blinking. It was Moira, sounding very much like herself or at least as she had been lately. "Where *are* you?" she asked plaintively. "I thought you'd at least be there at eight in the morning. Especially today!"

I racked my brain, trying to remember what was special about today, whether I had anything more than Patsy to feel guilty about, but I hadn't spent the night there and had only been up early to meet Sal. I'd had breakfast at Ma Fischer's to gather my thoughts before heading over to Brady and it was an hour later in Boston anyway so what was the big deal? Then it hit me. It was Tuesday and she'd had her follow-up appointment with the miracle worker at Mass General this morning. "Call me!" she commanded before hanging up.

I didn't know the details about her first meeting with the doctor at Mass General and had a dim recollection of her telling me about some tests to come but that was all. I figured in one way or another this would involve my spermatic inadequacies, but there would be plenty of time for that later. Besides, I still didn't know how to handle the Patsy question. The fact that she made no demands and took me exactly as I was with no suggestions for improvement acted as a strong aphrodisiac and I wondered idly if she knew it, if this was part of a plan. Instead of pushing the envelope, she acted as uninvolved as men generally did in a relationship, but it seemed real to me and this could actually be the reason she wasn't with anyone else. This was the way she wanted things to go. I made a mental note to call Moira later and went in the next room to dress for work.

Sometime during the night the wind picked up, howling around the sides of the house and getting in among the rafters and bringing with it wet, heavy snow. Weather always had a distinct personality in Milwaukee, sometimes mocking, sometimes gentle, but always different from any other place I'd lived. Weathermen lined up for jobs at our television stations because unlike, say, Phoenix or Los Angeles, the weather here interested them. Unlike cities where they took some cute redhead, sent her to correspondence school, and called her a meteorologist, in Milwaukee all the weathermen had PhDs, taught at universities, and published papers on updrafts and other abstruse subjects. They were serious people who considered a specialty in weather systems to be a calling, something worthy of dedication and study. Whatever the city might lack in other areas, Milwaukee was the big leagues when it came to weather and everyone knew it. The city repaid the local meteorologists for their passion by plastering their faces on the sides of buses and running promos for them during evening drive time. It was the weathermen, not the anchors, who were in demand. They all had fan clubs and were booked months in advance for charity events. It was a dream job, especially when it snowed.

I leaned against the window, feeling the glass like a cold compress against my forehead, and saw a wall of snow making its way like a foreign army south and west from the park and up the boulevard toward downtown. I imagined the storm in its infancy up north in Canada and then slowly gaining power as it swept down over the Upper Peninsula of Michigan, across the lake, heading for the Milwaukee shore. We'd bear the brunt of this one, though Chicago would have some weather too as it headed south. Now the trees outside were bent nearly horizontal from the wind and the storm seemed like an invading army, an unstoppable force that would be stupid to deny. Still, at daylight men would be out with shovels digging out their cars and before that, the city's plows would be on every street in town, because in Milwaukee the single greatest sin, guaranteed to end a mayor's political career, was being in the way of a man getting to work. This extended to the home front. It was a serious offence here to leave your sidewalk covered with snow and ice after a storm. If even a day went by, a city official would be at your door with a ticket and a summons. Milwaukee was a city that went by the rules and liked them; it had always been that way.

I got back in bed and noticed the clock read three a.m. "What is it?" a muffled voice asked. For a moment I was confused. Had Moira somehow reappeared without my noticing? Then I remembered. After dinner, Patsy had come back with me instead of taking me to her house as usual. She hadn't stayed over before and I had wondered if it would feel strange, if she would. If making love in another woman's bed would inhibit her in some way. But Patsy was thankfully immune to such feelings, and since she was, it turned out I was as well. In the past, I might have wondered if this meant I was sick, but I no longer worried about such things. Patsy had said our affair was just what it was and all that it was. That is, we were. And tautological as that seemed, I had decided she was right. Anything beyond the immediate reality of the moment would be our creation and without saying anything we'd decided we weren't going to create anything new right now.

"It's snowing," I said and kissed the blanket where I thought her head should be.

"It does that in winter," Patsy said. Then we went back to sleep.

The morning was different. We moved slowly, bumping into each other without apology, as if the kitchen were strange to us. Yet Patsy had spent hours there drinking coffee with Moira and, after all, this was my home. Eventually we got settled in the window seat and sat there together watching the storm.

The wind had brought cold weather with it and because the snow was wet, it froze in place before the plows could move in, making the boulevard a skating rink with cars rolling by sideways or doing donuts as they careened on their way. From our vantage point it looked balletic rather than terrifying, and we watched the slow drift of cars as one and then another slid inevitably into the curb, a tree, or another car trying valiantly to get out of the way. It was a graceful, beautiful dance and at that speed unlikely to cause too much trouble or inconvenience.

"It's like us," Patsy said dreamily.

"The cars?"

"No, well, yes, the sliding into something, maybe a crash," she said. "No one intends for it to happen, it just does and in its own way it's both beautiful and damaging."

"Do you always think in metaphors this early in the morning?"

"You bring it out in me," she said. "It could be a good thing."

I had to think about that for a minute, why it would be good, but before I could respond she was putting her dishes in the sink and walking out of the room. I looked back at the cars sliding and thought they could have avoided it all by not going on the ice in the first place, but that was no way to live. Staying inside where it was safe just because you were afraid to take chances, afraid of a fall, a crash. Which may have been what Patsy meant.

I reached Moira later in the morning at her father's house. Before speaking to her, I had to chat with the old man for a moment, sensing as I always did in his flattened As disapproval of me and the life I'd chosen for his daughter. I could see him in his braces and highly polished shoes, hand pushed into his waist, chin held high as if to avoid the scent of others, and I didn't like him in imagination any more than I did in life. Though an unpleasant word was never spoken, I knew the feeling was mutual. Finally, Moira came on the line. "I thought you'd never call," she said, still sulking.

"Sorry," I said. "It's been crazy around here. I didn't get your message until it was too late to call and now it's snowing."

"Andy, do I give a shit?" Moira said. It always shocked me when she was vulgar, made me think she was someone else, that I might be. It was hard to reconcile that tone with the woman I had fallen in love with, the woman I'd married, the woman who had waited for me at the law library—all the stories, myths, and legends that make up any relationship. I wondered if through some strange telekinesis she could see me over the miles, read my body language and know that I was committing adultery.

"I thought you might ask how I was," she continued. "That you might show some fucking interest in your wife instead of the goddamned snow."

She had a point. I wondered if her father was listening to our conversation and what he'd think of me now. Or what my mother would have thought. I didn't consider myself an amoral person, but it now seemed that I wasn't feeling what I should be. No matter who had left whom in the first place, we weren't really separated. "I'm sorry. I didn't mean the snow was interesting," I said, backtracking. "And of course I care how you are. I assume you're having a great time in Boston, seeing friends, going to the BFA and good restaurants."

But Moira wasn't mollified. "Did you just call me to fight, is that it? Does it make it easier for you?"

I wasn't sure what she meant, what would be easier, so I didn't pursue that. "No, of course not. Really, I'm sorry. What did the doctor say?"

She let out a deep breath as if talking to me was right up there with the labors of Hercules. Then she said, "Dr. France says he needs to interview you to be sure."

I see London, I see France came to mind, a children's rhyme. What was that all about, I wondered, but I had to stay on message here. "Sure of what?" I asked. A gray Chevy was sliding sideways down the street, the driver waving his arms ineffectually, as if that might have some deterrent effect on two tons of steel.

"Of what's wrong, of course. Are you okay, Andy?"

I was never sure when people asked this if they were asking if you were okay in a temporal sense or if there was a question of your okayness in relation to the cosmos, the great scheme of things, and you were demonstrating some essential fallibility. But most often I assumed people meant nothing at all. "I just meant did you tell him that we've already been through all that, the tests and examinations? Did you take your records along when you went to the appointment?"

"He said he needs to do his own exam, his own lab work, that there are lots of mistakes in labs." Which meant the good doctor didn't trust the rubes out here on the prairie and, more important, had allowed Moira to hold out hope that there might still be something wrong with me. Somehow this didn't sound right, however. I found it hard to believe a doctor, even a Harvard doctor, would possess Moira's snobbishness. Milwaukee had a university, a medical school, surely her doctor knew this, but there was no point in pushing things long distance.

"I'm in the middle of a case, Moira. I may have to go to trial."

"You mean with that gangster, the one with the tattoos and the earring? That's your case?"

"Not my only case, but, yes, he's one of my clients. Anyway, it doesn't matter who it is, you know that. It's my job. I can't just drop everything and come to Boston to have tests I've already had because some doctor at Harvard doesn't trust the labs in Milwaukee."

She was quiet for a moment. "I just thought this was important to you, Andrew. I thought I was."

Calling me Andrew was bringing in the heavy artillery, but I held my ground. "That's ridiculous. Of course you're the most important thing to me." I wasn't sure this was true, but it was the kind of thing you said under such circumstances.

"And our baby?"

"I know," I said. "But let's face it, Moira, we might not have a baby and that's okay. We've been trying for two years and you don't want to adopt so that's the fact, or could be, might be. People live perfectly good lives without children, maybe even better ones sometimes. Certainly richer."

"Well, I can't," Moira said. Then the phone went dead in my hand.

It took time to get downtown because of the storm and once I did it was almost impossible to wedge myself through the door of my office because of the boxes of documents blocking the door. "I'm sorry, Mr. Simonson," Sherry wailed. "They just kept coming and coming and Mr. Williams told me to put them all in there."

I climbed over the accumulated debris to sit at my desk and look at the mass of paper Cindy Braithwaite's lawyers had sent over. Because of the problem with Moira, the storm, and my growing involvement with Patsy, I had almost forgotten Frank's legal problems and Sherry was sensitive enough not to mention my inattention. Now it didn't matter because the case was impossible to ignore any longer.

The reason lawyers called this phase of a lawsuit discovery was borne out here. The idea was to ask for literally anything you thought might yield something of interest, typically letters, memos, diaries, phone records, the works. The strategy of the other side was to snow you with worthless material in return. You want diaries, we'll send you diaries *and* letters from Cindy when she was at sleepaway camp in Eagle River, report cards, her high school yearbook, notes and cards sent home from college, phone records of the whole family going back ten years but, hey, that's not all. We're also sending along other things that might interest you, tax returns, tickets from the homecoming dance, a pom-pom from a forgotten football game as well as copies of a certificate of merit earned at a square-dancing school in Wauwatosa as well as another from a cheerleading camp in Oconomowoc.

The thought of going through all this was exhausting, especially since I didn't know what I was looking for, except for the tapes Cindy had mentioned that supposedly included Frank's statements of undying love. But the tapes weren't hard to find. John Alexander had given them their own file and indexed them as to date and time. It made you think Cindy wasn't much of a romantic since despite her protestations of a broken heart she'd apparently had the presence of mind to record conversations with her lover going back two years or so.

I picked one at random and put it in the machine. A woman's voice came on that was easily recognizable as Cindy's. "I don't think you love me," she said playfully. "You're gone so much now."

Frank sounded bored or distracted. "Sure I do," he said. "I just got to take care of things here."

I made a note to ask him where he'd been when this conversation took place, though I wasn't sure I wanted to know what things he'd needed to take care of.

"Someday I'll wake up and you'll be gone," Cindy said now.

"Bullshit," Frank said. "What are you, on the rag or something?" Always the romantic, I thought, but then he said, "I ain't going nowhere. Don't worry about that."

That much was true. After all, he was the one who threw her out. I thought about the brunette with the finger waggle and made another note. "Sure, I know that," Cindy said, maintaining the babydoll tone in her voice. "I just mean you won't want me anymore, that you'll get tired of me and then where will I be?"

Frank's voice called out at someone named John to wait for him. Then he was back, tense and impatient. "Look, I don't know what you're talking about, okay? I'm always going to take care of you. You got nothing to worry about, but I gotta go. I'll call later." And the phone went dead.

So that was what they had, though I suspected there was more, maybe something specific he'd said in a similar vein when he was under pressure. Of course any of it could be interpreted in various ways. We could claim Frank had merely been making small talk, saying what she wanted to hear, that no one could seriously think he'd take on the support of a girlfriend he'd clearly thought very little about. And yet. Who could say what was going on in Frank's mind or what a jury would consider serious, assuming this ever went to court. I'd be kidding myself to think of him as a model client and it was unlikely we could find any group of citizens who hadn't heard of his father's mob connections.

Which meant the smart move would be to get a figure out of Alexander, negotiate it down as far as possible, settle, and walk away. There was only one problem with that: the other side didn't want to settle. Alexander and Arthur Braithwaite and Cindy had all made that clear. So the question was, what did they really want? What did they want, that is, that Frank could give them? The idea that humiliating a minor league hoodlum like Frankie the Pin could really be important to a high-powered downtown lawyer didn't make sense to me, but I couldn't imagine what more could be going on that I might be missing. That would be the job, understanding what I'd been missing in all this so far.

There was a slight brushing at the door and Tom Williams looked in. "Jesus," he said. "Where the hell am I supposed to sit?"

"Beats me," I said. "Guess we'll have to go the bar to talk."

When we were settled at Donovan's, Tom lit a cigarette and looked at me seriously through the smoke. I recognized this as the set-up for one of our meaning of life talks. We'd had these since high school and often they stood in for the fist fights we should have had. Since our friendship was too important to fight about, we settled for philosophy.

"Andy," Tom began.

"Yes," I said.

"Don't interrupt."

"You haven't said anything. You addressed me by name and I responded."

He looked to see if I was kidding, then said, "Quit fucking with me. I'm serious."

"Okay, sorry. I'm all ears."

But then he sat silently for a few minutes, smoking and drinking his beer. Finally, I broke in. "Is something wrong?" I said. "Girl trouble?"

"Jesus Christ," he said. Then he was quiet but not for so long. At last, he looked at me and said, "Do you really want to be a lawyer?"

The idea that your preferences actually made a difference in life was relatively new to me. Having grown up on the edge of poverty, I'd basically gone where I was pushed professionally and so far it had worked out. I discovered early I was good in school so pursued that eagerly. Then when I found kids at Princeton who were not only smarter but had better preparation than I did, I got into the habit of spending all my free time studying to keep up. The same formula worked at Yale, though by that time I had caught up with the young geniuses from Bronx Science and Groton. Keeping my head down and working hard yielded a sort of grim satisfaction and I had an aptitude for it, so I seldom thought very much about what I'd rather be doing or would prefer to do. In my life it had never seemed like an option.

"Actually, I'd like to be a millionaire playboy," I said. "But all the spots were taken when I applied. What are you talking about, Tom? I went to law school, passed the bar. I'm a lawyer. End of story. I'm supposed to like it too? I don't know a single lawyer, here or anywhere else, who actually enjoys what he does. It's a living, though. A good living, I might add. I like that."

He nodded. "It's just that you haven't been in much lately and when you are your mind's somewhere else. Then there's this goddamned case."

I knew what case he was talking about. "Don't tell me you're still getting heat from the partners about that."

"Not exactly," Tom said. He drank more beer and sighed. "I just don't get it, why do you want to represent Frankie the Pin? And where did your wife go and why are you fucking her friend?"

I had no idea how he knew about Patsy and was immediately self-conscious. I did what I often do in these situations and acted outraged. "What are you, Ann Landers?"

"I'm your oldest and best friend and I genuinely give a shit about you, that's who I am," Tom said. "So that brings me back to my original question. Is this what you want to be doing in life? And do you really want to do it here, in Milwaukee, in this firm?"

He had a point. I had come back to Milwaukee, supposedly having triumphed over my past life and had found it less than satisfying. People were happy to see me, and some seemed impressed with where I'd been and what I'd done, but essentially it didn't matter much to anyone and I had to admit that was disappointing. Things are seldom what you expect at the outset, of course, so there was nothing unusual in that, but it did raise existential questions. I had nothing to complain about and I knew it but despite making more than enough money to live well, I hadn't anticipated how unhappy Moira would be with Milwaukee. Moreover, while I didn't expect my law career to rival Perry Mason's, doing wills and contracts wasn't what I thought I was preparing for. In time, I supposed I might be assigned something more interesting, but how much time, that was the question. In a part of myself, I knew this was why I'd agreed to represent Frank but that hadn't turned out well either. Which brought me back to Tom's question.

"Am I in trouble? Are you having to backstop me to the point that it's putting you in a bad place?"

"No," Tom said quickly enough to make me think I'd hit on the truth. "I just want you to get your office straightened up, settle Frankie's case, and get back to the widows and orphans so I don't have to worry about you." He laughed to show he wasn't completely serious or completely kidding.

"I'll think about it," I said, not bothering to explain that settling Frank's case was turning out to be more complicated than either of us had originally imagined. I said nothing about Patsy and didn't ask how he knew but I assumed that meant we were common knowledge, which in Milwaukee couldn't be a good thing. If Moira-was ever coming back. Then we drank more beer and watched basketball on television until ten o'clock after which we both went home.

The wind had lessened by the time I went to bed, but I couldn't sleep. Images of Moira and Patsy and Tom and Frank interfered with one another, seeming to engage in imaginary dialogues to no particular purpose. Perhaps owing to my unusual upbringing I didn't possess some of the more conventional attitudes about home and hearth. That is, despite the fact that I was sleeping with Patsy, I knew I still loved Moira and felt loyal to her. I'd never had an affair before and hadn't been seriously tempted. Still, for me, sexual constancy and loyalty weren't always the same thing. To put it another way, I knew guys who were terrible husbands and providers but would never have thought of sleeping with another woman. That wasn't a justification; it was just the way I felt. Moira had gone away for her own reasons and Patsy and I had fallen in together. The fact that neither of us felt especially guilty about it tended to argue against our relationship lasting beyond this discrete period of time. And yet I was fond of Patsy; there were things about her I'd be sorry to lose.

Now it struck me in an almost physical way that this was the longest Moira and I had been separated since our marriage. In the past, friends had joked about our being joined at the hip but there was truth to it. It wasn't that either of us felt an obligation to spend all of our time together but that was what we had done. No separate vacations, not even many friendships we didn't share. We could claim this trip was no different than going home to visit her parents and see old friends, but we both knew it was more than that. She'd been gone more than two weeks and if it went on much longer people would start to notice. In fact, judging from Tom's comment some people had noticed already, which made sense because Patsy and I hadn't been very careful. I didn't know what to think about people gossiping, if I cared or what I would say if anything embarrassing developed. But I knew I didn't want to leave Moira. I wasn't essentially a passive person, waiting aimlessly for life to happen to me, but now I had a significant secret I was keeping from my wife. I wondered if she had secrets as well and if that's what was really going on here, what we were talking about to the extent we were talking. Secrets. I drank a cup of tea in the kitchen, alone at three a.m. Then I went back to bed and slept.

The next morning, I was up and out of the house early. I always liked Lake Park but especially early in the day, before it was descended upon by the daily horde of kids, nannies, joggers, lovers, and bird-watchers who were there on a daily basis year-round. Even in winter there was a stateliness about the winding footpaths, the deserted tennis courts with their metal fences standing in for nets, the covered English garden in the center of everything. It was something Milwaukee did well, parks and public spaces, making beauty available to the common people, a tradition stretching back to the German socialists who had settled here in the nineteenth century. And it wasn't just the parks. There was also a great zoo and the garbage was always picked up on time. Taken together all this spoke of an ethos, shared values, and in this the parks had a role, being large open spaces reserved for the relaxation of exhausted working men after their days on the factory floor were done.

There was no one like this around the park at this hour and Lake Drive was the high rent district. But I liked to think of the workers anyway, even as I was aware of the faint smell of burning cinders coming from somewhere behind me along with the soft pop-pop of the skeet shooters down at the range on the lake. It was all one with the damp mist and wet leaves underfoot as I headed for the pavilion, white pillared and welcoming, where I'd have breakfast and read the paper before going out to face the day.

Moira and I had married right after I finished law school and I always told people it was because I liked being married, which was true as far as it went. But now, with her gone, I found myself enjoying being single, at least temporarily. Patsy made few demands during the day and I was free to get up early or late, eat cold pizza for breakfast, watch junk sports at all hours and, as now, amuse myself alone in the park. I didn't really think of myself as a solitary person, preferring solitary pursuits, but now I found myself considering it. What if Moira didn't come back or we weren't able to work out whatever was really between us? I had heard cautions about growing old alone, but I was only in my thirties so old age wasn't real to me. I didn't think of any of this as being permanent but for now I was enjoying this new way of life.

I was in the office before nine going through the mountain of material Alexander had sent over. Despite Williams's disclaimer of the night before, I had taken his questions as a warning that I'd better become more regular in the office. I doubted my ability to wrap up Frank's case unless the other side had a drastic change of attitude, but I needed to work it just the same. This morning I discovered that the tapes I hadn't heard were much the same as the one I'd listened to the day before, no smoking gun there, but when I examined their witness list I felt a chill. All the names were familiar except one Maureen Somerville who was identified only as a friend. When I called Frank, however, he seemed unconcerned.

"Little Maureen," Frank said. "Friend of Cindy's. So what?"

I felt like wringing Frank's neck. Sometimes that wiseass tone got to me. I wished that just once he'd take responsibility for his actions the way everyone else had to do, but it wasn't going to happen here. I was his lawyer and one interpretation of that was that I was his hired shit catcher. I took a deep breath and continued. "Look, it's one thing for Cindy to say you promised to take care of her. It's something else to have a witness corroborate it."

"Corroborwho?" Frank sounded drunk but I was skeptical. He'd been in enough court rooms to understand what the word meant.

"Say she heard you say it, support Cindy. Did you ever say anything like that in front of Maureen? Could she have listened in on a phone call? What I'm saying is, does she have anything that can be used against you?"

"Lots of people have something against me," he said. "Jesus Christ, how the hell do I know what's going on with Cindy's friends?"

Something told me he wasn't being completely honest but then that wasn't new. More unusual would be the times Frank actually told me the truth about anything. I bored in. "Okay, fine, but I'm being very specific here. I'm not asking about the whole East Side. Just one woman, this Maureen Somerville, whose existence I first became aware of twenty minutes ago. How about her?"

"Okay, I used to go out with the bitch," Frank said grudgingly. "Go out my ass. I used to fuck her, all right? That's how I met Cindy, through her, so she's not crazy about me, Maureen."

I could feel the walls closing in. We now had not one but two angry ex-girlfriends joining forces to nail Frank. Not for the first time I thought I had been stupid to take this guy on as a client. I had been bored and thought it would be interesting to represent a gangster, even a small-time gangster. My friend Tom, to whom I owed my job, had tried to warn me against it but I was such a hotshot Ivy League lawyer that I thought I knew better and now I saw that I didn't, hadn't, and wouldn't. Whatever it was I had hoped to prove by getting involved in this case, I'd only succeeded in showing I was an arrogant fool.

"That's great, Frank," I said. "Really great. And when exactly did you intend to tell me about your relationship with Miss Maureen? I'm supposed to be your goddamned lawyer, right?"

"I never intended to tell you, okay, because I didn't think it mattered every skank I ever spent a night with. And I still don't think so. Your job is just to get me out of it, so don't fuck with me, Counselor."

I guess I was supposed to be scared and historically I might have been, but something moved deep inside me and instead I was angry. "Don't fuck with you, Frank?" I said. "That's actually kind of funny because the real problem is who you've been indiscriminately fucking and then expecting someone else to clean up after you, that's the problem. And I'm going to do the best I can because that's what you hired me to do but from now on I'm telling you to expect me to be in your face if there are any more surprises. So instead of trying to intimidate me you'd better start figuring out how you're going to explain all this to your dad. He doesn't get it and neither do I. The difference is he cares about you and I'm just a lawyer on a case."

No one I knew would have called me spiritual, but I began to have the odd feeling that some kind of transgenerational communication was going on involving Moira and my mother with me as the conduit. Not that I believed they were actually talking to one another, but the thoughts and feelings I was having seemed somehow to originate with them in my mind, to have historical resonance. It reminded me of an experience I'd had at school. Sitting in the vaulted lounge of the student union, I suddenly became aware of urgent voices, though no one was sitting near me. In time, I located the speakers, a couple involved in a lovers' quarrel across the room. Somehow the conversation had traveled over the room's high plaster ceiling and come down upon me, like voices out of the ether.

Unlike that conversation, however, this concerned me and I vowed to keep listening.

It wasn't quite as simple as wondering what Mom would have thought about what I was doing. I thought I knew that. But it was related, which might simply have been a way of me asking myself what I was doing and why. When I was growing up we didn't really have religion, or at least not anything others would have recognized as that. Every Christmas Eve we went to the Episcopalian church on the corner and on the odd Sunday when there was nothing else to do and the apartment seemed especially depressing we'd attend the Unitarian potluck and get into vigorous arguments about the fate of the world with the do-gooders there. That was the extent of my religious education, but I still would have said Mom was moral, that how you acted and treated people were the most important things to her.

I had never sensed any particular warmth between her and Moira, though Mom wouldn't have said a word to me against my wife. I just had the feeling she wished I had married one of the working-class girls I had gone out with in high school, that Moira was a bit uptown for her taste. It was bad enough that I'd gone off to the East in the first place, but she worried that I'd taken those values to heart. Mom tended to take people pretty much as they came, but she distrusted rich people. She assumed that they must have done something unethical to get the money, which was ironic given her moneyed youth. Still, it was the way things were and Yale was all about money, Skull & Bones, Bill Buckley, and George Bush in roughly descending order.

Going there was one thing. An argument could be made for a good legal education, which even she would admit I'd gotten. What made it worse was that to Mom all the unhealthy influences in New Haven and later the North Shore seemed to have adhered to me in some fashion because of Moira and our way of life. The house on the lake, the car, the law firm. It was all a long way from the floor-through on Frederick Ave. with a coal furnace and Salvation Army furniture where I'd grown up.

What's more, instead of defending the downtrodden I spent my life helping the rich avoid income taxes. In her mind it all had to do with eastern influences and what made it worse was that she never said a thing about it. I just knew. This wasn't fair to Moira, of course, which made it all the more strange that I was now imagining communication beyond the grave between the only two women I'd ever loved.

As close as I had been to my mother little of what she said on this subject resonated with me now. There's been a lot of nonsense written about a sense of place but the truth was I'd always felt like an outsider in New Haven and Boston. It was an important reason I'd come home. If I was honest, however, I'd admit that for me little had changed. Not that I didn't feel a bond of sorts with Milwaukee, but I knew that going away had made me different. If I'd felt set apart in New England, back in Milwaukee I understood that I was no longer just a guy from the East Side. If, like Tom Williams, I'd been content to go to school at Marquette or in Madison, I might have had the kind of social network he did, the old friends you'd gotten drunk and chased girls with at odd hours on forgotten weekends; the hairdresser with the impressive bust who had been your secret girlfriend; ballgames, brat festivals, motorcycle conventions, even all-nighters preparing for exams with a study group that rarely studied but somehow always passed just the same.

If I'd have stayed home I would have had all that along with friends from law school who had come back to Milwaukee to join firms, whose wives and kids knew each other and went to the same church potlucks and fundraisers, who bowled in the leagues their fathers had on Tuesdays, went to Summerfest on warm summer nights, gathered at Super Bowl parties in the same group they'd formed twenty years ago, and in the end would be buried in plots owned by their families for decades in Forest Home Cemetery. Milwaukee was famous for *gemutlichkeit*, good fellowship between people whose families had lived in town for generations, who were born there and seldom moved further away than Oconomowoc or Mukwonago at any point in their lives. It was either boring or comforting, depending on where you sat, but whatever it was I didn't have it.

Ironically, I left home in the first place because my mother encouraged me to get out of town, to see the world, breathe in the rich elixir of life and not be stifled by all that was narrow and conservative about Milwaukee. In addition to her suspicions of the rich, paradoxically she also worried that I'd become as provincial as my friends if I stayed at home. Like most people, she was a mass of contradictions. She wanted me to see the world and remain unchanged. As goals go, this was as good as most and just as unrealistic.

Finally, to add to the mixture of forces and ideas that had taken me away, there was some kind of identification with my long-dead father who'd grown up in the Pacific Northwest and left at sixteen on a tramp steamer, determined to avoid the fate of his father who had owned a furniture store, married his high school sweetheart, and died young. I thought I'd suffocate if I stayed in Milwaukee so like Dad I left home. But rather than a whale-ship being my Yale College, Yale was my Yale College. It was where I met my wife before we went away, spent time in Europe and the Far East and eventually came back to America. But in the end no matter where I went I ended up back home as I always feared I would. I hadn't found my father in my travels and the fact was Milwaukee wasn't any more provincial than any other medium-sized midwestern city.

The lasting effect of Yale, the East, and world travel was to make me stand out among my old high school friends who now danced around me as if I'd care if they used the wrong fork or were ignorant about wine and cheese. It made me sad, but there was nothing to do about it. The essential fact was that who I was always had little to do with where I happened to be living.

Since Mom wasn't married or otherwise encumbered while I was growing up, I became, in what seemed at the time a normal way, her stand-in husband, accompanying her to a variety of events as disparate as gallery openings and war protests when we might more logically have been going to the PTA or school Christmas pageants. Like most children I didn't question this. It was just the way childhood, or at least my childhood, was. But this didn't prevent me from knowing that things hadn't come easily for my mother and that the grim fatalism with which she viewed the world was the result. This may not have been a bad accommodation for her, but it was an unusual backdrop for childhood. She generally expected nothing from people, unless it was the worst. Still, she was willing to be surprised and kindness invariably brought forth her beautiful smile and life-long friendship for the person involved.

Understandably, I had adopted much the same attitude before meeting my wife. She was beautiful, rich, and her interest in me was so unexpected that Moira was able to upend the habits of a lifetime, leave Cambridge, and move west. I now realized I hadn't understood what a wrench that had been for her. And now she was gone, except for the sense in which she was always present to me emotionally. It was a contradiction, but at the moment there was nothing pressing, nothing being asked of me. Neither she nor Patsy were making demands and I had become morally lazy as a result. As my personal life tilted and became unbalanced, I had let things slide in the office. I knew this wouldn't have worked had Moira not left town. Whatever else she was, she was had never been lethargic. I didn't always like that in her, but I respected it.

For her own mysterious reasons she'd decided she needed a child to complete herself, not wanted or desired but actually needed a baby in some essential, physical way. It was vitally important to her to become pregnant, to gain weight and become unattractive, to experience the pain of natural childbirth and then be rewarded by something that was magically and uniquely hers. It was this that eluded rational argument and made adoption impossible for us, sensible as it might seem as an alternative. Someone else's mixture of DNA and history wouldn't have satisfied the urgency she felt. It wasn't the same for me, but now it came to me with the force of a punch that in the same way Moira needed a child, I needed her, even if what I truly needed to avoid was the conflict that might result in our breaking apart.

If this meant going to Boston and consulting experts after more conventional approaches had failed, so be it. It was a pain and a distraction for me, but I knew if I wanted the relationship with my wife, I'd have to make peace with her eccentricities, just as she had to accept mine. Without having thought it through, I knew I'd end up going to Cambridge and seeing a new set of geniuses, regardless of what I might think I knew about Harvard or fertility. I wanted Moira, or at least I wanted her more than I wanted anything else and I needed to want something. I needed that badly.

But before I left for Cambridge or anywhere else, I had a case to work on. The judge had set a trial date for January and before that I had to wade through the pile of tapes and papers Alexander had sent over, examine the witness lists again, interview anyone I thought might help or hurt Frank, and read through the interrogatories on my desk.

I sometimes thought the whole art of law was finding new ways to distract and confuse the opposition while appearing innocent and upright in the process. Interrogatories and the whole discovery phase of a case were a good example. The endless, meaningless questions lawyers posed to one another, often to appease demanding clients, which nevertheless needed to be answered. I felt like responding to the ones Alexander had sent by shoving the whole pile out the window, but that would have been futile as more would inevitably follow. I looked warily at the first package and read:

INTERROGATORY NO. 1: Identify ethnic extraction of Frank Pignatano.
INTERROGATORY NO. 2: Describe ethnic extraction of majority of American crime organizations.
INTERROGATORY NO. 3: Agree that Frank Pignatano is a convicted felon and was incarcerated at Green Bay penal institution.
INTERROGATORY NO. 4: Agree that Frank Pignatano is son and heir of Salvatore Pignatano, head of a Milwaukee crime family.
INTERROGATORY NO. 5: Describe Frank Pignatano's marital status.

INTERROGATORY NO. 6: Agree that Frank Pignatano lived in unmarried state with Cynthia Braithwaite between 2002 and 2005.
INTERROGATORY NO. 7: Describe discussions between Frank Pignatano and Cynthia Braithwaite regarding family planning during this period.
INTERROGATORY NO. 8: Describe promises or commitments Frank Pignatano made to Cynthia Braithwaite concerning future offspring resulting from their relationship.

It went on like this for ten or fifteen pages. It was all bullshit, but I responded to each interrogatory, saying they were prejudicial or unduly burdensome or overly vague or violated my client's constitutional rights because I knew that virtually none of this would ever surface in court and I knew Alexander knew it too. The idea that Frank's being Italian or a former prisoner meant he'd promised to support Cindy was ludicrous, but I supposed Alexander had to write these things to satisfy his client just as I had to object to pacify mine. It was the way the game was played and we were professionals. It interested me that he'd brought Sal into the case. We were never going to agree that he ran a large crime family, but I wondered if Alexander and Braithwaite would want to depose him for some reason. I made a note to call Sal and mention it.

In any case, the interrogatories could have been worse. Sometimes you asked for papers or letters and the response was to direct you to an unlighted warehouse in Oak Creek with drainage problems and rats scurrying down the aisles. You want files? Go find them, and in the past I had complied when this was necessary. Alexander had done what he needed to, but within the protocol in cases like this he'd shown respect and consideration.

I finished reading and responding to the interrogatories and then headed out to a grade school on the North Side where I'd been booked to talk to a third-grade class for career day. What I'd just spent the morning doing was actually worthy of a third grader but if experience was any guide they'd be more interested in knowing why I didn't dress as well as Sam Waterston did on television.

It didn't matter. The drive out gave me time to think, time I never seemed to have in the cluttered elegance of my office. I took a route through the city rather than chance the central freeway, which seemed permanently under construction. Urban renewal was a catchphrase here and had been for the last three mayors, but nothing ever seemed to change. There was a new convention center and basketball palace downtown, but once you got into the neighborhoods, especially on the North Side, all you saw was block after block of empty storefronts, weed-covered lots where dealers had once shown new Buicks and Oldsmobiles, cut-rate furniture stores with signs screaming no money down, and houses with asbestos or aluminum siding chevroned with rust and graffiti. Old men sat in tires sleeping off drunks and sullen kids stood defiantly on the curb giving passing motorists the stare that told you not to even think about stopping. It worked; no one ever did. Still, I saw, or thought I did, something else in their looks and it made me feel even more fortunate than I usually did to have escaped to my comfortable life where I earned more in an afternoon than these people saw in their monthly welfare checks. And while it was the most ordinary insight in the world, it seemed remarkable to me now, as if I'd won a raffle even if I knew the truth was I'd worked hard and raised myself far beyond what might have been expected of me, that I actually deserved what I had.

Even if that was true, it was hard to feel these kids deserved their lot in life, that a vacant expression on a shabby street was what anyone deserved. It was equally impossible to believe that they'd be able to do as I had and wouldn't instead end up in Fox Lake, Green Bay, or some other reformatory. No one ever dreamed of spending their lives in hopelessness and despair. I'd gotten away, but not so far that I didn't remember that bleak feeling and the sense that nothing better would ever come. This was what I saw all over the small angry faces on the curb as I drove by. Maybe their parents deserved this or some of it but the kids didn't. That haunted me.

The school was on the northwest side of town, a substantial brick building that seemed out of character in the neighborhood wedged in as it was among strip malls and new subdivisions advertising homes "From the 200s." The idea of a house in Milwaukee that wasn't on Lake Drive costing this much was something I was still getting used to, but the money had to come from somewhere and there seemed to be an unlimited supply of management trainees and consultants waiting to move in and set up their Weber grills at the first opportunity. When I was growing up, Milwaukee was a shot-and-a-beer town filled with blue-collar workers employed by Harnischfeger, Schlitz, or Allis-Chalmers as their fathers had been, as their sons would be. There were Friday night fish fries at neighborhood taverns and Sunday picnics in the city's parks. Sometime in the last fifteen years all this had changed and now Milwaukee could have been any sprawling city, pushing beyond what had previously been its limits. Whether this represented an improvement wasn't clear, but the developers didn't care.

It had been a while since I'd been in an elementary school and I'd forgotten the size differential, the drinking fountains barely three feet off the floor, the urinals in the restroom I had to practically kneel to use. I checked in at the office and in a few minutes a tiny pig-tailed girl named Jessica came, took me by the hand, and led me to the classroom. It was a nice touch and made me wonder why adults never held hands as a way of saying hello. Shaking hands didn't really accomplish the same thing. Jessica and I didn't talk but feeling the child's sticky fingers in mine and seeing her trusting smile gave me a ghostly understanding of Moira's desire to be a parent.

The teacher, Miss Clock, took over when we got inside and looked as if she could use the break career day would give her. We shook hands and she turned to the class.

"This is Mr. Simonson," she said, then wrote it on the blackboard. The kids all intoned "Good afternoon, Mr. Simonson."

Looking at the twenty-five freshly scrubbed faces in front of me I was immediately struck by the contrast with the kids I'd seen on Fond du Lac Avenue driving out. There were two black kids in the class but they looked like all the rest in their clean T-shirts and jeans. But sentimentality didn't work here. People who've never taught don't understand what goes into holding the attention of a group of children for an hour, so I played it safe, talking briefly about who I was, where I worked, and what I did there on an average day. Then I asked for questions. A red-haired boy in the front row raised his hand and asked if I knew any gangsters.

Mrs. Clock interrupted to say I wasn't a criminal lawyer, but I cut her off. "Actually, I do," I said, thinking of Frank. I knelt down and looked the boy in the face. His skin was so fair it seemed translucent in the afternoon light and there were pale blue circles under his eyes. His mother had spit-combed his hair and his jeans were creased. His lips seemed to quiver now as he looked up at me. "How do you know about gangsters?" I asked.

The boy stammered as he spoke. "The TV," he said simply.

"You saw some gangsters on television?" I wondered if he meant he saw something on the news about a drive-by or had just watched one of the crime shows on the tube. It might even have been that he'd seen teenagers with tattoos and baggy pants in the mall, but he wouldn't appreciate the subtle differences between fact and fiction. "Did that scare you?"

The boy nodded. It was an awful thing to be small and scared, to feel there was so little you could control in a world that was dark and frightening. I knew about that; I remembered feeling the same way. I put my hand on the boy's shoulder. "It's okay to be scared," I said. "I'm scared of them too."

The boy looked amazed. Then he laughed, a tiny hiccoughing sound that set off the rest of the class, so ludicrous did it seem that I'd be afraid of the things that frightened them. Even the teacher smiled. After that, I was home free. All the other questions were about the kind of car I drove and whether I had a big house.

Driving back to the East Side I thought about what I'd seen that afternoon, the angry kids in the ghetto, the scared third grader in the suburbs, which were really two sides of the same thing. I wondered if we ever really got over fear or just learned to handle or medicate it as we went about our business. But before I was able to resolve this in my own mind I was home and the phone was ringing.

I met Patsy later at Kalt's and was surprised how relaxed and pleasant it was considering what had gone on that morning. Not that she would know, but I did. One of the things I liked about Patsy was that she wasn't attuned to every raised eyebrow or despairing sigh or that if she was, she didn't let on. If it wasn't for the sex I would have considered her an ideal companion, a pal or close friend. But sex had a way of altering things. "I talked to Moira today," I said.

Patsy nodded and lifted one of the ornamental tankards to see if it opened, which it did. Kalt's didn't do things on the cheap, though the mixture of heraldic knickknacks and red checked tablecloths could be a bit distracting if you thought much about it. "I assumed you'd be talking," she said. "I mean, you're married."

She said this in a monotone as if it had no significance to our relationship. "That could change," I said, not knowing why I said it.

But Patsy didn't take the bait. She shook her head. "You're not the type to divorce, Andy," she said decisively. "You're more the till-death-do-you-part type, teeth in the same glass, the whole nine yards."

I disliked being categorized, even if she was right. I wanted to be less predictable, maybe a little bit dangerous. "Maybe, but I'm not sure Moira is."

Now Patsy looked interested. She smiled, her narrow face looking oddly diabolical in the dim light. "Oh, really? Do tell."

I shrugged. "There isn't much to say except that she's really serious about wanting a kid and so far it's not happening."

Patsy looked disappointed. Scandal, intrigue, even discovery of what we were doing together would have been exciting, but children didn't interest her. "I don't have personal experience there," she said drily. "But I hear it takes two and you guys were trying, what, a year? It always seems weird to me to say you're trying, which means you're screwing with intent and on a schedule when the time is right and all that."

"It helps to have a sense of humor," I said.

"I never got the feeling Moira thought it was very funny," Patsy said. This was sensitive ground since we'd first met because she was Moira's friend. Even with her advanced moral sensibilities Patsy usually knew to steer clear.

"You're right about that," I said. "Anyway, there are things you can do if you don't get pregnant."

"You mean jerk off in a glass and transfer it to a petri dish?" Patsy made a face. "You really want to do that?"

I knew that talking tough was her way of avoiding emotion, but as usual she had asked the relevant question. I drank some beer and ate an onion ring before answering. I had this nice easy relationship with Patsy that worked for both of us. We maneuvered around our schedules and got together when we could, each understanding if something came up. There were no hurt feelings, no tense phone calls or accusations if one of us forgot to get in touch. We didn't keep track of who had called last. I could have characterized it as a mature relationship, but the truth might have been that neither of us cared enough to yell, scream, and throw things. This bothered me more than I generally admitted to myself because I wanted to think if love mattered, sex did too. And that if I was sleeping with this woman and caring more for her than either of us said, then I should be honest about that. But honesty meant different things to Patsy. It meant taking care of yourself and not worrying about the consequences. I didn't know about friendship or what it meant to be sleeping with a friend's husband. I wasn't sure if she would consider herself the proximate cause if my marriage broke up, but it seemed that someone should take responsibility for something. Yet for me to interrupt things now and insist on a new understanding would be to set us on a new path that neither of us wanted.

"I don't know," I said. "Maybe. I guess I'm willing to go out there and be tested again by the geniuses at Harvard."

"No doubt they've scaled heights in reproductive science our guys can't even imagine," Patsy said. "Trust me, I went to school there. I know how they think."

I smiled at her ironic tone because I felt the same way. I wondered again why I didn't love this woman more, given the consonance of our ways of looking at the world, why love never came into it with us and who might be scared by it. "That's Moira's point," I said. "Anyway, I'll be gone a few days."

Neither of us raised the question of what might happen after that, which probably was the reason we could go on this way. Still, even if it was inevitable, I knew giving up Patsy would be a wrench and not something I'd do easily. She'd never said a thing about it, but I knew the same was true for her. Which was all the more reason not to broach the subject. Timing mattered and I knew enough to know that pushing the issue now would be the worst timing imaginable. Unless it was simple cowardice on my part.

Patsy drank more beer and ate a piece of sauerbraten. Then she pushed her plate aside. "Why don't you come over to my place tonight?" she said.

I was up earlier than I needed to be and went to the pavilion where I sat on a steel chair on the veranda of the gazebo looking at the lake. There was a nice lift to the waves this morning and the water was aquamarine, reflecting the cloudless sky. I had slept at Patsy's but then awoke at five feeling restless and left without waking her to walk up Kenwood in the near darkness to the park. I was flying to Boston today but my plane didn't leave until late morning and I could have stayed for breakfast. It wasn't even that I didn't want to. I just liked the way things had been between us the night before and wanted to hold onto that.

After a while, I left the veranda and started walking vaguely in the direction of Mom's house. The air was clear and cold and the bare maples lining the streets could have been telephone poles as I made my way up Park Place away from the lake toward Hackett. When I got to the house, I climbed to the attic and surveyed the stack of paintings I'd left on the floor the last time I was there. I knew there would come a time when I'd have to wade through all this, even throw some away, but I was still discovering new things, periods of artistic development I hadn't known about, and that was interesting. Near the leaded windows on the east side of the room I noticed a pile I hadn't moved and looked to have been there for some time. I knelt down and lifted the pictures, unearthing some dust and a few dead moths. I shifted the stack to the left and as I did noticed that beneath the dun portfolios there was a pile of notebooks that I hadn't seen before. They were composition books like those you'd buy at the university bookstore with mottled black and white covers. I picked one up and recognized Mom's familiar slanting hand and the date, April 11, 1990. Fifteen years ago. It seemed like an eternity and for a moment I couldn't think where I'd been then. College, traveling in Europe? I wasn't sure, but it was odd thinking of her now, as if she were still alive, at least here in the writings in this book. Feeling vaguely like a voyeur, I began to read.

> It's my birthday, 42 years old, an age I now realize I never thought I'd reach or at least not in good health and conscious. By this time in their lives my parents had both gone, as had my brother and two uncles. Yet here I am, healthy enough, relatively solvent; the mortgage paid for another month, still working and as pleased as an artist can ever be with her work. I haven't kept a diary since I was a girl, but I saw this book at the store and decided to start one now, the new year, another beginning. I was at the university to have lunch with my friend Sylvie who much to her surprise just received tenure and wanted to celebrate. I hadn't been over there for a while as I tend to avoid the academic artists, but I was impressed with the new studios. You'd have to be half-dead not to be productive in those places with their high windows, white walls and perfectly modulated air conditioning. Still, there were no students around and when I asked, Sylvie smiled and said, "I guess they're all home doing conceptual art." A joke, but probably true. She did introduce me to one of her colleagues, Alfred Koenenberg, a sculptor who said he was

familiar with my work and liked it. This seems unlikely since he's only recently arrived here from the East, but I was flattered. I wonder if he was flirting with me. It's been so long that I wouldn't recognize it if he was, but on my birthday it's a pleasant thought.

I put the book down and shook my head. I remembered Koenenberg, though I couldn't remember when he'd come into our lives. I had been home on vacation from somewhere and this odd-looking man had appeared, probably in his middle fifties, bald with wire-rimmed glasses and small insistent eyes. For some reason he was wearing black bicycle shorts, though it was January and ten degrees outside. Mom had introduced us in an offhand way and I noticed Koenenberg left quickly, but I didn't think to question this at the time. Mom had many odd friends and I assumed he was just one of them.

The idea of someone flirting with my mother was oddly disturbing, though it was hardly fair and now well after the fact I wondered why she'd never had boyfriends while I was growing up. She was a strikingly attractive woman, with bright blue eyes and long black hair and when she was younger she'd been thin and long-waisted. Her taste in clothes was early Salvation Goodwill it was true, but she had a sense of style and could make the drab skirts and blouses she bought at the thrift store seem interestingly disheveled with the addition of a crimson scarf or African beads. Every boy thinks his mother is beautiful, but mine actually had been, in her own way, so while I'd never considered it before now it seemed odd that there had been no men around all those years. Whatever the truth, why should I feel compelled to defend her honor twenty years later against a middle-aged artist in bike shorts? There was no good reason, but the possibility of sexuality in my mother was upsetting, a selfish impulse on my part but real just the same. I read on.

May 15, 1990. So quickly Alf, as he likes to be called, has become an essential part of my life. A few weeks ago he started coming over in the afternoon when he was done with classes, often with his wife Deidre, a strange little woman with an impossibly curled pile of hair on her head and large horn-rimmed glasses obscuring her face. She never said a word and after one or two visits she stopped coming, though Alf continued to appear without warning one or two afternoons a week. Sometimes he'd bring wine and we'd sit at the kitchen table looking out at the garden, drinking and talking. I was immediately comfortable with him even with his odd get-up, the bike shorts and tight jersey year round, though he told me he didn't often ride a bike. He has an interesting history, having emigrated from Cologne when he was ten as part of the children's crusade Hitler allowed out of Germany for publicity purposes. Like many of those kids, he never saw his parents again and was raised by emotionally distant Londoners who Alf said tolerated him only for the stipend they received from the government. When immigration restrictions were lifted after the war, he came to New York to study at the Art Students League, and was even there for a few of the years I was, though we didn't know each other. Then he taught for a while at Cooper Union before coming west. It's an intriguing story, but not as interesting to me as Alf himself with his barrel chest and intense expression. I wondered vaguely why he kept coming over until one day he leaned over and kissed me, a long lingering kiss, his tongue caressing mine.

And then I understood right away and realized I'd really known all along. That afternoon he picked me up and carried me into the bedroom in his arms, an oddly gallant gesture that seemed incredibly funny to me and I started laughing uproariously and couldn't stop. This seemed to bother him. He put me down and looked at me seriously, "You think this is funny?" he said. "You think I am ridiculous?" And though it was kind of ridiculous, it was in a good way and I enjoyed being absurd and unexpected since everything I'd done for years seemed now to have followed a script. But he looked so hurt that I had to control myself. "No," I said. "You're not ridiculous. You're the opposite. You're wonderful." Then he smiled and

> we made love right there in my little room with the crocheted quilt I'd brought from Kentucky so many years ago, with pictures of Andy and his father looking down at us from the bureau and I wanted in the final instant to take them down, to spare them this, but then I couldn't because I was part of whatever Alf was doing to me and I lost myself in him and just came and came and then came again.

This was too much for me to read. I flung the book away and sat there in the dusty attic feeling violated even though nothing had happened to me. There was just something about being close to my mother in this way, even if in this writing she was another person, a person who'd been living this particular experience decades ago. It didn't matter. What I'd read bothered me in a new and intimate way. It seemed invasive, a means of undermining what I thought had been our shared experience of a time exclusive to us. Now this Alf was there in his weird glasses and bike shorts, his head buried in my mother's hair and private parts bringing her to orgasm repeatedly. This was something I didn't want to know about, but now I did know it and there was no way to banish it and go back to the certainty of the past. This was the new past and thus the new present and I'd have to adjust to it. Cautiously, I took up the book again and flipped through it. This volume carried through 1990 into 1991 with each subsequent book being labeled from this month and year to that one and so forth. The diaries continued until 1995 when they stopped abruptly. I would have to read further to find out why, but I wasn't up to it today and I had to catch a plane.

As I walked downstairs, I wondered why Mom had left the books there among her art portfolios in the attic. Even in illness it would have been possible for her to destroy them and in the process shield me from knowing these things about her. Apparently she didn't want to shield me, but why would it be important to her that I know about her romance with Koenenberg? I didn't even know if he was still alive but whether he was or not, this seemed so provocative that I wondered if she'd been angry and perhaps felt I had neglected and abandoned her. While I could admit as an adult that there was really nothing wrong with her having an affair, even with a married man, it didn't change the fact that I felt there was. I was no prude but her diaries offended me because of their insistence of her as a sexual being. It was an assault on my vanity since the diaries made clear I hadn't been all to her I thought I was. I wasn't sure if this changed everything I felt about my mother, but it changed something. Shaken by my discovery, I descended the stairs, seeing no tenants and was glad for this small solitude.

In the cab on the way to the airport, I wondered about Alf Koenenberg, whether he was still alive and in Milwaukee. If so, I knew I'd be paying him a visit.

Logan Airport seemed to be in a perpetual state of construction, as if after completing whatever had been done before, the architect had afterthoughts and tore it all out, like a seamstress rethinking a line. I had gone in and out of the airport dozens of times and it was never done and wasn't done now. My plane had come into an area that seemed oddly like a warehouse or a hangar and the other passengers and I wandered about confusedly until we were able to figure out where we were supposed to go. This compounded by the so-called Big Dig that had torn up central Boston made it a labor of hours to get to my father-in-law's house in Cambridge. I'd told Moira not to bother picking me up, but it hurt my feelings that she'd taken me at my word. I wanted her to be there, waiting anxiously at the gate, perhaps with a funny sign welcoming me to Boston. But there was no one except the usual morose limo drivers looking for a fare. I picked up my suitcase and walked to the subway to catch the blue line into town.

Moira had grown up in a comfortable home on one of the small streets off Brattle, a few minutes from Harvard Square. I'd visited her there once or twice when I was in law school and had been acutely aware of the difference in our backgrounds. Even though she insisted it didn't matter to her, it mattered to me. It was one of the reasons I'd bought a grand house on Lake Drive in Milwaukee before we could really afford it and encouraged her to remodel and update however she pleased. I wanted her to feel that at least in this way Milwaukee was the equal of Cambridge. Needless to say, it hadn't worked out as I had hoped.

Now I prepared myself mentally as I approached the house. It had been a strange day, starting with the night at Patsy's and then the discovery of my mother's new life revealed in the attic diaries. I wasn't sure how much of this I wanted to share with my wife. She was already competitive with Mom and sometimes mocked me for viewing her as a secular saint, which wasn't quite true but close. It was important to Moira to do her part to disabuse me of this, to point out what might have seemed to be obvious flaws in my narrative about my mother. Moira wasn't proud of this tendency and admitted it was ridiculous to be jealous of a person who was after all dead, but she couldn't help it. If I told her about the diaries she'd not only be shocked but would certainly use the new information as ammunition in future arguments. I wanted to avoid that.

Just as I was about to knock, however, the door opened and Moira was in my arms, her hair soft and perfumed against my face and suddenly everything I'd been thinking before, all the discomfort and confusion, was gone. "I'm so glad you're here," she said over and over. "I missed you so much." I had missed her too, but it wasn't that simple, as things never are. I decided not to say this, not to say anything. I was tired from the day and whatever needed to be said could be said later, if it had to be said at all.

Edward McQuaid was waiting in the breakfast room when I came down the next morning. Moira's father and I had never hit it off and I could tell from his frozen expression that things were unlikely to change now. His family had been lace curtain Irish not far removed from the shanty towns formed by immigrants in Boston and Cambridge in the late nineteenth century and my father-in-law found it hard to understand how anyone could reject his largesse, especially by moving to Milwaukee.

When he had first gotten involved in politics, Eddie had initially been rewarded with a no-show job at City Hall but then picked up a law degree at some diploma mill and the next thing anyone knew he was a principal in some important real estate deals downtown, all of which had landed him in this comfortable home on the right side of town with fresh lilies in the dining room along with a maid and cook in starched uniforms. It wasn't to my taste, but you had to be impressed by the way Eddie had risen in life, even if he never lost the flattened vowels that hinted at his beginnings.

I sat down and drank the orange juice someone had kindly left for me. I was acutely aware that we were alone in the room. "So how you doin' out with the shitkickers in Wisconsin?" Eddie began.

I smiled. "Still kicking. You ought to come for a visit. You might like it. We've got a big lake, universities, professional sports, running water, the works."

Eddie clearly didn't consider the possibility of his venturing west of Route 128 worth talking about. "What they paying you out there?"

I told him and he seemed surprised, though not impressed.

"Time I was your age Moira's mother had popped out three already," he said, a not very subtle reference to our inability to conceive.

"Well, you've got a lovely family, Sir," I said.

We sat for another few minutes but there was really nothing more to say. The maid brought eggs and bacon and I ate. Then Eddie got up and left the room without another word. Fifteen minutes later Moira appeared and we were on our way to the hospital for our appointment.

In the car as she was maneuvering around Harvard Square, Moira said, "Now, I know you're not exactly excited about this, but I want you to be open to what this man says, okay?"

"Why wouldn't I be open?" I said.

"Because you assume they're all Harvard assholes who think they're better than you are. You resent that."

"It's not true?"

"You went to Princeton and Yale law so what do you care? Anyway, it doesn't matter," Moira said. "We're just trying to get medical information. Dr. France is an authority in his field."

I could have argued that the man in Wisconsin was also supposed to be an authority but there seemed little point. I'd come all this way to please Moira so why raise objections now? As it happened, however, I liked Dr. France immediately. He was a rumpled man, perhaps fifty, with glasses that had been mended with adhesive tape sliding down his long nose and an off-center smile. His thinning hair hung down over his forehead and his hands were as small and delicate as a child's.

"Please," he said, indicating a side chair in the office. "Sit. I've enjoyed meeting Mrs. Simonson so I appreciate your coming all this way when you have excellent doctors in Milwaukee."

I wondered if the man was a diplomat or if he really felt this way. In any case, he put me at ease because he didn't look like a Harvard man or at least not my idea of a Harvard man, which was after all based on a very small sample. When we were all seated, France said, "The first thing I need to tell you is that I don't know if we can help you or not. It's important to say that because some people are so desperate to conceive that they just can't deal with the reality that some of us can't." He looked at each of us in turn to make sure this was sinking in.

"I think we've got that," I said. "But we wouldn't be here if we didn't think there was a possibility."

"Right," France said, "and as I was telling your wife at her last appointment, I do think there are some things we can look at that may not have been explored by your doctors before."

I wasn't sure if this was a dig at Milwaukee doctors or not but decided not to be sensitive about it. We were here, we'd see what this man had to say. "How long can you stay in Massachusetts?" France asked.

I wasn't sure what my travel plans had to do with anything. "I have a law practice," I said. "I'm actually in the middle of a case, but I came out because this seemed important to my wife."

Moira squeezed my hand at this and in that moment I felt a rush of optimism about her and our life together. France nodded, "Well, let's get to work then. The first thing is that we need to have you examined by a urologist."

"Don't you do it?" I asked. "The exam, I mean." I hadn't seen a urologist in Milwaukee and wondered why it seemed important here.

France shook his head and smiled. "I'm a gynecologist and a fertility doctor but we always have men talk to a urologist before beginning any course of treatment." He said this in a matter-of-fact way but I had the feeling he was surprised that I'd asked, surprised that the excellent doctors in Milwaukee hadn't suggested this step before. Now France nodded his head slightly, though neither Moira nor I had said anything. Then he continued, "But before you go off, there are just a few things I'd like to tell both of you, probably things you already know, but bear with me." He looked at each of us again and Moira nodded, as if this was part of an agreement they had.

"Go ahead," I said.

"First of all," France said, "women have a relatively small window when it comes to optimal times in the month when they can conceive. We say this rhythm is symptom-thermal and during this period eggs will last for about forty-eight hours, sperm slightly longer, say seventy-two. This is when we have women take their temperatures and wives call their husbands to come home from the office right away because the time is right." He smiled a small tight smile to let us know what he thought of this, a small joke, then continued. "But there are all sorts of reasons people can't conceive in addition to bad timing, having to do with childhood illnesses, scarring of the fallopian tubes, STDs or endometriosis, which causes scarring in the abdomen that's enough to stop sperm getting to the tubes."

It was a lot to take in all at once. "And you've ruled all of that out?" I said.

"For the most part," France said. "We're going to do a hysterosalpingogram, which just means shooting dye into the uterus and then an x-ray study, in which we use fluoroscopy as we watch it drain, what some people call a fill and spill." He smiled again. "But I don't expect this to show us anything new."

"Okay," I said. "What problems do men have?"

"Again, these are things for the urologist to look at, but in addition to sperm count there's the motility and morphology of the sperm. Are they moving? Are they dead?"

"Sperm die?"

France seemed amused by this. "As we all do. There can also be an excessive white blood count, which indicates an infection, and if the sperm are alive are they moving in the right way, are the head and tail in the right places?"

"And you can affect all that, maybe change it?" It sounded a little like a medical video game but I decided not to say this.

"Sometimes," France said.

I liked his modesty but wondered what he might be holding back. "What else?"

"In a small percentage of cases, perhaps 10 percent, there's no explanation, or at least none we can find. A related problem can be emotional disturbances, which often go along with all this. Women get impatient, men get angry, sometimes performance anxiety is involved. It can all affect a couple's ability to conceive."

"I think we've been there," I said.

France nodded, as if Moira had filled him in before our visit. Oddly enough I didn't resent her allying with him because she needed support and he didn't seem invested either way. "Not unusual," he said. "Common, in fact."

"What if all the tests show she's okay and so am I, what then?"

France nodded. "We have some experimental procedures we can try, but let's get all the tests done first, especially since you have time constraints. Once you've seen the urologist and I've examined Mrs. Simonson further, we'll get together and talk. Does that make sense?"

Everything this guy said made sense to me and for the first time I understood why we were here. Moira was different in France's office, even if he wasn't offering guarantees and she seemed more willing to accept reality. I had the feeling for the first time that whether she was able to get pregnant or not, we could go on. My coming to Boston had meant that much to her. She leaned over and kissed me on the cheek. "See you at lunch," she said.

I had never seen a urologist before. I assumed it was something that awaited us as we moved on but was for older men or those with a specific problem. For now, my prostate was quiescent, waiting quietly to expand, and in the meantime patiently shepherding those sperm, motile or not, where they needed to go without any help from me. It made me vaguely uncomfortable to think that there was extensive interior microscopic movement going on but then I'd never been adept at the sciences.

All this aside, I wasn't prepared for the urologist to be a small dark woman about my age with her hair tied into a bun. She introduced herself as Dr. Bardwell and sent me to the lab to produce the necessary fluids. When I returned she gave me a prostate exam, her small fingers expertly exploring the dark recesses of my body. Then we sat in the examining room and she asked questions.

"Multiple sexual partners, Mr. Simonson?"

"Ever?" I said, but the doctor didn't crack a smile. She'd heard all the urologist jokes and while she didn't seem rushed she wasn't in the mood for levity.

"Just the past two years," she said.

"One," I said. There was no point in lying to my doctor.

"In addition to your wife?"

I nodded. "In addition to my wife."

If Dr. Bardwell was shocked by the idea that I'd been unfaithful she didn't show it and I decided she saw much more egregious instances of misbehavior than mine on a daily basis, but it didn't matter. We weren't friends. She was gathering information. "Any venereal disease, in you or your partners?"

I was momentarily insulted on Patsy's behalf but the doctor was waiting patiently. "No. None that I know of anyway."

She made another note. Then I told her I'd never had cancer, that my father hadn't either, as far as I knew, that I masturbated occasionally and had my first sexual experience at fifteen with our cleaning woman. This seemed to interest Dr. Bardwell marginally. "Any pregnancies?"

"Not with her," I said. I thought of Edith, a short, squat woman who for mysterious reasons had conceived a crush on me. One day after washing the floor down, she came into my bedroom where I was reading, raised her skirt and lowered herself on to me. We didn't talk then or later about what we'd done and continued to do nor had either of us mentioned it to my mother, but she intuited it somehow and in a few months Edith was gone, never to return. "My high school girlfriend got pregnant," I said now. "She had an abortion."

Dr. Bardwell raised an eyebrow at this and went on writing. Then she looked up. Her coat had fallen open revealing nice brown legs extending from a puce skirt. "Our lab's pretty efficient," she said. "I'll put a rush on this and we should know more in a few days. You'll be here over the weekend?"

I nodded and she asked if I had any other questions. "I do," I said. "Since my high school girlfriend got pregnant doesn't that rule me out as far as infertility is concerned?"

The doctor looked at me with an expression that mixed patience and incredulity. "Absolutely not," she said. She checked my chart again, though I wasn't sure what she could see there that she didn't already know. "You're thirty-five now and, what, seventeen then? That's a lifetime in reproductive science, Mr. Simonson. Also," and here she hesitated. "We don't know that the child would have been yours."

I was stunned. It had never occurred to me that Janie Hamilton could have been sleeping with someone else. Convincing her to spread her beautiful legs for me had taken months of cajoling. Now, eighteen years later I felt as if I'd been cuckolded.

My expression must have revealed some of this and the doctor smiled for the first time. "Don't worry," she said. "I'm sure your girlfriend was faithful to you."

I laughed. "Sorry," I said. "Stupid of me."

"Human," Dr. Bardwell said. And I liked her better immediately. "Have you told your wife?" she asked.

"About what?" I was thinking of Patsy but she could have meant Janie or even Edith. That was a conversation I didn't want to have.

"The pregnancy," Dr. Bardwell said, as if she was coaching a recalcitrant adolescent, which in a sense she was. "It could be helpful."

I nodded. "But this is confidential, right? Doctor-patient and all?"

Dr. Bardwell nodded and got to her feet, her coat moving rhythmically around her small body. "Of course," she said. "But think it over. That could be an important part of the conversation."

That conversation would have to wait. When I found Moira she was standing outside the hospital cafeteria, shifting from one foot to the other. "Let's get out of here," she said. "I can't stand hospital food."

I didn't have feelings one way or another about hospital food but was happy to leave. "Where do you want to go?"

She smiled in a way I hadn't seen in some time. "If we stay around here I've got a feeling you and my dad might kill each other."

"I don't know what you mean," I said. "We had a perfectly civilized conversation this morning at breakfast."

"Right," Moira said. "But how about getting in the car and driving out to Northampton for the weekend. I can show you where I went to school."

We crossed Storrow Drive and turned onto Route 2 going west on what some people still called the Mohawk Trail, though Indians hadn't been spotted in Massachusetts recently. The highway was an alternative to the organized madness of the Mass Pike and cut across the northern part of the state running all the way from Cambridge to Williamstown and into New York. It was more scenic than the southern route and in places meandered a scant ten miles from the New Hampshire line. The area was poorer too with empty mill towns on the route filled with abandoned factories where shoes and fabric had once been made. Once past Route 128, which girdled the Boston area, the landscape changed with heavy forests on either side of the road and Mount Wachusett rising in the distance on the left. We passed the towns of Harvard, Leominster, and Fitchburg, where I had once lived for a few months in another life. Gardner, the chair city, where generations of Ivy Leaguers had their mementoes fashioned without knowing it, passed below the highway, and then we were approaching route 202, what people called the alimentary canal because it ran between the towns of Athol on the north and Belchertown on the south end. When a former governor had been in office, the standard joke was that there were three towns in Massachusetts named after him, Endicott, Peabody and Athol.

But that was then and I was in a good mood as I turned south and drove past the huge Quabbin Reservoir, which had been created in the thirties by flooding three small revolutionary era towns in order to provide water for the city of Boston. Some people in this area were still angry about this and you couldn't really blame them. The legend was that if you drove by the Quabbin at night you could hear the voices of ghosts crying out in protest, but this morning there were only scattered bird calls and the occasional truck left at the side of the road by hunters or ice fishermen. As we drove down the hill, Moira reached over and we drove through Amherst holding hands.

I had been in Northampton before but hadn't mentioned it to Moira because I was dating a Smithie at the time whom I'd met walking on the Rhode Island shore while I was in law school. The romance hadn't lasted but I had always liked the town, especially in contrast to Amherst, so neat and prim you could almost imagine Emily Dickinson walking to the market in her straw hat. Northampton was, despite Smith's presence up on the hill, a working-class town, with lots of sooted red brick and abandoned store fronts, some of which were being bought up by wealthy young New Yorkers looking for a deal.

Unlike Pittsfield and other New England towns that had tried to modernize, Northampton still had the traditional curved main street downtown and angled parking with no meters. This would probably change in time but so far the Northampton Renaissance, as locals called it, hadn't gone beyond a few wine and cheese shops, a funky bookstore, and some fairly upscale restaurants. It was still a place where you could buy a house for relatively little, take your dog into the ice cream store, and buy pierogies, kielbasa, and hero sandwiches as easily as fresh brie and bordeaux. It was what gave the place its peculiar charm.

We parked and walked down Main Street and back again looking for a place to eat when I heard someone call my name and looked to see Bill Chandler, still tall and stooped as I remembered him from New Haven, waving at me from a sidewalk coffee shop. We shook hands, I introduced him to Moira, and then I said, "Now is when we each ask the other guy what he's doing here, right?"

Bill smiled. "I don't know about you, but I live here, right upstairs in fact."

I looked up and saw new floor-to-ceiling windows and some blond wood worked into the brick that had been there before. "Lofts?" I said.

"I'm not that hip," Bill said. "It's just an apartment, but a big one. I got a great deal because the guy who owns this place had just gutted and restored the upstairs and wanted some of his investment back right away."

"Nice," I said. Moira had been shyly hanging back during the conversation. Even though we'd met when I was in law school she hadn't known a lot of my friends and Bill was a year ahead of the rest of us. Now I took her hand. "Moira's practically a native," I said.

Bill nodded knowingly. "They all come back to Mother Smith," he said, "lovely and smart. It makes the town a nice place to live. But the last I heard you were working in Boston."

I told Bill I'd left the public defender's office, moved back to Milwaukee and joined a firm, that we were just here on some personal business and to visit Moira's family. "I thought about going that way, Boston, I mean," he said. "I had some good offers. I can't even say I'm a small-town guy, but I came here for a weekend and it just seemed too good to leave."

"You work here?" I asked, looking around. I vaguely remembered seeing a courthouse. Northampton might be the county seat. "Doing what?"

Bill smiled and handed me a card. "Check it out," he said. Printed neatly on the card was: "William Chandler, attorney at law, wills, estates, personal injury."

"You cover the waterfront," I said.

He laughed. "Hey, whatever works. It's a small town. If I was smart I'd get into immigration law, more and more cases like that with the tobacco fields up the road bringing in labor. But the fact is I'm too busy right now, or at least busier than I'd like to be. Why don't you and your beautiful wife move here? We could be partners."

I couldn't tell if he was kidding and there was no telling what Moira would think of the idea, but on this mild winter afternoon with a blue sky overhead and people in heavy sweaters and Birkenstocks going past it seemed more attractive than going back and defending Frankie the Pin.

"Watch out," I said. "I might take you seriously."

Bill wasn't smiling. "I'm completely serious," he said. "My home phone's on the back of the card. Go for a walk, have dinner, and give me a call later if you think there's even a chance you'd be interested."

Moira and I didn't talk about Bill's offer or even about Bill afterwards, but I felt oddly pleased to have seen him, to have been able to take a part of the past and fit it in here. So much of my life had been compartmentalized—either between Milwaukee and New Haven; my mother, Moira, and Patsy; my absent father and trying to figure out how to be a man and what kind of man I wanted to be—that everything fit into its own discrete segment, separate and away from everything else. Now, suddenly, this seemed like an enormous burden. I remembered as a boy having an old cigar box that I hid under my bed with various adolescent treasures in it, an old coin, a photograph of my father, a baseball card commemorating Warren Spahn's three hundredth win. I used to take it out when I was feeling bad and look at each item, hold it, and the process would work some kind of mood magic for me. But then I had gone away and when I came back the box was gone. The attitude I had taken toward aspects of my life, the sense of obligation toward Mom, my ambivalence about Milwaukee and the law, even the dalliance with Patsy, was like that cigar box, each giving momentary satisfaction but little more. My mother used to talk fondly of what she called my "enthusiasms," which was another way of saying I couldn't be satisfied with anything for long. It had seemed as if disillusionment might be my life's work but walking in Northampton that afternoon it seemed possible that what I already had, just this, might actually be enough.

The air was soft and moist and as we made our way with no particular purpose up the hill, past the town library and then down Green Street, the small shopping area that bordered the Smith campus, looking in the windows of the shops in a desultory way at old lace, Victorian jewelry, and rare books without stopping to buy or inspect anything. Young women in trench coats went by, walking fast with earnest expressions on their faces. Unlike Wisconsin, no one smiled or said hello. They'd all mastered the hard straight-ahead stare, as if they were dodging muggers in Manhattan rather than walking in a small New England town on a midwinter afternoon. Their exaggerated seriousness made me feel old.

We walked past the Smith theater and the faculty club and the small house where a movie had been made with famous actors years before and then we were standing facing Paradise Pond, supposedly named after a comment by Jenny Lind on her honeymoon.

"There was a story that if a girl took a guy here in moonlight he'd propose," Moira said now.

"Too bad you're already married," I said.

She smiled. "Actually, I always avoided this place because the guys I dated at Smith were such losers."

This surprised me. As beautiful as Moira was I'd assumed she had many chances before me. "Why'd you go out with them?"

She shrugged. "There wasn't a lot of choice. There were these mixers with Amherst and UMass, but the guys were always disgustingly drunk by the time they got there. And townies weren't really an option. It kind of made sense that some of the girls just turned to each other. It was a process of elimination, you know, gay until graduation."

"Not you, though?"

Moira shook her head. "No, but some of the girls never went back and Northampton became a big lesbian stronghold with a gay bar and city council person."

"Impressive," I said. "So that's why you were in New Haven staking out the law library. Why not go to Harvard, closer to home, after all."

I was teasing her, but Moira didn't seem to mind the banter even if she didn't join in. She spoke in a kind of dreamy voice as if she was talking about someone else. "A girl friend from school lived there. I probably wouldn't have thought of it on my own."

There was something sad about the whole dating dance, the pressure to put your life in order before you reached twenty-five. But Moira's determination to meet an acceptable man and marry him hadn't necessarily been a bad thing. The Yale law library was probably better than a singles bar. I just wanted to believe in fate or serendipity, something a little more romantic than what Moira was describing. On the other hand, she could have stood in the lobby all afternoon and never met anyone, so there was some chance involved.

We left the campus and walked by the small pristine chapel on Elm Street that someone had gifted to the school. Then past what served as the Smith Student Center and on down the block where we saw a man in a tan raincoat planting a for sale sign in front of a small Victorian. Like many others in the area, the house was painted yellow with dark blue shutters and a green door. It was the kind of house that you'd simply never see in Milwaukee, too prim and well-preserved somehow, redolent of a well-behaved past.

Now the man noticed us. "Used to belong to the college," he said, though we hadn't asked. He was wearing a bowtie beneath the raincoat and a homburg hat. "The younger professors used to live here and some of the grad students, I guess. But they don't need it anymore." He looked at me approvingly. "Any chance you kids would be interested? It's not even on the market yet, I could give you a good price." He smiled now. "Name's Abe Allen," he said, and offered his hand. "I handle some of the real estate for the college and the Clarke School, too." He nodded at the hill across the street and the school for the deaf that spread around it.

The day's cold was beginning to work its way through my overcoat, but the fact that I'd only been in town for two hours and had already been approached about a job and a place to live seemed to have karmic significance. It was nice to feel wanted. "We'll walk through it with you anyway," I said.

So we did, admiring the wood floors, high molded ceilings, tiled fireplace, and small window panels tinted red and green in the living room. The kitchen was functional and the bathrooms were ancient, but it was impossible not to be charmed by the house, by its lack of pretension and the wide openings from room to room suggesting space that really wasn't there. There was a modesty about it that echoed the town's zeitgeist, a quiet confidence just beneath the surface charm, suggesting character and fortitude in the face of suffering. When we left I took Mr. Allen's card and added it to Chandler's in my wallet. I didn't know why I'd agreed to look at the house but I was glad we had and I could tell Moira liked it too.

"We're not really looking for anything," I said as we shook hands.

Mr. Allen smiled and replaced his hat on his head. "I wasn't either when I came here thirty years ago with my wife, rest in peace," he said glancing toward the sky. "You never know what will happen, though. No harm in looking, am I right?"

"No harm at all," I said. "Thanks for your time.

At dinner, Moira said in a dream voice, "It would be a sort of a compromise."

"What would?

"You know," she said, not answering directly. "It's not Boston. I mean, it's really not, you have no idea. But it's not the Midwest either, right? And your friend is here."

I wouldn't have thought of Northampton and the Pioneer Valley as a compromise between Boston and Milwaukee, but in a strange way she was right. Big cities have more in common with one another than with nearby small towns. My law firm had relationships with others in Washington, New York, and San Francisco but nothing in between. It was a world away from Northampton or Dodgeville, Wisconsin. I'd never lived in a small town and had no idea what it would be like, but I was willing to extend the fantasy a bit further, especially since it had put Moira in such a good mood. "What would you like about it?" I asked.

161

We were sitting in Wiggins Tavern in the Hotel Northampton. The windows were frosted over and someone was playing Rodgers & Hammerstein standards in the lobby. It was a scene that might have evoked old Bing Crosby movies if it weren't for the fact that we were taking a brief respite from a fertility workup in Cambridge. Moira smiled and sighed. Her hair had fallen over her eyes and she had a gamine look about her that was irresistible. "Everything," she sighed.

"You hate Milwaukee," I said helping her along. Sitting here, it seemed impossible that the somber old houses on the East Side even existed, that every neighborhood wasn't filled with small Cape Cods and Victorians painted yellow and white, and that the streets weren't named Elm and Maple and Common.

She nodded. "I don't actually hate it," she said. "It's more of a contextual thing, feeling out of place all the time. That's what I hate."

It was hard to believe Moira would ever feel out of place anywhere in her perfect haircut and stylish clothes, but I knew it was true, just as it was true that she was shy.

Like most people, I'd assumed before meeting her that good looks and money would make anyone feel self-assured. "And you wouldn't feel that way here?"

She looked amused. "Andy, I went to school here. I lived here for four years."

"That's different, isn't it? Being a student in a place? Being a wife and mother in a small town might be kind of isolating, even if your parents were nearby."

"If I ever am a mother," Moira said.

This was the first time I'd heard her express any doubt on the subject that didn't have to do with Milwaukee physicians or me.

"Dr. France seemed reasonably optimistic." She nodded and drank more wine. Then she looked at me directly. "I have to tell you something, Andy. Something I should have told you before."

This seemed like a good time to say nothing, so I sipped my beer and waited. Outside, students were running up and down the street yelling at one another. It was Friday night and weekends were the same in any college town. I patted Moira's hand to reassure and encourage her.

"You know I went to this private girls' school," she began. "Miss Porter's?"

I couldn't see what this had to do with anything but I wanted her to keep talking. "I remember," I said. "In Connecticut."

"Well, the only time we saw boys was at these mixers on weekends when everyone got horribly drunk or if we went down for a football game."

"In New Haven?"

"Or Princeton sometimes," she said. "Well, on one of those weekends, I met a boy from St. Paul's." She hesitated and I saw tears in her eyes."

"It's okay," I said, though I had begun to sense that maybe it wasn't.

"It's not that I was that wild," Moira said. "I didn't usually go anywhere on the weekend and I never saw the boy again, but that one time I did and we stayed out very late and I got pregnant."

Her last words were a hushed whisper and then silence settled on the table. I could hear glasses clinking and silverware hitting plates on other tables. The buzz of conversation was all around us and the piano player was doing his best Mary Martin imitation. A number of possibilities occurred to me in that moment but I went for the obvious.

"What happened to the baby?" I asked. Moira looked out the window and dabbed at her eyes with a napkin. "There was no baby. It was just so impossible. I was only seventeen and Daddy would have killed me if he knew."

"You didn't tell your father?" I was surprised, having been regaled for years on stories of how close they were, how accepting old Eddie was of everything Moira did.

"I couldn't. He would have been so disappointed. Anyway, one of the girls' fathers was a doctor and he knew someone who did abortions, so I just went to New York for the weekend and had it done. It was all very clean and safe, no complications. Then I was back at school and I never told anyone."

Which raised the question of why she was telling me now, speaking in a precise fashion uncharacteristic of Moira, biting off the words clean and safe in a way that was almost surgical. Obviously there had been unforeseen complications. I sat for a moment thinking over what she'd said. It occurred to me that it was odd that I'd never wondered about this possibility before. But it was congruent with my image of my wife. She was too perfect, too poised and beautiful to picture in a back seat with a panting preppy on a football weekend in Princeton. I had wanted Moira's experiences of men to begin and end with me and now that I learned they hadn't I found I was more relieved than disappointed. In my own way I'd been unfair to Moira by putting her on the pedestal and making her more virginal than she'd really been, than anyone could be.

"Does Dr. France know?" I asked.

She nodded. "That's why I'm telling you. I lied about that too. I didn't just meet him. He was my ob-gyn so he's known all along. What he told me then was that there was a question about whether my ovaries had been scarred during the abortion and if so whether they'd heal themselves in time."

So Moira's resistance to following through with a work-up in Milwaukee wasn't really about hick-town doctors—or not only about that. It had more to do with getting home to the kindly doc who'd treated her all those years ago and knew her history. In some sense, I'd been manipulated but rather than being angry I felt compassionate. I knew how hard it was for Moira to come clean about this, to reveal herself to this extent, and how much France's support mattered to her. She had been acting superior and above it all back in Milwaukee but actually the opposite was true.

Now it was coming out on her turf in this little restaurant with showtunes playing in the background. But it didn't matter to me because for the first time I understood how she felt about all this. "So that's why you haven't gotten pregnant?" I said.

"He's not sure," Moira said. "It doesn't help, but apparently some people get pregnant even if there's scarring. It takes longer, I guess, and sometimes those fertility treatments . . ."

"Nice of you to let me in on all this," I said.

Moira took my hand. "I'm really sorry," she said. "It could all still work out Dr. France says."

Or, I thought, you could just walk away from the whole thing, figure you could live a long and complete life without children. But for Moira it was a chink in the armor, an imperfection, and it was hard not to sympathize with her for losing that. Perfection was a heavy load to carry around with you and to Moira adoption would similarly indicate to others something lacking in herself. I thought of Eddie Pockets back in the breakfast room bragging about having three children in his twenties, flaunting his fertility and how ironic it would be if he knew the truth about his darling daughter.

I considered telling Moira my secret in exchange for hers, but without knowing why I held back. There'd be time later and enough had been said tonight. We sat at the table for another ten minutes not talking. Then I signaled for the check.

"Are you mad?" she said.

I took her hand and palpated it. "I sort of think I'm entitled to be, considering all the crap you put me through about the shitty doctors in Milwaukee," I said. "But it turns out I'm not. Still, I'm glad you told me. No matter what happens after this, it helps."

We stayed over Saturday night in Northampton, both because the hotel was nice and to avoid more contact with Ed McQuaid. Walking around town and browsing in the shops at Thorne's Market, it was a pleasure to hear Moira laugh again. I hadn't seen her so relaxed in months and Milwaukee seemed a long way off. On Sunday I had breakfast with Bill Chandler and he told me more about his practice.

"It's not that intense," he said, "not what you're used to. People out in the country take their time about things. I'm not into criminal law and almost never have to go to court. But most of the time I actually feel like I'm helping people, giving them advice on things that matter. That's kind of refreshing after Yale."

I told Bill I'd call and that afternoon we drove back to Cambridge. On the return we took the Mass Pike in order to make better time. The holiday was over.

I was leaving in the early afternoon on Monday so Dr. France worked us in during his morning hours. I had the feeling he'd talked to the urologist and knew more about my checkered past than he was letting on, but he said nothing about it during our appointment.

"We put a rush on the labs," he said, "but it didn't tell us much more than we already knew. Beyond the fact that you two have been trying for quite a while there doesn't seem to be any reason you absolutely couldn't conceive."

A careful choice of words often hides an ineluctable truth. "What about the scarring on my ovaries?" Moira asked and I was grateful she'd brought it up.

France blinked his eyes then smiled sympathetically. "I'm glad you discussed that," he said. "We don't know if that's why you've had trouble or not, but it's a complicating factor."

"What's next?" I asked. I thought it was best to cut to the chase since I was short of time.

France shrugged. "It's really up to you. If you go on as you have been, there's a chance Moira will become pregnant, maybe sooner than you think."

"A good chance?"

"I'm not an oddsmaker, Mr. Simonson. I wouldn't say it was good or bad because I just don't know. It could happen."

That didn't sound terribly optimistic. "And what if we go the other route and try in vitro?"

France smiled again and ran his fingers through his hair. "That would allow us to bypass the scarring issue but we're not absolutely certain that's your problem."

"What else could it be?"

France got up and walked to the window. I had the feeling he was tired of me asking questions but was too polite to tell me to go away. "We don't deal in sure things here. If nature was allowed to take its course some people simply wouldn't have families. Presumably, they'd accept that and move on with their lives. As it is, science has allowed us to help some people who would otherwise be unable to conceive. It's expensive and time-consuming and doesn't always work. Sometimes it results in multiple births that present the parents with other problems. Some of the children aren't perfect, as none of us are."

The way he talked about it, pregnancy didn't sound like a completely desirable outcome; but I knew he had to be cautious. "Maybe we need to think about this some more," I said.

France nodded. "That's a good idea," he said. "I'll be here if you need me."

Moira drove me back to Logan in time for the plane. As I was getting out of the car I turned to her and asked, "Are you coming back home soon?"

She kissed me on both cheeks, her breath warm on my face. She was more beautiful than I could ever remember her being. "I think so," she said. "I'll call you."

Coming home was complicated. I had mixed feelings about my trip east, even about the idyllic two days in Northampton, which made returning to good gray Milwaukee less inviting but comfortable in an old shoe kind of way. There was the familiarity of Mitchell Field with Billy's airplane flying nowhere in the terminal and all the Wisconsin kitsch assembled for the visitors who meandered through on their way somewhere else. The idea that Milwaukee was all cheese, kielbasa, and Harley-Davidson motorcycles was briefly diverting, but then the sinking feeling hit, the sense of my feet actually sagging in the quicksand of my past along with the knowledge that rather than clarifying anything about my life, the trip to Boston had just made things more difficult.

Perhaps because of this I drove directly to the office rather than going home. I was sitting at my desk going through the mail and messages that had accumulated when there was a knock on the door and Tom Williams came in and sat down in my clients' chair. "How are things in the East?" he asked. "Moira ever coming back?"

"She said maybe," I said. "We had a good weekend, though."

"I assume you didn't mention your girlfriend?"

I smiled. "I just couldn't find a good time to do that. I did get offered a job, though, if things don't work out here. An old friend from law school is running a one-man operation in western Mass. Says he could use a partner."

Tom didn't respond directly to this. Instead, he pointed at the pile of tapes and files on the floor. "While you were gone, I took the liberty of catching up on your case, hope you don't mind."

"God, no, but I'm surprised. Things slow upstairs, or are the higher-ups really that unhappy with me?"

"Neither. I was just curious, but I listened to those tapes and I can't see the other side has much of a case. Why won't they settle?"

I shrugged. "I think they just want their pound of flesh. The girl's father thinks Frank dragged his daughter's name through the mud, ruined her reputation, the whole nine yards. People aren't often willing to spend a lot of money litigating about principles, but this guy doesn't care about money. If he did, he'd take an offer from us."

"You could ask the judge for summary judgment," Tom said slowly. "You wouldn't be risking much."

What this meant was just going to the judge and laying out all the facts on both sides and asking him to decide. Basically, Cindy was saying she and Frank had agreed that Frank would support her if they broke up, if not for life at least for a long time. But in Wisconsin to prove palimony you needed to provide an enforceable contract, which meant a meeting of the minds and it was hard to see how anyone could think Frank and Cindy had that. "Interesting," I said. "You think I could get a win that way?"

"It's worth a try," Tom said. "I don't like to think of Frankie the Pin in front of a jury, know what I mean?"

I thought of Frank in his duck's ass hairdo with his collar turned up over a leather jacket and had to agree. We could try to dress him up but it would take a magician to make him look presentable, no matter what he was wearing. "The tapes are inadmissible," I said. "If they were phone messages it would be different because that would constitute consent. The thing that bothers me is that the other side knows this, but they still won't settle. It makes me think I'm missing something."

"Like what?" Tom said.

I shrugged. "I don't know but the whole thing just seems kind of illogical. I understand people being angry and insulted but I don't get why Frank came to me in the first place, why the old man didn't just make the girl an offer she couldn't refuse."

Tom smiled. "I'm not sure that happens outside of the movies but say you're right. Why didn't the old man get in anyway and what's it to Braithwaite in the end, know what I mean? His daughter's well rid of that little shit so why isn't he happy?"

"Maybe I should go back and talk to Sal," I said. "They listed him as a potential witness in discovery and I don't know why."

"Good idea," Tom said. "Anyway, do what you can to figure that out but I'd like to wrap this up as soon as possible, okay?"

I sensed some urgency in his voice but didn't think he was telling me what to do, just trying to be a friend. What's more, he was right. The only person I hadn't talked to was Maureen and I didn't expect much to come from that. I made a note to call Frank's father in the morning. "I'll give it some thought," I said. "Thanks for coming by."

He got to his feet. "Don't mention it," he said. "I've got to admit some of those tapes were fun to listen to. She was really trying to hold his feet to the fire and meanwhile Frank's shtupping some showgirl in Vegas. Not many gangsters in my practice these days."

By the time I was done returning calls and writing letters, it was five o'clock and a magenta light was coloring my windows. I'd been up early to catch the plane in Boston and felt light-headed now, but it seemed too lonely to go home. It occurred to me that I hadn't talked to Patsy in four days, had left no messages and received none. Though it was part of our unwritten agreement not to have these expectations of each other, it seemed odd.

I knew I could call, invite her to dinner and pick up where we left off, but something made me hesitate. It seemed like an opportunity to actually think about what I was doing and perhaps go in a different direction. I sat in the gloom of my office studying the Matisse reproductions on the wall and wondered if there were still quiet streets like that in France where you could go to escape. But of course that was the beauty of art. It didn't matter if such things were realistic as long as they were real in the painting. It probably had something to do with so many artists having terrible lives. The world could never measure up. Better to stick to apples and pears and old churches.

Around six, my phone rang. I waited for Sherry to pick up but she must have gone home. On the fifth ring, I answered.

"I'm guessing you were going to call," Patsy said brightly. She wore irony like an overcoat. "You must have gotten tied up in some very heavy Law and Order kind of legal thing and couldn't break away, right?"

"Something like that," I said. "How are you?"

Instead of going to Kalt's we met at a Chinese restaurant just over the city line in Shorewood. The food wasn't very good and the owner, a small Taiwanese, came by the table every few minutes to make sure everything was going well, but the place was quiet and we weren't likely to see anyone we knew there.

"So how was Boston?" Patsy asked, getting right to it. She was wearing a green turtleneck that forced skin into her neckline making it appear she had a double chin. Even so, her jaw seemed tense.

"You mean, how was Moira? She's fine. She asked about you."

"I assume you didn't tell her we've been sleeping together since the day she left town."

I had been around Patsy enough to know that this kind of in your face comment usually covered anxiety, so rather than feeling attacked

I was sympathetic. "I didn't think mentioning that would be helpful," I said.

She nodded and I was aware of a pulse in her forehead I hadn't noticed before. I should have realized before that this would be difficult for her, that she was making an effort to be nonchalant, but I hadn't, not really. Sympathy was one thing, but empathy was more important. Maybe for the first time I wondered if I'd been fair in taking her at her word about our affair, about not expecting anything from it, from me. The greater likelihood was that she wanted what anyone would from a relationship but had learned to temper her expectations through hard experience, to demand less and then perhaps be less disappointed with what she got. It was actually a lousy way to live. I reached across the table and took her hand. "I'm sorry, Patsy," I said. "I know this isn't easy."

I stopped speaking because I realized how lame this sounded, how far from anything relevant to the problem it was, but I was stuck with my own language, my own sense of things, my own weaknesses. I hadn't fallen into the affair only because it was easy but because it was there and I was curious. That didn't say much for me, but it was the fact. I had always liked Patsy and been attracted to her, but I hadn't bothered to take seriously the complications that would follow. The fact that she'd made light of that didn't let me off the hook. I should have known. It was as if sleeping with her were an itch I'd decided idly to scratch and that wasn't good enough for her or anyone else.

Fortunately, Patsy was disinclined toward confrontation. "Don't worry about it, Andy," she said. "It's not your fault. I got in over my head and I guess I hoped you would too. That I'd be so irresistible you wouldn't be able to help yourself." She smiled and shook her head. "People handle these things more gracefully in the books I teach but I'm not up to it." She wiped her eyes but the pulse seemed to have quieted down. "So what happens now?"

I could have asked her what she wanted but it didn't really matter what she wanted and she knew it. "One thing I figured out in Boston is that I still love my wife," I said. This sounded stupid but had the benefit of being true.

"Who wouldn't love the beautiful Moira?" Patsy said. "And look at the competition." She spread her arms. With her red eyes, nose and turtleneck I had to smile.

"It's not a competition."

"Damned right, it's not," she said. "No contest. Don't get up, Andy." She said, standing suddenly. Then she leaned over and kissed my cheek. "See, the problem is that in my own fucked-up way I really love you."

And before I could say anything she was going out the door.

I don't know what I expected from Maureen, but it wasn't what sashayed in when I deposed her the next day. I wasn't sure how she and Cindy knew each other, but I was pretty sure it wasn't from Holy Angels. Small and busty, Maureen had jet black hair and a long nose that just prevented her from being beautiful. She walked in the room with Alexander following a step behind, did a slow take on the conference table, the stenographer, pointed at me and said, "Let me, guess. You're the lawyer, right?"

It was unusual for people being deposed to show attitude unless they were criminals and used to being questioned by attorneys, but Maureen was one of the most self-composed witnesses I'd ever interviewed. Instead of using the table for protection, she sat in the chair next to me, crossed her legs carefully, and looked at me directly.

Normally a witness would sit with her lawyer but Alexander took a seat at the end of the table, a small smile on his face. "Okay with you, John?" I asked.

He shrugged. "Whatever you and Mo want to do. I'm just listening."

Maureen was obviously a woman who was accustomed to the admiring stares of men. I was a little surprised that she'd given Frank a tumble, but I didn't say this. I asked if she wanted water or a soft drink. “I’m fine,” Maureen said. “Let’s just get started, okay with you?”

Her confident manner was surprising, but I wasn’t put off by it. The opposite, in fact. I found myself wondering about her relationship with Frank, so I started there. “Miss Somerville,” I began.

“Please,” she interrupted. “I know you guys are all formal and everything, but call me Maureen, okay?”

“Maureen,” I began again, “I’d like to ask you a few questions about your relationships first with Frank Pignatano but also with Cynthia Braithwaite. So just to begin, do you know these two people?”

“Sure,” Maureen said. “It’s why I’m here, right?”

“And are you aware,” I went on, “that until recently they had a personal relationship with one another and lived together on Hackett Avenue?”

“Sure, I was aware,” Maureen said. “Because Cindy took Frank away from me when I was in the hospital having surgery. Not that he was that much to take or to lose, to tell the truth.”

I didn’t respond directly to this but I wondered why Cindy would have listed her as a witness. “Do you consider Cynthia Braithwaite to be your friend?”

Maureen smiled. “Some friend. She stole my boyfriend after I introduced them, but, yeah, she’s kind of a friend, I guess.”

I considered asking what kind of friend she was but decided against it. No point in alienating the witness. “And have you had detailed conversations with Cynthia about her relationship with Mr. Pignatano?”

“What are we talking about here?” Maureen said now. “I didn’t ask her how they did it or what he liked. Actually, knowing Frank, I didn’t have to ask. But we didn’t talk about nothing like that.”

“I wasn’t referring to their sex life,” I said. “What I meant was did Ms. Braithwaite ever talk about how she saw her future and specifically whether it included Mr. Pignatano?”

Maureen laughed. “I ain’t sure that lowlife has a future. There are some people in town he’s pissed off big time. But girls always want to know where things are going with whatever guy they're with, so yeah, Cindy did talk about that. I figured she was out of her mind."

I nodded and made a note on my pad. "When she talked about the future with Mr. Pignatano, what did she say?"

Maureen sighed and rolled her eyes. "All this hearts and flowers bullshit, how they'd be together always, crap like that. As if her old man was ever going to let that happen."

"What did Mr. Braithwaite have to do with it?" I asked. This was something I hadn't expected.

She smiled knowingly. "You're kidding, right? Arthur has something to do with everything that girl does, even with her trying to piss him off by going with Frank. I mean, Arthur's out at the country club with all his buddies from Yale and the law firm and Cindy's doing the dirty D with Frankie at some club on the East Side. What do you think he had to do with it?"

It occurred to me that the principals in the case might actually be the fathers rather than Frank and Cindy, and that I was wasting my time here. Alexander hadn't said a word, sitting silently at the end of the table and making a note or two. Normally, lawyers would caution their clients or object to something the examining attorney might say, but Alexander seemed amused by what was going on, which was puzzling.

I sat back in my chair and looked at each of them in turn. Then I decided to backtrack. "Did Miss Braithwaite ever tell you that she and Mr. Pignatano were going to be married?"

Maureen wrinkled up her forehead. "I don't know if she ever used the word," she said. Then, more decisively, "No, she wasn't really into marriage when we talked. She just said she'd nail his ass if he tried to dump her." Now she looked around the room and smiled. "I guess she did that pretty good, right? I mean we're all here."

There was something to that, but I didn't respond directly. "And did you ever hear Mr. Pignatano say that he intended to marry her, take care of her, or provide for any children that might result from their relationship?"

Maureen sat quietly for a moment as if considering both what she had to say and what she wanted to get on the record. Then, quietly, she said, "I never heard him say nothing like that."

I was having trouble understanding why I was even interviewing Maureen. So far everything she'd said seemed to support Frank, not Cindy. I looked over at Alexander again but he was giving nothing away, so I tried again. "Well, then, did Miss Braithwaite ever tell you that Mr. Pignatano had promised her these things?"

Maureen shook her head. "Like I told you before, the only thing she ever said to me was that he'd better be there for her or she'd kill him," Maureen said. "Which is actually pretty funny when you think about who he is, but I guess you don't fuck with Arthur Braithwaite either."

This was going nowhere but I wanted Maureen to keep talking if it was going to support Frank's version of things. "And what do you think Ms. Braithwaite meant when she said Mr. Pignatano should be there for her?"

Maureen looked at me condescendingly. "It's pretty obvious, ain't it?"

"I'm not a mind reader, Maureen. What I might think it meant could be very different from what Miss Braithwaite actually intended. You were there, I wasn't."

Maureen nodded. "Okay, sorry. But how do I know exactly, except I know she didn't mean for him to throw her ass out of the house and hold onto all the furniture she bought for them. She didn't mean that, all right?"

From what Maureen had said, she'd be nearly useless as a witness and as far as I could see the only point of the tapes must have been to distract or intimidate us. "I have only one other question," I said. "Do you have anything personal against Mr. Pignatano? Is there any reason you'd like to see him punished either for what he did to Miss Braithwaite or what he did to you?"

Maureen crossed her legs again, showing an impressive amount of thigh. She smiled at me alluringly. "I'm not that way," she said. "Frankie and I had some good times together. I leave it at that, okay?"

DEFENDANT'S MEMORANDUM IN SUPPORT OF SUMMARY JUDGMENT

I. Introduction

For approximately two years, between 2003 and September 2005, defendant and plaintiff shared an abode at 2720 N. Hackett Avenue in the city of Milwaukee. During this time they lived virtually as husband and wife though most living expenses, such as rent and food, were provided by defendant. Plaintiff alleges that certain promises were made by defendant regarding continuation of this arrangement, including but not exclusive to costs of living and provision for any eventual child resulting from this union. Defendant disputes this version of the facts of the case and states that no such promise of future support was made or implied. Had such promises been demonstrated by plaintiff either through contractual evidence or records of verbal assent, this lawsuit would not have been filed.

II. Summary Judgment Standard

> Summary judgment is appropriate when there is no genuine issue as to any material fact and the moving party is entitled to judgment as a matter of law. In this case, discovery has yielded no evidentiary data to support plaintiff's claims and defendant requests dismissal of the lawsuit.

There was more but it hardly mattered. This was the gist of the case and I was in at six drafting the document, having run it by Tom Williams and Frank the night before. "Should I call John Alexander and give them a last chance to respond before I give this to the judge?" I asked Tom.

"Fuck them," Tom said. "They had their chance."

"I'd have been willing to pay the bitch to go away, know what I mean?" Frank said. "But I didn't promise her nothing. Trust me on that one. And her old man always hated me."

I continued to have the nagging sense that I was missing something, that Alexander wouldn't have gone this far if he didn't have more to nail Frank with than he had given me, but the rules of evidence required him to show us everything he had and as far as I could tell, there was nothing beyond vague protestations of love that weren't worth anything in court. I wasn't absolutely sure Cindy was lying, that Frank hadn't said he'd support her and any child she had that was his, but if he had, she couldn't prove it.

The tapes were neither conclusive nor admissible and while Frank was cocky he hadn't been stupid enough to write anything down. I still didn't understand why a good lawyer like John Alexander would agree to go ahead with this, but the point of my motion was to find out. Arthur Braithwaite was a partner in his firm and lawyers took all kinds of cases, good and bad. People sued other people every day for no other reason than that they were furious and wanted their pound of flesh. It was frustrating to put this much time and effort into something and have to admit it had all been pointless, but that was the practice of law.

I put the motion in an envelope and called for a messenger to take it to the courthouse. The way these things worked, it could be a couple of months before the judge responded, but it was hard to believe he'd want to waste his time and the state's money over something as insubstantial as the action Cindy had taken against Frank. Yet it had taken weeks of two lawyers' time already so it was conceivable that it would go on out of some unseen momentum we'd built up. Selfishly, I hoped the thing would go away. It would make it easier for Tom and he'd stuck his neck out for me. But as I looked around my office I had the strong feeling my time here was limited anyway. I swept a pile of papers into the wastebasket and left the office.

Then because I had nothing else pressing, I retraced my steps to Little Italy and Sal Pigntano's office in back of the bakery. When I walked in, the same secretary was at her desk typing. "Do you got an appointment?" she asked.

I said I didn't and she sighed and said she'd check. In a moment, the door opened and Sal invited me in. He was wearing an Armani suit, which made me wonder if he was going to court, but I didn't say this. He offered me coffee and we sat again in the Breuer chairs.

"I didn't really expect to see you again," Sal said.

"I just asked the judge for summary judgment," I said. "There really isn't much in the case against your son, but I keep thinking there must be more than I'm seeing here, that I'm somehow in the dark. Then I saw your name on the witness list and decided to ask you if you knew what was going on."

"Smart," Sal said, without answering the question. Then we sat silently drinking coffee.

"So?" I said finally. "What am I missing?"

"It could take the judge, what, six weeks before he rules and then whatever he says will be in the papers, right? Not good. It's one of those things, even if you win you lose. Everybody does."

"Right," I said. "My point exactly. So why are we going through all this and what am I doing in the case? Why not get one of your own lawyers on it and hold their feet to the fire? I don't get it."

"Frank and I aren't that close," Sal said. "I've probably messed around in his life too much already. I thought it would be good to let him handle this himself."

"You can see how well that turned out," I said. "Not just because of Frank; I don't really know much about palimony. I'm supposed to be doing wills, contracts. Frank hired me because we knew each other in high school. Even so, I don't see why the other side won't take a payout. It doesn't make sense."

Sal nodded and drank more coffee. Then he said, "You're probably not aware that Arthur Braithwaite and I know each other."

"Milwaukee's a small town," I said, to keep him talking.

Sal nodded. "Sure, but I mean, Arthur and I go back, way back. Surprised?"

I was. I didn't see Sal at the Towne Club and Marquette law wasn't exactly Yale. "Tell me more."

Sal licked his lips and looked at the ceiling, a small smile on his face. "We actually wrestled against each other in high school. He went to MUS and I was at East. I won."

Milwaukee University School, I remembered. Preppies with long blond hair in London Fog raincoats. The place was gone now, swallowed up by some other school. "No surprise there," I said. "So what?"

"We got to know each other a little, went to some of the same parties, you know . . ."

"Slumming?" I said.

"They figured the public school girls would put out," Sal said. "Actually, it was the other way around. I got with Arthur's sister for a while. Pissed off his dad, I can tell you that." He shook his head at the memory but I could tell he didn't mind annoying rich people who likely looked down their noses at Italians.

"Okay," I said slowly. I had a glimmer but I still didn't really know why he was going down memory lane.

"Her name was Charlotte," Sal went on. "I called her Char, liked her a lot for back then, thought she had class, you know. Anyway, Char got pregnant and they sent her out of town so that was the end of that."

No legal abortion in Wisconsin in those days so rich girls were sent away to fat farms or nunneries or worse. I knew the drill. But what did that have to do with Frank and the lawsuit? "She had an abortion?"

Sal shook his head. "No, they were Catholic like me, so that was out of the question. She had the baby with some nuns down in Illinois. I wanted to marry Char but that wasn't going to happen. They never even let me see her again."

In its own way, it was an amazing story. Sal Pignatano, the all-powerful crime boss, loses out in love to North Shore aristocrats. "What happened to the baby?" I asked.

"You met her," Sal said. Suddenly, everything became clear and I wondered how I could have been stupid enough not to suspect it until now.

"Cindy's your daughter," I said. "No wonder Arthur was ripshit that she was with Frank. History repeating itself. And incest to boot."

Sal nodded. "You could look at it that way."

"And Braithwaite did, so that's why he won't settle."

"You got it."

"Do they know, Frank and Cindy, that they're actually brother and sister?"

"No one else knows except me and Arthur. When Char cracked up, they sent the baby to live with Arthur and his wife who couldn't have kids. He raised her as his daughter."

This seemed like a rather callous way for Sal to dismiss his ex-girlfriend, but now I understood why he had held back rather than putting pressure on Arthur. Still, understanding this didn't make things any easier or show a way to resolving the lawsuit. "Thanks for telling me," I said.

"Lawyer-client privilege, right?" Sal said and winked.

He wasn't my client, but close enough. "Right," I said, and left the office. It was a lot to digest for one day.

Finality is not an easy gig. It might work for other people just to walk away from situations or relationships, and making a clean break of things seemed appealingly sanitary. But it wasn't my personality. I called Patsy but when there was no answer, it occurred to me that this was her long day at school, with classes in the morning and office hours all afternoon. I don't know how I knew this since she never talked about her job as anything but an occasional nuisance, but somehow it had stuck in my mind. I seldom made an appearance on campus but there seemed no harm in it now. There wasn't much left to ruin. One nice thing about college campuses is that people there actually like messy personal situations as they provide the fuel for months of gossip and backbiting. Anything to get you through the long Wisconsin winter.

I parked my car in the underground garage and walked across the quad to Patsy's building, which looked like a bunker, probably meant to turn away hordes of protesting students when it was built back in the sixties. Patsy wasn't in her office, but the department secretary said she had seen her going to the library earlier in the day, so I retraced my steps and wandered around the carpeted rooms looking for her. I had almost given up when I recognized a black hank of hair spreading across the top of a desk in the corner and found her fast asleep on a pile of books, her face paradoxically fresh and open in the reflected light in the carrel. For all the times we'd slept together I'd never really watched her before, never seen her without her wits about her and the flash of irony in her eyes. I thought of going away and leaving with just this for a memory of her, but dinner the night before hadn't been satisfactory for me and I assumed it wasn't for her either. Besides, it wasn't as if we'd never see each other again. We had to figure out a way to feel normal when Moira came back.

Just for the moment I didn't allow myself to seriously consider the possibility that my wife wasn't coming back.

I put my hand gently on Patsy's arm and she stirred. "That's not your most seductive move, Ace," she said, suddenly awake. Then she stretched and smiled. "But I'm glad you came."

We walked back across the quad and sat facing each other in the union café. The coffee was lousy and it was anything but quiet, but the rush of students all in a hurry to get somewhere seemed to insulate us so we could talk. "I didn't feel very good about last night," I began.

She nodded but didn't say anything right away. She reached across and took my hand. For a moment I felt self-conscious, as if someone would see, but then that went away and I didn't care because Patsy didn't and it didn't matter. We sat like that for a few minutes, then she leaned back in her chair.

"I don't know how to do this," she said. "You're too likable to hate. I can't even really blame anyone but myself for getting involved because I was involved from the first time I saw you. You had that tall, geeky look I can't resist, and, oh yeah, you're married to someone else. That's my rule, always fall for the guy who's unavailable. Anyway, if I didn't want anything to happen I should have walked away right then."

Her description of me wasn't exactly flattering but at least she was smiling. "So you were plotting this all along?"

She laughed. "I never plan anything, you know that. I just knew it would happen given space and time, and it did. So who's surprised?"

She had her irony back, which was an improvement over the night before when she'd seemed tense and sad. "That still doesn't answer the question of what do we do next. It'd seem weird if you just disappeared from our lives, didn't call when Moira comes back."

"She's coming back?"

"I hope so," I said. "She didn't say anything specific about it."

Patsy nodded and drank some coffee. "I've got a radical idea," she said. "Why don't we do nothing until there's something we need to do? She might just stay out there in Massachusetts, send for her stuff. End of story. It could happen, right?"

This left a lot unsaid but much of it was probably unsayable. What was truly radical about Patsy's idea was how messy and inconclusive it was. It didn't allow me to wrap everything up neatly and file it away as I did most things. Still, it appealed to me because there was a kind of implied consistency in it. Our relationship had never made sense long-term. I knew I was letting myself off the hook by allowing things to meander this way, but I decided not to worry about it. If I needed to be called to account for my behavior at some point, Patsy or Moira would take care of it.

"What do we do in the meantime?" I asked.

"Lunch sounds good to me," Patsy said.

Rather than declaring itself, sometimes an ending sneaks up on you and it's only after the fact that you realize it's happened. It occurred to me that this was the situation with Patsy. Nothing more was said at lunch. We didn't discuss plans to meet later because we both understood there would be no more intimate dinners at Kalt's, movies at the Downer, drinks at the Tuxedo, or nights together at her house. It was the opposite of a dramatic conclusion and while it made me feel glum, I knew there was no rational reason to feel this way. Ending was the best possible solution for both of us.

I walked around the park and then retraced my steps and drove to the office.

Things were quiet when I came in, or as quiet as they ever got in the middle of the day. There was the hum of a hundred computers, ringing phones, and subdued conversations going on in the offices I passed, but that was all. My secretary's desk was empty and when I checked, I saw two clients had called wondering where I was. There was also a message from the doctor in Boston, asking that I return his call.

Predictably, France wasn't in when I phoned so I did paperwork until dusk filled the room. As much as I disliked this part of the law, working on plans for the end of peoples' lives suited my mood today. At six, the phone rang.

"I'm sorry to call so late and bother you at work," France began.

I told him it was no bother and asked if there were any new developments, though I couldn't imagine what might have changed in two days. "It's not that," France said, "but your wife came in this morning and we discussed your situation. I wonder if you two have talked?"

I didn't want to admit to an outsider how infrequent our contacts were, especially since for the moment I wasn't feeling estranged from Moira. "I've been out," I said. "It would have been hard for her to reach me."

"Of course," France said, as if this were the most natural thing in the world. Even over the phone the man seemed incredibly ill-at-ease. I thought of him as he'd been in his office with his unkempt hair and small hands. I doubted he made a practice of calling patients privately, especially long-distance quasi-patients like me. I didn't know how to interpret his hesitation so I said, "Why did Moira come in exactly?"

France seemed relieved that I'd broken the silence. His tone of voice changed and became brisk and businesslike. "Of course she'll need to talk more with you, but she indicated that she'd like to go ahead with more aggressive measures," he said.

"Because she thinks she won't get pregnant otherwise?"

"Well, you've been trying for some time," he said. "It's understandable that she'd be frustrated. Moira indicated to me that she'd like closure."

This made sense. What all the tests came down to was that Moira might or might not become pregnant the old-fashioned way but there was no certainty and Moira was all about certainty. Success wasn't guaranteed with in vitro fertilization either, but it was an option open to people like us with money, time, and the willingness to challenge nature. This didn't conform to the stoical acceptance of fate I had grown up with, but I'd crossed that line long ago and there was no point in pretending otherwise. "I'm not sure anyone else can give you that," I said now, a feeble protest.

"Philosophically, I agree with you," the doctor said. "But in my experience if couples take this step—with all the expense and inconvenience involved—and still don't become pregnant, they're more able to leave it behind and move on."

If you're going to discuss philosophy in the late afternoon who better to do it with than a Harvard man? But it was really beside the point. It was nice of France to call, but Moira had been driving the pregnancy issue from the start and this wasn't likely to change. "I'll talk to Moira," I said, feeling embarrassed. "Assuming we do go ahead, what's the next step?"

"I gather expense won't be an issue," France said. I didn't contradict him but I wondered if my father-in-law was in on this. Still, money was the least of my worries at this point. "But you would have to be here for the procedure."

"You mean visit Cambridge again?"

France cleared his throat again. Momentarily, I felt bad for the amount of discomfort this man was suffering on our account, but no one was making him carry Moira's water. She had known that by the time we connected I would have talked to the doctor and she wouldn't have to break it to me about in vitro. It did seem kind of unilateral, sort of my-way-or-the-highway, but that was Moira. "I was actually thinking of a longer period of time," France said. "It's very hard to proceed with only one patient in the clinic."

I was beginning to understand why Moira had asked her old friend to handle this, but instead of feeling manipulated it made me feel tenderly toward her. "You mean I'd have to move there?"

France cleared his throat again. “I really can’t advise you what to do,” he said.

But he just had. “I understand,” I said and after repeating that I’d talk to Moira, I hung up.

Despite what I'd told France, I didn't call Moira immediately when I got home. Instead, I ordered a pizza and ate it standing at the kitchen counter while drinking beer and looking out at the small white lights of Lake Park. It reminded me for no reason of a half-remembered flight I'd taken years before when I had flown south from New Haven to visit Duke's law school. I remembered looking at the darkened countryside from the window of the small plane I'd caught in Hartford. From the air, there was an innocent charm to the towns and villages passing beneath the window, with their neat streets laid out in horizontal patterns lined with little yellow and white lights. It obscured what I imagined to be the tawdry reality of life below, the used car lots and fast-food joints, the run-down houses and shotgun shacks with cars up on blocks in the yard, the drive-through liquor stores and worse. Of course I had gained my knowledge of the South from Erskine Caldwell, Carson McCullers, and Faulkner. I knew a whole region couldn't be populated by misfits, killers, and misogynists no matter how memorable they were. I assumed the South was really like everywhere else I'd been; that a serene appearance masked a turbulent life roiling beneath the surface.

None of this had much to do with Lake Park, which was as beautiful in the light as it was charming in the darkness, but I viewed the past few months of my life with a certain ambivalence and marveled that I'd been able to hide my misdeeds from Moira as well as I had. It was some comfort that I wasn't the only one concealing something. While I'd been carrying on in secret with Patsy, my wife had hidden the facts of a back-alley abortion and thus the true nature of her relationship with France. Perhaps we were even, though keeping score this way didn't seem to bode well for our relationship unless you believed secrets were necessary in marriage, a way of remaining private while still sharing your life with someone else. I was learning what I needed to know gradually and things seemed to be coming into the open. There would be decisions to be made, both of us knew that, which might have been why I put off calling Moira.

The gloominess I felt that night had dissipated by morning, replaced by peaceful resignation. As I had expected, there had been no response to my petition to the judge for dismissal, but while the widows and orphans remained, someone had thoughtfully left my calendar clear this morning. I had a slow breakfast at Fischer's, read the papers, and ignored my cell phone, which buzzed irregularly. I knew there were things I needed to do but I was infected by a kind of languor. The sun was out and there seemed to be no hurry about anything. Finally, I left the restaurant and stood out on Farwell Avenue looking at the traffic moving toward downtown. It was nice not to be a part of it.

I remembered my conversation with Sal the day before and knew what I had to do. I put in a call to Alexander who picked up quickly.

"Andy," he said. "I was just thinking of you."

"Great minds think alike," I said. "I need to talk to your boss."

"You want to talk to Arthur?"

"Yes," I said. "I mean I need to meet with him. Alone."

For a moment, Alexander said nothing. It was unconventional to bypass the lawyer and try to talk to the client directly and Braithwaite wasn't even the client of record, just as Sal wasn't. Alexander said, "I'll call you back."

I'd been to Alexander's office before when we met in the large conference room for discovery, but Arthur's office was even grander than this, as befit a partner in an important and prosperous firm, with windows showing the sweep of the Milwaukee River going north and City Hall rising majestically just south of us. There was a floor-to-ceiling bookshelf with a rolling ladder to help reach the top shelves and a diploma wall that looked more than a little like Sal's. Arthur was sitting behind a desk the size of a battleship but when he rose to shake my hand I noticed a Parkinsonian tremor in his thin right hand. He looked shrunken, his collar gaping around his neck and thin gray hair arranged to try to disguise a growing bald spot. I had to remind myself that he must be exactly Sal's age.

Two club chairs in blue leather flanked Arthur's desk and now he gestured me toward them in a courtly way. "Well," he said, when we were seated. "Mr. Alexander said you needed to see me even though I'm not a principal in your case. May I ask why?"

"Because you're driving the case," I said, jumping right in. "As I'm sure you know, palimony cases seldom make it to court. They're settled as a rule by one party satisfying the other with a cash settlement, but you've refused even to discuss this. So my question is, why won't you settle? What do you want?"

I had thought Braithwaite might be insulted by my frankness or at least act insulted, but he just nodded and when he spoke it seemed to have nothing to do with what I'd said. "She was beautiful," he said softly. "I wish you could have seen her at seventeen. Small, blond, blue eyes and the picture of innocence. She never had a bad word to say about anyone."

For a moment I didn't know who he was talking about. It didn't sound like Cindy but then I realized he was reminiscing about his sister. There was nothing to say about this, so I kept quiet, waiting for him to make the point. He shook his head now, trying to rid himself of the memory.

"Then that bastard got to her, that dago sonofabitch with his greasy hair and smart mouth knocked her up and we had to send her out of town and she was never the same. You know how old she was when she died?"

I shook my head no. I could see the man was suffering and I empathized with him for this but I had to remind myself not to feel sorry for Braithwaite, to stay the lawyer in the case. I wasn't his friend. "I'm sorry for your loss," I said.

He ignored this. He had no use for my sympathy. "Thirty-four," he said. "And it was a blessing. We didn't know her in the end. Such a beautiful girl," he repeated. "I assume you've spoken to Pignatano or you wouldn't be here, so you know all this already."

I nodded. "So I have to ask you again, what do you want? Nothing can bring back your sister and as far as I know Cindy's unaware of any of this. She thinks she's your daughter, am I right?"

"Sins of the fathers," Braithwaite muttered now and I wondered if I was going to be able to get anywhere with him, his grief was so profound, his anger so deep seated. It was likely Alexander knew nothing of this either so even if I could understand Arthur's feelings, his revulsion at Frankie and the idea of history repeating itself, what could I possibly offer that would make him whole? It might be that summary judgment was my only hope and that my visit to Braithwaite had been a waste of time. We sat for another five minutes without saying anything and then I rose to leave. I offered my hand and Braithwaite took it in his. Then he looked up, his eyes watery with tears.

"You ask what I want," he said. "I'll tell you. I want that lowlife and his son to burn in hell. That's what I want."

"I understand," I said. "I do, but realistically you might have to wait a while for that. My question is what do you want now?"

A day went by, two days. I made plane reservations to return to Boston and turned my attention to cases I'd been ignoring while I was involved with Patsy and the Pignatanos. I kept turning over in my mind my visit with Arthur Braithwaite but could come to no better conclusion than I had when I sat in his office. Money was no salve for the kind of tragedy his family had endured, but at least now I understood what was really going on, the subtext, which is often more important than whatever reality seems to be at issue. Then after a week, I got a call at the office from Sal Pignatano's secretary, asking if I could come down to his office at my convenience. Sal and I had gotten to be friendly, but I still felt unable to say no to him so obediently I retraced my steps to Brady Street.

This time I passed right through the bakery and no one seemed to notice or care, went to the small building in back and walked inside. The secretary was sitting at the table reading the paper. She picked up the phone and whispered into it. Then she turned in my direction and said, "You can go on in."

Sal was sitting behind the desk wearing a tan cashmere jacket over an open-necked burgundy shirt. On the sofa was Maureen Summerville, though she seemed different than before. She smiled when she saw me, but the gum-chewing cockiness I'd observed during discovery was gone. She seemed composed, even elegant, in a gray suit with a lavender scarf tied around her neck. I hadn't expected to see Maureen in Sal's office, but I wasn't taken aback either. It could have been that I was past surprise in this case or simply that seeing her there made sense in terms of the way things had developed.

Sal indicated Maureen now and said, "I believe you two are acquainted?"

"We've met," I said. "Actually, I wasn't aware that you knew Maureen, though I knew Frank used to be a friend of hers."

Sal smiled, amused apparently by my delicacy. "I've known Maureen since she was a teenager," he said. "But she's only come to work for us recently."

I wondered what kind of work she could have been doing for an organized crime boss, but it didn't really matter at this point. "Does Cindy Braithwaite know about this?"

Sal smiled again. "There was an accommodation with Cindy that we were able to make," he said. "Arthur was more difficult, but I think your visit with him made a difference. We had dinner the other night, first time I'd seen him in years, and I think he may change his mind."

"Do tell," I said. "When I saw him he was in no mood to settle."

Sal nodded. "Basically, I ate crow, said I was responsible for everything and apologized. It's not going to bring Char back but there wasn't anything else I could do. Arthur doesn't need money."

"So it's all going away?" I asked, relieved. "My friend at the law firm went out on a limb with his partners or I wouldn't have been allowed to get involved with this. Is there still really a lawsuit at all?"

Sal ducked his head and ran a hand through his hair. "I hope not," he said. "I'm sorry if this got you in trouble with your employer but actually you made this happen. If you hadn't tried to talk to me and Arthur, I think we'd be going to court and that wouldn't really help anyone."

What it all came down to in the end was that Sal, the Mafioso kingpin, far from breaking legs or leaving a horse's head in the bed, had prostrated himself before Arthur Braithwaite, who had all the cards. This seemed right in some essential way. I didn't really see why a simple apology should satisfy Arthur, but it seemed as if it had. Maybe he was just tired of the whole thing and exhaustion had trumped outrage.

I looked over at Maureen who still hadn't spoken. "Were you really going to testify for Cindy against Frank?" I asked. "Or was that all an act too?"

She glanced at Sal who nodded almost imperceptibly. "Sure," she said. "Frank did promise to take care of her and I knew about it. Her old man was being a real pain in the ass, putting pressure on me so I said I'd be a witness, but I didn't feel good about it even then because, you know, Cindy's going to be fine. Rich people always are. She was just pissed off because Frank dumped her, but that's Frank, you know? Why make a big deal about it?"

"And now you're working here?"

She smirked. "Yeah, and I'm really busy." Then she got to her feet and left the room.

Then Sal and I sat facing each other across the big desk. There wasn't a paper or book in sight, but he swept his hand across the glass surface as if it needed to be cleaned.

He shrugged and raised his hands in a gesture of resignation. "With kids, you do what you've got to do. Whether you like it or not." It seemed odd to hear him talk about Frank as if he'd thrown a baseball through a neighbor's window but in his mind it was the same thing.

"So we're done here?"

Sal nodded. "Looks like it. I appreciate what you did, I want you to know that. You'll be paid for your time." He gestured toward the credenza behind him. "I could write you a check right now."

I didn't tell him that I was happy to have the distraction the case provided, that the work I was doing at the law firm bored me to death and I liked the slight hint of danger that accompanied his son, whether it was earned or not. "Never mind," I said. "I don't handle billing, but someone at the office will be in touch. They're very good about collecting." I meant this to be ironic but Sal didn't seem amused.

"Of course they are," he said. "Big firm like that, they'd have to be."

There was no reason for me to feel put off or deceived. The goal in a lawsuit was always to settle because it was a certain outcome while going to court carried with it uncertainty, no matter how solid your case might seem. What's more, witnesses tended to be malleable. They'd lie, forget crucial details, or withhold information without warning; it went with the territory. I wondered how much of the truth about all this John Alexander had known, but there was no point in going down that path. I admired Sal's willingness to go to Arthur to resolve the case. This didn't change the fact that his business involved breaking the law on a regular basis. Sal's cashmere jacket, hand-made shoes, and fine art on the wall didn't change that. Still, he'd been decent to me and I was relieved to see the end of all this.

Representing Frank Pignatano may not have been the best decision, but I knew it wasn't the worst either and from the firm's point of view, I had won. There was comfort in that. What's more, taking the case had served the function of making me understand that handling wills and estates was not going to work for me in the long term. Since the firm had no need for another litigator, this likely meant my days there were numbered, regardless of Tom Williams's support. And despite the undeniable intrigue of Sal and his gang contacts, I didn't really think I'd fit in either as a prosecutor for the district attorney or working the other side of the street as a criminal defense lawyer.

This might have made me feel insecure, but it actually had the opposite effect. I stopped in the bakery for a hard roll and sat chewing it in the car while deciding on my next move. Then without knowing how I knew, my direction seemed clear, even foreordained. I put the car in gear and drove.

Alfred Koenenberg lived in a house with a peaked roof and faux wood siding on Bartlett, not far from the North Avenue bridge. Most tenured professors at the university had houses farther up on the East Side toward the lake or even in the northern suburbs, but it made a kind of sense that Koenenberg lived down here, given what I'd learned about him in Mom's notebooks.

The house itself was small and rundown but not out of character for the neighborhood, which seemed disinclined to make much of itself and stood out after the garish rehabilitation of Brady Street.

The yuppies hadn't discovered Bartlett yet and there was a good chance they never would. An empty garbage can stood in Koenenberg's driveway and a stack of newspapers still in their plastic wrappers were piled next to the door. Apparently, Alfred wasn't big on keeping up with the news.

No one spends much time at home anymore so I didn't really expect to find him in, but when I rang the bell Koenenberg answered almost immediately, as if he'd been watching for intruders, which I certainly was and meant to be. The question would be why, why after all these years would I care what he and my mother had done, but the ineluctable truth is that in some strange way I imagined I had come to defend our family honor. I was there representing my dead father, whom I'd never known, and my mother who as I saw it had been callously tossed aside by this bush league Casanova.

We stood on the stoop facing each other for a silent moment, neither sure of what to say. I'd built Koenenberg up in my mind as a seductive heartbreaker, but the little man facing me seemed incapable of that. At least ten years had gone by since I'd seen him, but he hadn't changed much. He was wearing his signature bike shorts, a little hat with the brim turned up, a fleece pullover and severe wire-rimmed glasses. His gray hair was cut short to his skull and it looked as if he hadn't shaved in a week.

"I'm Andy Simonson," I began finally. "You knew my mother . . ."

"I know who you are," Koenenberg said, interrupting. "I've been expecting you." His tone was not hostile but neutral, businesslike, as if I'd interrupted some important experiment he was conducting in the lab. What is it you want, exactly, he seemed to say.

Then, as if he intuited my indecision, Koenenberg stood back and gestured me inside. The vestibule was filled with a racing bicycle, helmet and a variety of sweaters, coats and shoes, but the living room where we sat down was as spare as the entryway had been cluttered. There were just two chairs facing each other on a bare wood floor.

"Your mother was a remarkable woman," Koenenberg said. He

didn't offer to make tea, as if to acknowledge that this wasn't that kind of visit. "I miss her."

What he said was true, but often people who had hardly known my mother said similar things. Even Sal Pignatano had talked about her ability as an artist. Koenenberg's characterization had the odd effect of irritating me more than if he'd made a snide remark because it wasn't the kind of thing that deserved an offhand comment, some forgettable compliment. My mother was more unique than that. Just like all mothers are to their sons. But rather than take umbrage, I said, "You probably don't know, but she kept a journal. Actually, a series of journals, composition books, diaries, and you're all over them."

Koenenberg didn't respond immediately to this or even show interest. He took it in, a small, satisfied smile on his face, as if women all over Milwaukee were writing about him and there was little he could do to prevent it. "This I didn't know," he said. Then, quickly, "But it's okay."

Suddenly, I was angry. "Who are you to say whether it's okay or not? You were a married man and you didn't give a shit. You seduced her and then you dropped her when it was convenient for you. God knows about your wife, what she thought. Okay, my ass."

Koenenberg seemed more amused than threatened by my anger. "The journal said this?" he said. "I, a seducer? Interesting."

I had to admit, looking at this nondescript man in bike shorts in his run-down little house, that it was hard to imagine him in the role I'd assigned. And yet there were my mother's diary entries, the chronicling of her multiple orgasms, the amount of herself she'd given over to this man or allowed him to take. Despite all this, however, I felt my anger begin to ebb. "I might be exaggerating a little."

Koenenberg smiled in a kindly way. He held his thumb and forefinger an inch apart. "Just a little," he said. "Too bad, though. At my age, I wouldn't mind seeing myself in a new way. To be honest, it would probably be an improvement."

"I think my mother was in love with you," I said.

Koenenberg nodded somberly. I liked the fact that he took it seriously. Love was serious. If I'd learned anything from the events of the past few months, I'd learned that. Even Cindy's fury at Frank's behavior spoke in its own way of the power of love, misdirected as that might have been. "I hope so," he said, "because I loved her."

Then what happened, I wanted to ask. Why had the entries in the notebooks stopped suddenly ten years ago? I remembered he had a wife, that Mom had mentioned her in passing. But that didn't seem like much of an impediment at the time and this house seemed empty, not just empty in the sense of people not being home, but uninhabited in an odd but tangible way. Looking at the strange little man before me, it seemed incredible that he could ever have been the focus of my mother's romantic yearnings, but who really understands anything about human attraction? Not knowing what else to say except what was on my mind, I finally asked Koenenberg what had happened between them.

He shrugged expressively and puffed his lips. "I don't know," he said. "The air went out of it all of a sudden. Sometimes things just end. I don't know why, but they do, at least they seem to for me."

This seemed a bit philosophical, not to say dishonest, assigning something mystical to human motivation and putting people into passive roles. "Did you get tired of each other?" I persisted. "Was that it? Or was it your wife?"

Koenenberg smiled again. "It was my wife who pushed me toward your mother to begin with," he said. Then he laughed. "That surprises you, but it's the truth. She said she thought it would be good for both of us and she was right about that, but I think really she just wanted to get rid of me."

"A good idea?" I thought of Moira and the impossibility of her ever encouraging me to have an affair with another woman, how furious she would be if she knew what had been going on with Patsy.

Koenenberg nodded. "Weird, right? But that's the way she was.

We were kids in the sixties and she didn't think you should own anyone else, know what I mean?"

I'd heard about this. Open marriage, free love, flowers in your hair and swimming nude at Woodstock, though not from my mother. She was the same age as Koenenberg but had spent her life working dead-end jobs trying to provide for us after my father's death. Maybe the affair with Koenenberg was her way of revisiting all that, her private Woodstock. "Is she still alive, your wife?"

Koenenberg shrugged again. He was a big shrugger. "I think so. She took off a couple of years ago, left me a note. That was it, a note after more than thirty years. Not that I really minded, but it just seemed kind of cold. Every now and then she used to send a postcard, but it's been a long time so maybe she is dead." He pulled at his lower lip and wrinkled his forehead. "You'd think I'd hear about it, though."

He patted his knees and sat up straighter. "But you're not here for that, are you? You're here to defend your mama's honor. You want to know why I did whatever you think I did to her. Maybe you want to knock me down, eh?" He raised his fists in imitation of a boxer and I had to laugh.

"Kind of," I said, but whatever anger I'd felt had slipped away, lost beneath the floorboards of the dreary house on the forgettable street. Whether I wanted to admit it or not, I did feel something toward this man. As pathetic as it might seem, he was the one who more nearly than anyone else had taken the place of an older man in my life. He was the only one who'd been close to my mother over the years I was gone, a secret—what, lover, friend?—of whom I'd been almost completely unaware. It seemed like a lot not to know about someone. "Really, though, I'd like to know what she was like for you. Not as a lover. But in other ways. Not all that remarkable woman crap, but really, day to day, what did you talk about, what did you do? What do you remember?"

For the first time Koenenberg looked engaged. Not amused, not bored, but genuinely interested. He patted his knees decisively then looked at me directly. "You want to know what your mama was like, that's very good. We never know our parents, not really, not as people, just their place in our lives, their assignments. I'm the same with my parents but now they're gone and no one I know knew them. So I don't blame you; I congratulate you. This is good."

He hesitated again and looked at the floor. "The truth is your mother was an artist," he said and then held up his hand. "You think you know what I mean by that because you've looked at a few pictures and read some books, but you don't know. No one really knows except another artist. What I mean is that for your mother art was the only thing that mattered except for a few people—you, maybe your father when he was alive. Maybe me. But all the other things that most people worry about twenty-four hours a day, their houses, their cars, their jobs, who has more money, what other people think, all that to her was bullshit. She wore old clothes not to make a point but because she didn't care about clothes. She drove a car that broke down all the time; she didn't care. She didn't have a New York gallery representing her. So what? She never made a dime off her work. None of that mattered. What mattered was what she put on the canvas. And maybe because of that she was a good artist, a very good artist who deserved better than she got. She had taste and she could see what she was doing, even if no one else did. She had pride, she had self-respect and every other artist in town who was worth anything knew it and that was what mattered to your mother.

"From the time she got up in the morning until she went to bed at night, what was on her mind was her art. How to get down in paint and clay and metal and stone what she felt, what she saw, the impossibility of ever really doing that and the fascination of that impossibility. She liked how hard it was; she liked the fact that nothing she ever did satisfied her. And that's what was so great about her as an artist, as a person. That's it, that's what I thought of your mother, okay?"

If my mother had a gravestone, this was what she'd have liked to have for her epitaph, but there was no stone and I had no plans to erect one. We weren't monument people. Still, I was moved. We sat looking at each for other for a few moments without speaking. Then I stood and walked toward the door. What had needed to be said had been said and now we were done talking. In the open door, the wind from the street warming my head and neck, I turned to face Koenenberg who hadn't moved. He sat slumped in his chair, apparently exhausted by what he'd said. It had obviously taken an effort. There was an openness to his expression speaking of a kind of honesty we seldom experience with anyone but a lover.

"Thanks," I said. "That's what I wanted to know."

"No problem," he said. "It's okay. I'm glad I got a chance to say it. And I don't need those books she wrote." He patted his chest. "I got it all right here. I want her to be just the way I remember, and nothing else."

I was back on the sidewalk in front of the house. It seemed smaller now, the second-floor windows with their shades at half-mast looking like hooded eyebrows, the roof drooping over the eaves as if it were about to fall in the street, the flaking gray paint more obvious than ever despite the time I'd put in trying to touch it up. It was hard to disagree with Moira's judgment that the place was just looking for a decorous way to collapse without injuring anyone.

I thought of the promise I'd made my mother and what it had cost me. Time, money, nearly my marriage. I wondered why something as desperate as a deathbed request should have the reach it did, why beyond sentiment a promise made under those circumstances should mean more than any other. I didn't believe in god or an afterlife, didn't believe I'd be struck down if I went back on my word. Yet something held me back. How long should such a promise hold? What was the length of the contract? A year, ten years, a lifetime? And what were the terms measured in loans reneged on, bankruptcies filed, marriages lost, friendships ruined? What really mattered about the house was that it had belonged to my mother. It represented my only tie to a tenuous past, though looking at it now, tenuous seemed like a generous way to describe the place.

What it really came down to was something else entirely. I knew my mother, wherever she was, would understand if I just gave up, said the hell with it, I had other lives to live. While she was alive whatever I had done had finally been acceptable to Mom. I was her only son, as she would have said the apple of her eye, and could basically do no wrong. But none of this was really about her. It involved some obscure sense I had of keeping faith and doing the right thing. Following through on a promise seemed to be a value worth living by, but in this case it was turning out to be more a straightjacket than a guide.

What's more, my reasons for coming home now seemed ridiculous. I had returned to Milwaukee to show people who probably didn't care how well I'd done out in the world. How smart I was, how successful, what a beautiful wife I'd snagged, ultimately how superior I was to all the misguided losers in the neighborhood who hadn't gone to Princeton or Yale and were one up on me when we were kids. No one cared. There'd been no welcome home parties or intimate dinners with friends, no free tickets for the Brewers or the Bucks or the Rose Bowl.

Gossip is rewarding in that it creates the illusion that you matter to others. But the truth was that I didn't matter very much to anyone outside my family and realizing that left me free to make the next move. I'd been slow to admit this experiment in coming home hadn't worked but now Mom was dead and I'd screwed things up with Moira and the law firm. It looked like a good time to light out for the territories.

In a sense it was that simple: just walk away. There would never be a problem selling a house three blocks from the lake, regardless of its condition. Moira had insisted that I wasn't a landlord and now I understood that she was right. I liked the idea of being a lord of any kind, but I lacked the temperament for property management. I cared too much and yet not enough about my tenants. I had to bite the bullet and sell the goddamned house.

I climbed the stairs to the attic. Dust motes hung in front of my eyes and I had an air of expectation with no reasonable origin. It was if I'd wandered into another zone altogether. If the bottom two floors and those who lived there represented my mother in her public life, this was another part of the house, secret and sacrosanct, and yet this was the part that really mattered. What became of it all was up to me, whether to keep it or let it go. The stacks of canvases and the small books containing the record of her last love affair were no one else's business except for Alf Koenenberg and he'd said he didn't want to see them.

Which meant my last responsibility to my mother was just to make sure that what was private and personal remained that way. I gathered the composition books in my arms and walked downstairs and into the yard. Then I placed them in two equal piles on the flagstone patio and lit a match.

Once the fire had started, Ginnie came out on the back porch. She descended the stairs and walked over to me. "Who's bringing the marshmallows?" she asked. Then she noticed there were tears in my eyes and put her arm around me. "Sorry," she said. "Something's going on, huh?"

I nodded but didn't answer.

When the fire died down, Ginnie took me inside and made tea while we watched the guttering notebooks on the patio. "You want to tell me what was in those books that was so bad you needed to pollute the backyard?"

"Not really," I said. "They belonged to my mother. Old stuff."

Ginnie sat across from me and took my hand. She sipped Red Zinger then looked at me with concern. "Are you okay?" she asked in a way that spoke of a more intimate friendship than we had.

"I will be," I said. "Where's your roommate?" I hadn't seen her for a while but she'd always been quiet.

"Moved out," Ginnie said.

I'd never thought much about relationship problems for lesbians and now I felt stupid. "Did you two have a fight?"

"Not really," Ginnie said. "I'm just not completely sure I'm gay." She gave me what might have been a meaningful look, but as attractive as she was I'd learned something the last few months. I leaned back in my chair and looked sympathetic. "Too bad," I said, "but you're not going to have any trouble finding someone else, male or female. I wouldn't worry about that."

She leaned across the table and kissed me, a long lingering kiss, her tongue caressing my teeth playfully. "It could be you, Andy," she said. "Just so you know."

I was tempted but not stupid. "That's the nicest thing anyone's said to me in quite a while," I said. "But I'm getting out. I'd give you a great price on the house."

Ginnie smiled. "Not on an adjunct's salary," she said. "But thanks."

We sat quietly for a while, drinking tea and watching the smoke of the past rise over the backyard. Then I got up, kissed her on the cheek, and left.

I walked home in a light rain, enjoying the feeling of lightness I always get in wet weather, the sense of things coming clear, as if enlightenment is a possibility. I should have lived in Seattle where it rains all the time, but I was about to head in the other direction, which said something about my life.

When I got home there was an envelope taped to the door. On one sheet of eggshell paper, Patsy had written, "I can't do this. Call me."

I reread the note, admiring her slanting letters and the quiet demand of the last sentence. What would happen if I didn't call, if I just let it go instead? Her diction said I didn't want to know. I had to respond, but I wanted to gather my thoughts first because this wasn't what I'd expected. When we had lunch, Patsy had seemed sad but controlled. Now she couldn't do whatever it was we were doing, breaking up or stepping away from something temporary or just acknowledging what I thought we both knew in the first place. The trouble with these interpretations is they made things very convenient for me. I'd had a lover when I needed one and now I could just let Patsy go. No harm, no foul. And no need to inform my wife. It was easy; too easy.

When I called Patsy, however, she was brusque. She didn't sound hurt or sorrowful but rather strong and in command. "Meet me at The Coffee Trader in an hour," she said. Then she hung up.

When I got to the restaurant, Patsy was waiting and she looked different than I had ever seen her. Her hair was gathered severely in a bun and she was wearing a red pencil skirt and a black vest over a white shirt open at the neck. It was as if she was late for a business meeting rather than preparing for a poetry lecture.

I leaned over to kiss her on the cheek but she turned away, her mouth a tight line. I shrugged and took a chair. There was a coffee cup in front of her but I didn't feel like ordering anything. "What's going on?" I asked, getting right to the point.

When she turned to me it looked as if her eyes were wet but I couldn't tell if she'd been crying or was as angry as she appeared to be. "You're leaving town," she said. It wasn't a question.

"I told you the other night."

"Nice for you," she said.

Her saying it made me feel ashamed, as if by returning to my wife I was running away from something, which was ridiculous. I reached for her hand, but she jerked it away. "Come on, Patsy," I said. "We talked about this from the beginning. No one said anything was going to be permanent."

"Boys just want to get laid," she said. Her intensity was making me nervous. I felt a chill on the back of my neck, spreading to my shoulder blades.

"Not really," I said quietly. "I care about you."

"Bullshit," Patsy said. "Just be honest, for Christ's sake. You care about you."

It was true, but what was surprising or dishonest in that? "Sure," I said.

"And your wife."

Now I was getting mad. "Right, I care about Moira. What's your point?"

She took an envelope out of her bag. "Take a look," she said.

Inside the envelope were five or six pictures of Patsy and me in various stages of undress, another of me at her kitchen table in my underwear, the two of us with our arms around each other naked in bed. Nothing really outrageous but all incriminating. "You took pictures with a hidden camera?" I said, too stunned to say anything else. It felt as if we were in a movie, a spy novel, something.

"You can keep those to show your friends," Patsy said. "I've got copies."

I didn't often find myself at a loss for words, but Patsy's revelation went beyond surprise and had I wanted to say something, sound wouldn't come. In a grotesque way it was interesting to have been so completely wrong about a person. I looked at the photos again. They were perfectly focused, as if the camera had been mounted on a tripod and operated by some kind of remote switch. Who would have imagined Patsy capable of such technical sophistication? Against myself, I was impressed by her foresight and cleverness. Finally, I said, "What are you planning to do with those?"

It was an obvious question. Why take pictures unless you were going to use them? They weren't the kind of thing to put in a scrapbook and show the grandchildren in thirty years. I felt the chill return, but I didn't know what more to say. I wouldn't have imagined blackmail would be her style, but I'd been wrong before. A woman scorned and all that.

"That depends," Patsy said, cagey now.

The room moved around us, people coming in and leaving the restaurant, the palm frond fans on the ceiling eternally circling to no visible effect. "On what?"

"On what you do."

"Oh, yes. And what exactly are you expecting or demanding" She had me in a corner and was looking smug about it. At that point, I hated Patsy, though I couldn't blame her. She was in the power position and perhaps had been all along. "Do you want me to leave Moira, is that it? Do you want us to be married? What?"

"Don't flatter yourself."

"Okay. What then?"

"Simple. Tell your wife."

"About us?"

She nodded. "Unless there's some other bimbo I don't know about." Patsy stood and picked up her bag. "Tell Moira," she said. "Or I will."

After she left, I sat in the restaurant for a while, in a daze, getting it all in order in my mind. It's amazing how just when you think you've got your life settled in a way that makes sense something comes along to make everything impossible. I'd taken care of Frank and his palimony suit, decided to sell the house, made peace with moving back to New England, and confronted Mom's aging lover, but I'd clearly underestimated Patsy. I wasn't quite clear why she wanted Moira to know about us, whether it was out of revenge or triumph. Nor did I understand why she thought she was in a position to order me around. She'd made clear that she didn't want me back, even if that had been what I wanted. So why the kick-ass insistence on full disclosure?

I watched the fans paint shadows on the ceiling of the restaurant, feeling the light movement of air in the room, aware of tinkling music somewhere in the background and a line at the door full of impatient people waiting to get in, but I still couldn't move. As a lawyer, I understood there were always unforeseen consequences to your actions. But I had been arrogant enough to think I had a good sense about people, too, knew what they wanted and what they wanted from me. I had gone ahead with Patsy just because we both wanted to. I hadn't been dissuaded by loyalty to Moira; in fact, I felt entitled to the affair since she was the one who'd left town. Stupid, but there you were. It hadn't occurred to me that in the process Patsy would be hurt. Now she wanted me to hurt Moira or else. About the kindest thing you could say about my behavior was that I hadn't been thinking and today I wasn't inclined to be kind. Patsy hadn't given me a deadline but that didn't matter. The question was, what should I do now?

I needed to talk to someone and Moira was out of the question for the moment. I called Tom Williams but he'd left the office so I drove down to Donovan's and found him wedged into a corner booth. "It's a little early for you, isn't it?" I said, sliding in across from him.

"You know what they say," Tom replied. "It's five o'clock somewhere."

Suddenly I felt very middle-aged, tossing down drinks with my old friend while the sun was still high in the sky. It was like something out of an old melodrama, *The Man in the Gray-Flannel Suit* or *The Lost Weekend*, though neither of us were well-heeled Wall Street movers or entitled to world-weariness.

"I've got a problem," I started.

"Just like everyone else in the world," Tom said. "Why tell me? I'm not your godfather anymore. I'm lucky to still have a fucking job considering I recommended you to my partners in the first place. But just out of curiosity, what's going on?"

"You know about me and Patsy already," I said.

"Like the rest of the East Side or at least that part of it that gives a shit. You guys weren't exactly discreet. No out of the way bars or motels for you. It's dinner at Kalt's with a woman who's not your wife and then back to her house with your car parked in front all night. You might as well have put out an announcement for Christ's sake."

"I thought they only cared about that kind of thing in small towns."

"Milwaukee is a small town. That's why we love it, right? Everyone knows everything about everyone. It's just a good thing Moira's in Boston and no one here really knows her. If she was a Milwaukee girl you'd be shit out of luck."

I smiled at the high school expression. Some things never changed but he was right about Milwaukee being a small town with every neighborhood complete in itself. "I might be anyway. It turns out Patsy's quite a photographer."

Tom's whole posture changed at this. No longer lethargic, he sat up and lost the air of detachment he'd favored a moment before. Leaning forward, he spoke in a hoarse, charged whisper. "Pictures? You kidding me? Dirty pictures of the two of you? Slide them over here."

I shook my head no. "Sorry," I said, "they're not that good. You'd be disappointed. But they're probably enough to put me in divorce court."

Tom smiled broadly. "So, basically, you're fucked, my friend. What's she going to do with them? Send them to Moira? But that's so twentieth century. Maybe put them on YouTube, not that anyone who doesn't know you would give a shit."

I hadn't even considered the internet, but it was a great way to get back at rivals, casual enemies, and this went beyond casual. The whole idea of exposing your private embarrassments to thousands of strangers tended to put a different slant on the notion of progress. I wondered how Patsy would feel about broadcasting our affair to colleagues, students, friends. It seemed sort of like self-immolation and I had no idea why whatever she felt about this would bring it to that level.

"Jesus, she didn't say anything about that."

"Fine, so what did she say?" Tom asked. "I mean, she took the pictures for a reason, right?"

"She said Moira should know what's been going on and if I didn't tell her, she would."

Tom looked puzzled. "I'm still not getting it. She's doing this why, as a public service or something, so everyone will know what a scumbag you are? But the only thing she wants you to do is tell your wife?"

Tom seemed disappointed at the level of Patsy's anger, but I couldn't help that. I hadn't really thought about why she had gone to the trouble to take the pictures unless it was to protect herself. If that were the case, what would she be protecting herself from? And it was so premeditated. What had made her think she'd need protection? The idea of me being a threat took paranoia to a new level but for some reason the pictures, the placement of a hidden camera, all seemed oddly logical now.

The world of Frank and Sal Pignatano seemed to be bumping up against mine, something that hadn't occurred to me as being possible before. I'd enjoyed the illusion that I had escaped to a new higher level of existence and was above all that. But what was the difference, really, between Cindy taping her phone calls and Patsy planting a hidden camera in our love nest? If anything, Patsy was more Machiavellian than Cindy, something that would have surprised both of us.

"You thought this was just a harmless little affair with a hippie college professor who'd be cool about the whole thing, right? A little walk on the wild side and no harm, no foul."

He had me there and it was embarrassing. "I guess I did."

Tom shook his head ruefully. "I hate to be the one to tell you, Andy, but you're a real asshole. The sixties are a long time ago, free love, open marriage, wife swapping, all that shit. No one's really into it now."

He was right, though I hadn't exactly been thinking along those lines. I even loved my wife. I thought of an old poem by Dowson I'd read at Princeton. "I have been faithful to thee, Cynara, in my fashion." I loved Moira in my fashion, but what kind of a fashion was it really? If I was honest I had to admit that I loved her as long as it was convenient for me. When things got hard and she went home to Boston, I bailed and found Patsy. But self-flagellation was not going to help.

"Okay," I said. "So you're smart and I'm an asshole. What should I do?"

Tom shrugged. "You don't want to hear this, but you'd better call Moira and tell her what's going on. I don't know if Patsy's serious about showing the pictures or not, if she'd really follow through on this, but she sounds pretty crazy right now. You have to protect yourself."

Telling Moira didn't seem very self-protective to me considering what was likely to follow, but there didn't seem to be any good alternatives. "Over the phone?"

Tom thought this over for a minute. "It's impersonal," he said. "But the advantage is she can't shoot you over the phone, and neither can her old man."

Before I could think seriously about this, however, I got a call from Frank Pignatano. "I hear you're pissed my old man bought off Cindy," he said, getting right to the point.

I didn't think it was wise for the word to get around, even if it was true. "That's not really what happened," I said. "Who told you that?"

"No one told me," Frank said, sounding vaguely insulted. "Maureen just said you were out of the office in a hurry this morning and I figured it out. See, I know you, man. We go back."

I hadn't previously been impressed by Frank's sensitivity, but he was right. It just didn't seem to make sense to explain my negotiations with Arthur and Sal so I played along. Sal hadn't really paid anyone off, but this might have been his way to save face with his son. "You might have told me," I said now. "I mean, I'm your lawyer, or I was anyway."

"You're right, man," Frank said, sounding truly penitent. "Hey, I'm sorry, okay. The deal was going down and I was supposed to keep my mouth shut."

"Forget it," I said. There was no deal for Frank to know about and I knew Sal hadn't confided in him about the conversation he'd had with Arthur Braithwaite. He no doubt assumed there was no need to tell Frank anything and I agreed. "It's for the best," I said now. "I'm leaving town."

"I know," Frank said. "That dyke on the first floor told me. Maybe I'll buy the house from you, you give me a deal."

I was still looking for three months' rent from Frank, so I wasn't sure how he was going to buy the house. "You mean your old man would?"

"Same diff," Frank said. "Anyway, I hear you got other problems, with that hippie bitch you were seeing."

This was becoming disturbing. It was one thing for Tom to know about the affair, but the word seemed to be out in Milwaukee's underworld as well. I wondered if Patsy had already circulated the pictures. It was my fifteen minutes of fame, unappetizing as it might be. "You heard about that too?"

"Like I told you, man," Frank said. "I'm connected. I hear things, all kinds of things. I don't miss much. To make it up to you, maybe I could have a talk with her. You know, make the problem go away."

I felt the world begin to spin around. A member of a crime family was talking about making Patsy an offer she couldn't refuse. Patsy would probably find it both amusing and terrifying, but I wanted to spare her that. "It's okay," I said. "Don't talk to her, Frank. I mean, I appreciate the offer, but I don't want you to threaten Patsy in any way. Don't do anything at all."

"You read too many goddamned books," Frank said. "Who said anything about threatening anyone? I was just going to talk to her. I mean, I've been through this. I know how it is."

"Don't do anything, Frank," I repeated. It occurred to me that he might already have taken action, that Patsy could be in a meat locker somewhere in the Third Ward, but Frank just sighed.

"Okay, man. No problem. It's your funeral, but if you change your mind, just let me know." For perhaps the first time I felt sorry for Frank, sympathetic to him because he needed so badly to be the big man in his leather jacket, hanging with his crew down at Axel's or wherever the mob met these days. It was a burden for a guy who'd really been a failure at everything and needed daddy to bail him out when things got rough.

"I mean it, Frank," I said. "Thanks for the offer. I know you want to help but there's really nothing to do here."

"Okay, man," he said. "Drop in before you leave. We can have a drink."

I hung up the phone and looked across the table at Tom who was looking at me with a quizzical expression. "I assume that was Mr. Pin," he said.

"The same."

"And he's happy you got him out of the palimony thing, I assume."

"Actually, he seemed to think he was doing me a favor or his dad was. I didn't disabuse him of that. Let him think whatever he wants."

"Right," Tom said. He got up and stood over me, looking down. "Look, Andy, you're my oldest friend, we've known each other since grade school, but I have to say I'm worried about you. I mean, I've been worried about you all along with the Patsy thing. I kind of need to know you'll be okay."

I nodded and got up. We embraced clumsily like men who weren't used to such expressions of affection. Then I stepped back. "I'll be fine," I said.

"Really?"

"What choice do I have?" I said. "I'll be in touch."

Time went by. There are things you know in life, things you discover, and things you'll never know. I'd never know my father and I'd never be able to unmake or revise the childhood I'd had in Milwaukee. I didn't really know why I'd slept with Patsy, why I'd gotten mixed up defending Frank, why I'd let things deteriorate with Moira, or why I was giving up the life I had here to go back East and participate in Moira's passion for reproduction. I could provide reasons, but the truth was I'd let life carry me along like a branch on a river ever since Mom died. This might have been my way of grieving, but if so it was time now to let it be over.

Both houses sold quickly, as I suspected they would, in part because I priced them below market value. And my last days at the firm were quiet and uneventful. Moira and I spoke on the phone every day and as far as I could tell Patsy hadn't followed through on her threats to expose me, either locally or on the national stage. After thinking about it obsessively for a few days, I decided to roll the dice and not say anything because I couldn't see that it would serve any purpose beyond possibly yielding absolution if Moira didn't divorce me. I had done what I had with my eyes open and I'd accept whatever followed from that.

Before leaving town, I called Bill Chandler and told him I was coming through Northampton on my way to Cambridge and wanted to talk. Then I called Mr. Allen to see if the little Victorian we had walked through was still on the market. Moira and I had our first appointment set with France at the fertility clinic in four days, which would give me time to drive out and get settled. It might have felt like a defeat to give up on my life here, in fact it might actually have been a defeat of some kind, a failure of an idea anyway. But the reality was that while I might have felt disillusioned about Milwaukee or my relation to the city, I'd come to have a more mature view of who I was and what I needed as well as a clearer sense of who my mother had been and what I meant to her. My inheritance had yielded that much and more. Which couldn't be bad. Whatever my return to and final retreat from Milwaukee represented, I now found myself feeling more relieved than anything else at the realization that I no longer had anything left to prove and no one to impress.

The night before I left, I was sitting in my empty kitchen when I heard someone knock. In all the time I'd lived there, no one had ever come to call except neighbors wanting to borrow something and it was too late for encyclopedia salesmen, so I was surprised to find Alfred Koenenberg standing at the door.

He had an anxious look around his eyes. "You're leaving?" he asked.

"Tomorrow, but come on in." It was odd but I felt friendly toward the man. He was the only thing approaching family I had left.

"Perhaps for a moment," Koenenberg said and stepped through the door. "I don't want to intrude."

"On what?" I swept my hand toward the empty room.

He accepted a cup of tea and we sat at the kitchen table. "There is one thing I didn't mention the other day," Koenenberg said. He cleared his throat and looked furtively at the door before continuing. "I wanted you to have your anger. I believe in anger for young men; it is a good thing. And I liked the idea you held of my being a seducer of women. There aren't too many triumphs of that sort for men my age." He smiled quickly at his joke.

I nodded because even in my mid-thirties I was beginning to have a sense of what he meant. "I guess anger can be good," I said. "I never really thought about it."

"Yes," Koenenberg said. "Extremes are what you want." Then he hesitated again. "But when you said I deserted your mother, I have to tell you, that wasn't true. I loved your mother. I wanted to divorce my wife and marry her."

I let this hang between us for a moment. "You told her this?"

Koenenberg spread his hands. "Of course. She said you wouldn't allow it."

"What did I have to do with it?"

He smiled again. "To her, you were very powerful. Your approval was. I think maybe you don't know your own strength. Of course, it might have been an excuse. Maybe she just didn't want me."

The notebooks argued against this, but in retrospect I felt a pang at having denied my mother a chance at happiness as well as regret for having believed the worst of Koenenberg. Nothing was as it had seemed and now I thought the only constant in my life was that all of my assumptions had been wrong. The idea that I could have been this important to my mother was amazing. I had known of her love, even her sacrifice, but I wouldn't have suspected this.

"I'm sorry," I said. "I didn't know."

Koenenberg puffed out his lips. "Why should you be sorry because your mother worried about you? Anyway, it's now years ago and she's dead. I just thought you should know, even if you have to give up a little anger."

At the door, I offered my hand but he put his arms around my neck instead and held me to him. "I'm kind of sorry I'm leaving," I said. "Now we could be friends."

Koenenberg nodded. "We'll still be friends. I'll visit."

"I'd like that," I said, and then the little man was gone.

Two days later I was in western New York where I stopped at a roadside Howard Johnson's for breakfast. After eating, I stood beside my car, watching the traffic move past in a leisurely tableau but the road was lower than the truck stop and in the distance I could see purple flowers blowing in the wind among the grass of what might have been a marsh. My mind was clear, fresher than it had been in months. I had no idea what outrage might be waiting when I arrived in Massachusetts, but today it didn't matter. A cool breeze was against my forehead and my mind seemed clear. I must have had an odd expression on my face because an attendant appeared at my elbow. "Everything all right, sir?" the kid asked.

In that chilly morning with the sun overhead and the flowers waving in the distance, his question had a strangely calming effect. Against all reason amidst the uncertainty in my life, I suddenly felt more hopeful than I could remember feeling in a very long time. All the underbrush in my life had been cleared, imperfectly no doubt, but it was gone. An open field stretched in front of me.

"Yes," I said and nodded decisively. "Everything's just fine." Then I got in the car and drove the rest of the way into Cambridge that afternoon.

A month later Moira and I were sitting in the garden of our new home in Northampton. We had started the in vitro process and would need to make the trip east once a month for a while, but I'd made my peace with that. My father-in-law was quiescent about my return and our decision to move west rather than staying on in Cambridge. We hadn't told him in any detail about our visits to the hospital and to his credit he didn't ask. I'd set up in Bill's office downtown and already had a few clients. It was spring, buds on the trees and a few hesitant flowers in the grass. The streets were clogged with parents coming in for the end of school and graduation, which is why we'd retreated to our backyard on a sunny Saturday. Moira brought a pitcher of iced tea out to the yard and I was feeling pleasantly logy.

She sat next to me on the bench and then she said matter-of-factly, "You know, I heard from Patsy last week."

A burn began on the back of my neck, but I tried not to react. "I thought you'd probably be in touch. You were good friends." We hadn't discussed anything about the time I'd spent alone in Milwaukee, my decision to leave and what it might mean. Actions speak louder than words, I thought. I'd saved Moira the agony of returning to Milwaukee by selling quickly and getting a packing service to break down the house and send our things out here. What else was there to talk about?

"Really good friends," she said sarcastically. "She apologized, but I wasn't really surprised."

I didn't ask what she meant by this. "No?"

"They weren't very good pictures," she said now.

"I don't think quality was what she was after," I said. "At least she never put them on the internet."

"No," Moira said. "Probably not. Anyway, I don't blame you; you're a man, you're weak. And after all, I left town. I knew Patsy had a crush on you."

I didn't bother to quarrel with her characterization of my gender.

She was probably right, and I wasn't in a very powerful position. "Really? I had no idea before."

She was sitting with her back hunched over in the Adirondack chair, shaking her head. It didn't seem like the sort of conversation to have in such a beautiful place.

"Face it," Moira said. "It was a pretty shitty thing to do. For both of you to do. But maybe less for Patsy. I think she was actually in love with you."

This made it worse. I'd not only betrayed my wife but misled Patsy and took her at her word when she'd said the affair didn't have to be complicated. I believed her because it made things easy for me, but I should have known sex was always complicated. It was convenient for me to believe her rather than make an assumption based on my own experiences. Oddly, however, even in my moment of embarrassment I didn't really regret the affair. If I was honest with myself, I knew I'd enjoyed it as something more daring than I'd allowed myself before. Stupid, maybe, but daring too. And while I had never wanted to hurt Moira, I had a feeling I'd hurt Patsy more. I don't know if she had really been in love with me, as Moira said, but I knew Moira was tougher than she was, tougher than either of us were.

"It probably doesn't help much," I said. "But I'm really sorry. I never did it before, never wanted to, never wanted anyone but you."

"It's not okay," Moira said. "You don't get a pass on this and it's not the kind of thing you actually forget. We can move on, at least I think we can, hope we can, but it's going to be there between us." She stopped, puffed out her cheeks and breathed heavily. Then she turned to face me. "Just one thing. Do it again, and I'll have someone break your legs. I'm serious, Andy. I know people."

"You mean your dad does."

"Same thing," she replied. She was smiling as she said this, but I knew she was right and she might actually have been serious. It was hard to tell.

I reached for her hand and in that moment, I understood the last five years had mattered and were worth suffering through. Not just the affair, but the move back from Milwaukee, selling Mom's house, disappointing my childhood friend and the rest. In that sunny afternoon in the midst of this difficult conversation with my wife, I felt somehow cleaner, fresher than I had in years. Regardless of the results of the in vitro, with or without a child, Moira and I would be all right. That seemed like a certainty to me and in the end that was the only thing that mattered.

ACKNOWLEDGMENTS

I wish to acknowledge the contribution of Jandel Allen-Davis, MD, who shared with me her extensive knowledge of the treatment of infertility. I owe a debt to my friend David Cross, a partner at Quarles & Brady in Milwaukee, and his associate Lauri Rollings, for their patient explanations of civil procedure and the inner workings of large law firms. In addition, I'm grateful to my wife, Jean, and daughter, Jennifer, both of whom are physicians, for reading the manuscript and making perceptive comments that improved the book. Any mistakes with regard to either medicine or law in *A Milwaukee Inheritance* are of course due entirely to my imperfect understanding.

I am grateful to the National Endowment for the Arts and the MacDowell Colony for generously providing grants during the creation of this novel. I'm also grateful to Dennis Lloyd and Adam Mehring of the University of Wisconsin Press who, through their guidance and support, have given new life to my work.

Nothing is more valuable to a writer, however, than the love and steady support of friends. In that regard, I want to thank Joe Lucas, Bob Harding, Frank Gay, Barbara Wright, Diane LaPierre, Joanne Greenberg, M. K. Malik, and Dick Blau for their camaraderie and good humor. I am grateful.